THE BONE CAGE

The Bone Cage

ANGIE ABDOU

NeWest Press

Library and Archives Canada Cataloguing in Publication
Abdou, Angie, 1969-
The bone cage / Angie Abdou.

ISBN 978-1-897126-17-2

1. Olympics--Fiction. I. Title.

PS8601.B36B65 2007　　　　C813'.6　　　　C2007-902159-X

Editor for the Board: Suzette Mayr
Cover and interior design: Ruth Linka
Cover image: istockphoto.com
Author photo: Judy McMahon

NeWest Press acknowledges the support of the Canada Council for the Arts, the Alberta Foundation for the Arts, and the Edmonton Arts Council, for our publishing program. We also acknowledge the financial support of the Government of Canada through the Book Publishing Industry Development Program (BPIDP) for our publishing activities.

NeWest Press
#201, 8540–109 Street
Edmonton, Alberta T6G 1E6
(780) 432-9427
www.newestpress.com

NeWest Press is committed to protecting the environment and to the responsible use of natural resources. This book is printed on 100% post-consumer recycled and ancient-forest-friendly paper.

10　　20

PRINTED AND BOUND IN CANADA

*Dedicated to
the memory of Craig Roberts (1968–2006),
Canadian Olympian . . . every bit as heroic off the mat as on.*

I had so long suffered in this quest,
Heard failure prophesied so oft [. . .]
And all the doubt was now—should I be fit?
—Robert Browning,
"Childe Roland to the Dark Tower Came"

One

*D*igger has always been a good sweater. He's only just stepped into the sauna and already he can feel the itch of sweat behind his ears, around his hairline, along his spine. It's a natural talent his teammates envy, especially at a time like this. Digger, Ben, and Fly lie sprawled in the sauna—cutting weight for the Olympic Trial matches this weekend, freshly flown to Toronto from Calgary this morning. All three are veterans to this routine. First, they unroll the plastics—pants and hooded jackets they crumpled into stinking balls the last time they cut weight. Eventually, they'll pull the clothes on in the sauna, but first they'll get a bit of a sweat going. They procrastinate at this stage, slumping naked, staring at the steaming rocks. Once dressed, they do a few jumping jacks in the sauna heat to get things rolling. When the sweat flows fast, that's when they really start moving, running at first, then riding the stationary bike that's plopped right in the middle of the sauna. No matter how dehydrated Digger is, no matter how shitty he feels, he can always find energy to sit on a bike and move his feet in circles.

Rarely, though, does Digger have to go as far as the bikes. Half an hour in the sauna and half an hour jogging; that's all it takes to get him within a kilo of weight. If he doesn't eat or drink after, the last bit comes off in his sleep. He wakes up ready to weigh in. After weigh-in, he just starts slow, which works for him because he's slow in the morning anyway. Drink a little water. Jog a slow circle around

1

the gym. Progress to Gatorade. Try some light food. A banana at first, never an orange. Acid kills an empty stomach. If he's got a couple hours, he can be back to weight by match time.

Others aren't good sweaters. One look at most of the guys on bikes and a healthy person would never peg them for strong athletes on the verge of competition. Lips white and parched, solidified gunk stuck to the corners of their mouths, breath reeking of shit, eyes dried red, bones nearly visible under grey skin.

But it'd be hard to get a good look at them. They won't meet anyone's eyes. Not because they know how bad they look, not because they're in any way embarrassed, but just because they can hardly hold up their heads. All that's ricocheting in their minds is *half more kilo, half more kilo, half more kilo*. But they're so dried out by this time that they can't imagine where that half kilo will come from, can't even imagine where a tenth of a kilo would come from.

Digger notices that Ben and Fly don't look too bad yet. All three slouch naked on the sauna bench, plastics piled next to them, waiting. Digger and Fly look pretty sucked already. "Ripped," most people would say. "Sucking weight" is what wrestlers call draining the body's water so it's just skin and muscle. Bodies lean, every muscle clear. Digger's wrestling at eighty-five kilos, Fly at sixty-nine. Ben is up at the ninety-two kilo class. Big Benny. Guys there are rarely as lean.

"Chicks dig the love handles," is how he responds when the guys rib him for being chubby. He flexes his right arm with the tattooed Celtic band circling his bicep. "They like their men a little bulky," he says.

"Digger, you bastard. You're sweating already," Fly says, glancing up.

Digger doesn't look back at him. He's looking at his own arms, running a credit card down the length of the right one, scraping off the first layer of sweat. Now more sweat will come faster. Some guys use window scrapers or butter knives. Digger uses a credit card— always gold (even if it's an expired one with his mom's name on it). He sets the card on the bench and breathes in the hot cedar air.

"You shoulda seen him at the Commonwealths," Ben says into

Digger's silence, ignoring the fact that Fly might not want to hear about the Commonwealths since he was the only one of the three not to qualify. Ben only has two kilos to cut and is chattier than Fly, who still has eight. He jumps into his story with a grinning flourish. "So we're in Kuala Lumpur and we only got a coupla hours 'til weigh-in. We're all *waaay* overweight because our moron of a team manager got us there with no time to suck. What kind of idiot books flights the same day as weigh-in?"

Everyone has heard this story—all of each other's stories—dozens of times. Digger only sweats in answer to Ben's question. Ben doesn't leave space for anyone to respond.

"All the other teams already cut weight the day before and are ready to show up at the scales rested and clean," says Ben. "Then there's us, jet-lagged and just getting into our plastics. So we're all suited up and Victor, coach from hell, is about to take us on a run. No one is saying a word—hating life. Miz-er-a-bull. I'm cool and dry as a bone and still have five kilos to cut, so I'm knowing my day will be pure misery."

Digger swats him on the head. Ben catches his meaning and shoots Fly an oops-sorry-buddy glance. Ben's five kilos that day will be nothing compared to Fly's eight today.

"Then we hear this *drip drip drip*. Somewhere close. We're all in our own zone, all so wrapped up in our own foulness that at first we don't even look. Then the drip gets annoying, louder and faster. We can't help looking around. I'm the first to realize: *Holy shit, it's Digger!* He hasn't done a damn thing and the bastard's sweatin' so hard it's pooling up and running down the inside of his plastics. It's literally *pouring* out his sleeve. Now we're all staring at him, so the prick holds out his arm, smiles and watches the liquid run out of his cuff. Not just a *drip*, but goddamn Niagara Falls." Ben throws a scoop of water on the steaming rocks for effect. "That guy can sweat a kilo a minute, I swear."

"Yep." Digger says. He wipes a hand across the back of his neck, then flashes his liquid-covered palm to his two dry-skinned friends. "I was born to be a wrestler."

Two

Sadie belongs to the water. Only here, her body performs as trained. Heat tickles her neck, mingles with the cold fluid enveloping her. She's near the end, should be exhausted, but today she feels she could swim forever, motoring full speed at the water's surface. Hot, cold, pleasure, pain. She has no time to consider these sensations. One thought pulses: *Go, go, go.* A syllable with every stroke. Her biceps and triceps, her shoulders and her back, her hamstrings and her quads—all pulse. Will they fail her? Can they finish? Something in her doubts this body. *Rest.* Surely she needs rest. Even on this good day, her muscles whisper at her: *Enough. No more.* She blocks these thoughts. She can die later, can rest when it's over. Today means everything. Her body buzzes with this knowledge. Only the next two minutes matter. One swimmer's head is at her waist, lane five, and another swimmer's head is at her feet, lane three. But today she will win. Today her body takes charge. Two lengths left and the others will try to pull ahead, but no matter how hard they pull, she will pull harder. She will win. In her last length, one word fills her: *Happening.* It's *happening.* She pulls harder, kicks harder, as if watching her pain from the outside. With throbbing in her throat, in her ears, in her temples, she stretches and slams her hand into the wall, feels the timing pad give with her force. Her face whips to the results board: Number 1. Sadie Jorgenson. YES. She lets herself fall beneath the water, rips off her plastic swim cap, and feels the cold water run through her hair. YES. Such a short word with so much weight, taking up so much space. It fills her head, her lungs, her heart. YES. She is Victor Davis. She is Alex Baumann. She is Kornelia Ender. Kristin Otto. Mark Spitz. YES. Her legs pull together hard, boosting her torso out of the water, her arms above her head. Victorious.

Who gets up this early? It's cold. It's dark. It's five AM. Calgary winter, no less. "Masochists," she grunts, pounding the alarm. Sadie hauls herself out of her dry warm bed with its down duvet to pull on a damp swimsuit. Her eyes stay closed and grit scrapes the inside of her eyelids. Fatigue and nausea grip her gut. She squints her eyes open and grabs the suit hanging on her doorknob, peels it up over her body. This is an old routine, one she's been doing for fourteen years. Swimming: two times a day, six days a week, two hours per time. All adding up to a grand total that even she doesn't want to know. She should be used to it by now, but every day she hates getting out of bed just as much as she hated it the day before. Yet she keeps doing it, even on this February Monday, the week after she's won the eight-hundred-metre freestyle at the Olympic Trials. Only seven months until the Olympics, no time for a break. She reaches for her swim bag on the floor and slides out of the room without flicking on the lights. No celebration, or even rest, for her: the weekend's victory was a beginning rather than an ending.

She opens the fridge and shuts her eyes at the light assault. A pre-mixed smoothie in the blender container waits for her on the top shelf next to her father's six-pack of Guinness. Too early to be running the blender and waking her parents. Enough that they put up with a grown daughter in their house at all. Eating their food, running their hot water. *Only until the Olympics are over*, she tells herself, leaning against the counter and giving the plastic blender container a shake, sipping from it as she scans the contents of the fridge. The Guinness is a new habit. Her father had always been such a health food freak. Never booze in his fridge. She was the only kid she knew who wasn't allowed white bread. Even now, ordering a sandwich in a restaurant, she'd cancel if the waitress couldn't offer a whole-wheat option. "White bread's the devil's work"—her dad's sentiment turned into her catchphrase. And white flour wasn't her dad's only hang-up. She'd endured a wide gamut of phases during her swimming career—the eight-raw-eggs-a-day phase, or the twelve-honey-bee-pollen-pills-with-every-meal phase. She's happy he no longer gets up to make her breakfast before practice.

Imagining this morning's practice, Sadie remembers an old saying: the only thing more boring than being a long-distance runner is being a long-distance swimmer. And it's true: at least a runner has scenery. All a swimmer has is the bottom of a pool. And Sadie has memorized every line, every crack, every drain, every single wad of gum on the bottom of the University of Calgary pool, the pool where she's spent the last eleven years training, where she's swum thousands, maybe hundreds of thousands, of lengths. Still, she can't say she finds it boring. She forces down the chunks of half-blended banana in big gulps.

"Only boring people get bored," her mother would say when Sadie was young and complained of long, tedious practices. Not that Sadie's mother approved of athletics in particular; she just had an appreciation of excellence—and a good work ethic—in general. *Only boring people get bored* became the refrain of Sadie's youth, dragging her through those endless, repetitive workouts. An active imagination didn't hurt either. While she swam for the varsity team, she did a degree in English Literature, and all those stories pulled her through the two-hour mindless pool sessions—staring at the bottom of the pool while memorizing her favourite Yeats poem or re-inventing Austen novels, imagining Elizabeth dumping Darcy's ass at the end of *Pride and Prejudice*. But the more advanced she got as a swimmer, the less she allowed herself to play these time-killing games. Her life had narrowed, focused, until it was just her body and the water immediately surrounding it. Every practice required her full concentration. To be the best, to win, she had to pay attention to the minute details of every second, of every stroke.

And what was the point, if it wasn't to win?

Hand entry, body position, stroke count—each movement counted towards the overall performance. The more attention she paid during practice, the more she could count on these movements coming naturally during a race.

The milk sits heavily in Sadie's stomach and she knows she'll be tasting the smoothie again during her flip turns. She quietly sets the empty blender container in the sink and fills it with water.

I, Sadie Jorgenson, am going to the 2000 Olympic Games. I am an Olympian, she tells herself as she pulls on her fuzzy boots in the dark hallway. Others on her team had worked just as hard, had suffered the same early mornings, and wouldn't be going.

She'd trained with Bogdan since he was just a kid who bragged that he never messed up a workout by getting out of the pool to go to the washroom—a habit that carried over to his varsity years when he nicknamed himself Big Chief Yellow Cloud. Sadie wondered if he got away with this brand of humour simply because swimming was a sport pretty much limited to upper-middle-class white kids. Before Sadie's race at the trials this weekend, Bogdan hovered around her, shooting instructions into her ear—*start out nice and steady, no intense effort; remember, second half of the race is what counts; don't be lulled into anyone else's race; if they want to go ahead at the start, just let 'em—they'll pay for it at the end . . .*

"Aye aye, Big Chief," she'd answered with a sharp salute but then pinched his cheek when he scowled.

"Just keep your arms relaxed," he'd concluded, waggling his arms at his sides.

She never got a chance to talk to him after her race but watched his fifteen-hundred metre in dismay. His pacing was off from the first fifty metres, his face quickly growing red, his stroke more and more awkward and laboured. It simply wasn't his meet. Who knew why? Maybe he missed his taper, maybe he had a bit of a bug, maybe he ate the wrong pre-race meal, maybe his stars just weren't aligned. End result—Sadie was going to the Olympics without him.

"I'm going to The Show! Disneyland, here I come!" she'd laughed with her coach, Marcus, after the race, water still running down her back.

The Olympics weren't in Disneyland—they were in Sydney, Australia. Athletes mocked the parades and outfits of the Olympics, the intense media coverage, but at the same time craved the attention. Widespread recognition came only with Olympic gold. Every athlete's dream.

A dream that reeks of chlorine. If asked what reminded her of childhood, Sadie wouldn't answer baked bread, hopscotch, summer camp. Her childhood was scented with the heavy bleached fragrance of a swimming pool. Chlorine's toxic aroma so deeply soaked into her that it had become her natural perfume. In high school gym class, as soon as she broke a sweat, the pungent aroma of chlorine would swim around her.

"Ewww, something smells like a swimming pool."

"Just me," she'd admit, blushing under her chemically stripped hair. At least now it would be blonde for the Olympics, not green as it was for many of her school photos. Thank goodness for Bromine.

Twenty-six and swimming in the Olympics. She pulls a bright red toque down over her forehead, almost covering her eyes, and zips up her calf-length red parka, U of C Dinos blazed across the back. With a sigh, she steps into the dark, her boots crunching on the frozen snow, and heads to the swimming pool that is her life. Her high school alumni will see her on TV and wonder, "Isn't that the sleepy girl who always smelled like a swimming pool?"

"SAYYY—DEEE—YOU'RE—HERE!" Marcus belts out as she makes her way onto the pool deck. This is his standard shtick for all the swimmers. Each deep, booming syllable assaults the silent air.

"MI—CHAAAEL—YOU'RE—HERE!"

"JO-HAAAN—YOU'RE—HERE!"

"BEZ—ZAAAD—YOU'RE—HERE!"

He says it as if every one of them isn't always here, isn't here every single practice, every single morning, every single afternoon. It's the coach's job to be enthusiastic. Once they're in the water, it's: *Harder! Faster! Concentrate! Streamline! Kick! Think!*

But now, no one looks to the water, not until Marcus gives the direction at 6 AM exactly. Now, swimmers sprawl across the deck, heads resting on their gym bags, towels pulled across their faces, bags of ice on their shoulders. Sadie listens to the insistent ticking of the pace clock, the rumble of the heater kicking on, and wonders how long she has. She loves this limbo, lying on the warm pool tiles, still wrapped in the hazy protection of sleep, postponing the assault of the ice-cold pool water. The two hardest things: getting out of bed, getting in the pool.

Only the people who qualified this weekend have shown up for practice. Those who didn't win got the morning off. Sadie's body envies them as Marcus pronounces, "Start time." At the pool's edge, while pulling on a plastic cap that tears at her hair, she dips her toes in the water. Cold. She takes a deep breath and holds it while counting down—5-4-3-2-1—and forces herself to dive in against her will. She does the same thing after diving every time: swims half a length under water, exerting herself—moving her arms and legs quickly—to help fight the cold, then jumps up, breaking the surface with a splash. A quick breath, then three fast flip turns, feet over head, feet over head, feet over head. That's all the movement it takes to adjust to the water's temperature. Now she's awake and ready. A nice smooth front crawl back to the edge and it's time for her first set.

I might go on, naught else remained to do. So on I went, trips through her head as she imagines herself a late-twentieth-century incarnation of Browning's Childe Roland, the black line at the bottom of the pool her own darkening path.

Sadie does 4 x 800 metres on twelve minutes, a mild recovery workout after a weekend of exertion. Long strokes and smooth turns. With the lapse in intensity, Sadie returns to fictional worlds like she used to when she was just a varsity swimmer, not yet on the national team. But today it's not the world of Austen or Yeats. Today it is CBC Newsworld, and Steve Byron interviews her after

9

she pulls off a miraculous gold place finish in Sydney.

This has been a dream of mine ever since . . .

I want to thank . . .

I couldn't have done it without . . .

I just gave 110 per cent . . .

The clichéd speeches flow over her as she swims back and forth past the three wads of gum in her lane—two bright pink and one green, must be Clorets. As a Lit student, Sadie knew a cliché when she spoke one, but athletes' lives were governed by clichés. They not only talked in ready-made phrases but also wore them on their T-shirts, taped them to their walls. *The road to glory's paved with sweat. No pain, no gain. 1% inspiration, 99% perspiration. Just do it.* Why do you suffer? The pat answer—for her Olympic Dream—quickly forestalled further thought. The phrase echoed in Sadie's head, the words hollow from repetition. But she'd built her whole life—her very identity—on those two words: Olympic Dream. Now was not the time to question them. At moments, Sadie was aware that if she and her athlete friends were to delve deeper than the ready-made phrases, they might find it difficult to justify their quixotic lifestyle—a life where a twenty-six-year-old man can still get away with peeing in the pool and then announcing, "I Big Chief Yellow Cloud." Or worse yet, standing quietly close by your leg before whispering, "Does the water seem warmer than usual to you?"

Sadie expected a celebratory atmosphere at practice this morning, everyone puffed up with their new status as Olympians. Instead, it's quieter than usual, no sound but the echoing thud of a kickboard on the deck or the rhythmic splashing of water. For now, they're all quietly getting used to the idea of themselves as Olympians, immersed in relief at having made the first distance.

After practice, Sadie drives to her grandma's for breakfast, another of her traditions. In the tiny, glassed-in entranceway that reeks of lilacs and cigarette butts, she pushes 5-1-2, the code printed next to the name Eva Jorgenson.

"Hi Grandma, it's me!"

"C'm up." The door buzzes.

Sadie could've pressed any arrangement of numbers, said the same thing, and gotten the same response. The building is a twenty-storey seniors' high-rise, all single apartments. Each unit with its own little kitchen, its own little bathroom, and its own little half-deaf inhabitant. Every morning, Eva hangs a piece of cardboard painted with a green circle on her doorknob, letting the caretaker know she's awake and alive. Meals and homecare will be available when she needs them.

She's still a kick-ass cook and will now be loading the table with scrambled eggs, raisin toast, sliced grapefruits, homemade cinnamon buns, fried hash browns, and Saskatoon berry jam. Sadie pushes open the apartment door without knocking, welcomes the smell of fresh baked bread.

"For my starving swimmer girl," says Eva, setting a plate in front of Sadie, who's shrugging off her Dinos parka. The loose hanging sleeve of Eva's flowered satin housecoat drags through the ketchup on Sadie's eggs, but neither pays any attention. Eva rarely dresses anymore and her housecoats get brighter and looser all the time. Two bobby pins at each temple hold her short, uncombed hair off her face.

"Thanks, Gran! Flashy dress." Sadie sits down to the table, reaches for the butter, piles it thickly on one of the steaming cinnamon buns.

Eva is eighty-two now and breathes in shallow but loud gasps while she covers the six feet from her kitchen cupboard to the table, bringing Sadie a coffee with cream. She rests her hand on Sadie's head, "This head of hair. It looks like it's trying to escape from your head!"

Sadie brushes Eva's hand away, tongues a chunk of cinnamon bun into her cheek. "I like my hair. It's wanton and lascivious. Like Milton's Eve's. Responsible for the downfall of man!"

Eva shakes her head and moves to her own spot at the table, then leans on the back of her chair and sprays a long squirt of nitro under her tongue. "Enough of this stuff'll turn me into a bomb." She makes this joke daily. A rattle of phlegm comes in place of a laugh. Eva claims to have already eaten but pulls a small box of chocolates, the weekly gift from Sadie, from her housecoat pocket. She unwraps a small globe of chocolate and sets it under her tongue, letting it melt. Sadie refuses to nag Eva about her diabetes. The family doctor once told Sadie that Eva needed to pay attention to her weight.

"She hardly eats," Sadie had defended her.

"Sadie, you don't get to be that size hardly eating."

Sadie remembers thinking, *You don't get to be your size by hardly eating either, doc.*

The chocolates were Eva and Sadie's secret.

Neither speaks while Sadie devours her breakfast. She races to shovel food into her mouth. Eva claims to love the way Sadie eats: nothing wrong with a passion for food. She sits across from Sadie, chewing with her mouth open; Sadie can see chocolate making its way around her mouth. Finally, Sadie rises to take her plate to the sink, rinsing it under water though there's not a speck of food left on it. On the microwave lies a white doily trimmed with canary yellow. Her grandmother has obviously ironed and starched it. Another flecked with green rests atop the fridge. One trimmed with red sits under the teakettle. When Sadie was younger, these doilies were dresses for her Barbie dolls and wedding veils for herself and her friends. They were camouflage when she'd spilled nail polish and marked up the perfect white dressers her parents gave her for her thirteenth birthday. Now she reaches over and fingers the stiff edge of the yellow one.

"You can have all of those once you're ready to set up house for yourself."

Sadie drops the doily. "Subtle, Grandma."

Eva shifts her weight uncomfortably and puffs on her inhaler. "I hear congratulations are in order. Your mom tells me I'll be seeing you swim on TV this summer?"

"Yes," Sadie says. "I finally made the Olympics." She flattens the doily and moves to the table. "What a relief."

"Relief?" Eva makes a noise in the back of her throat. "Relief?

Is that all it is? Hardly seems worth all the trouble. Just for relief. I thought it must make you happy." She lifts the inhaler towards her mouth but then drops it on the coffee table at her side, fingers the neon pink flowers at her chest.

Happiness? Yes, once it was about that. Sadie almost says these words aloud, but Eva is still talking.

"If I want relief, alls I do is take an Ex-Lax."

Three

*D*igger and Ben walk the echoing nighttime hallways of the hospital, the fluorescent lights stinging their dry eyes. Digger holds a big bottle of water and Ben, whose curly, damp hair sticks to his neck and forehead, a jug of blue Gatorade. They're both pale and look weak—every movement an effort—but both look better than Fly, stretched out in his hospital bed, a sheet pulled up to his shoulders.

Digger had just finished checking his weight—84.98 kilos with twenty minutes to spare—when his coach, Saul, snapped at him. "Your weight good, Digs?"

Digger nodded, leaning against a cool cement wall and wiping his face with a rough towel.

"Well, go help Fly. Fucker's not gonna make it." Saul dropped a coin in the vending machine, grabbed himself a Coke, and waddled off without looking for an answer. Digger heaved himself off the cool wall and went to find Fly propped on a bike in the sauna. Fly looked like shit and smelled worse. His upper body hung limp over the bike's handlebars, arms and legs swathed in plastic. He didn't lift his head when Digger popped his face into the sauna, though he did seem to pedal a little faster at the burst of cool air.

"Let's turn this sucker up, Fly. Get your feet moving. Not making

14

weight isn't an option. Not at the Olympic Trials." Digger wrapped
Fly's head in a dry towel and plastic hood, then cranked up the heat
and stood outside the door, banging on the little window whenever
Fly's feet slowed. In the end, Fly did make it, weighing in at exactly
sixty-nine kilos.

Afterward, they walked by the vending machine on their way to
the water fountain.

"Mmmm, a Coke." Fly forced the words out of his parched
throat.

"Have some water first," Digger instructed, but he too felt his
taste buds twinge at the though of a cold, sweet Coke. Fly was already
popping coins into the machine. "Well, at least have some water
after. More water than Coke," Digger said over his shoulder on his
way to the change room. The next he heard, Fly had been carted off
in an ambulance.

Now Fly lies on his single bed, hospital bars up and intravenous tubes
inserted in both his arms. Digger and Ben pause in the doorway
before slinking to his bedside. Fly opens his eyes, but otherwise he
seems unaware of his friends. Only his eyelids have moved. He says
nothing.

"Look at that," Ben pushes out a loud bark of a laugh. "You're
not dead after all. They's just trying to scare us."

The room is lit with a painful, unnatural white light that shows
the salt dried to Fly's face, highlights the darkness around his eyes,
makes him look old. He seems oblivious to Digger and Ben and
stares blankly at the ceiling.

The reek of urine and antiseptic fills the air. Neither sits well
with Digger's post-weigh-in stomach. Still, it's an improvement on
Digger and Fly's rez room.

"See, that's how you got your name, buddy," Digger reaches as
if to pat Fly's hair but at the last moment forms his hand into a fist
and gives Fly a light bop in the middle of his forehead. Fly's stare
remains fixed on the ceiling. "All you do is eat shit and bother people.

Dragging us out to a hospital to console your dehydrated ass. All 'cause you couldn't keep your lips off the Coca Cola."

Digger knows how good the icy sugar rush of a Coke tastes after cutting weight, all that sugar sending an instant energy buzz to a depleted body. Cold, fluid sugar pouring down a dried throat. But he also knows that when the body is that dehydrated, it needs water, a lot of water, before wrestling with sugar. Fly knew better too. Digger's not surprised that Fly went into seizure. Surprised, no. Worried, yes. Fly's chances of wrestling in tomorrow's trials are not good.

Ben slides open the medical supply drawer next to Fly's bed. "Hey hey, looky here, a little lube." He puts several packets into his breast shirt pocket. "Might just need this for the post-tourney festivities." He kneels and rifles through the drawer for toys, while Digger watches Fly's face for movement or colour or anything, but Fly lies, covered and still, his eyes dim and unfocused.

Ben is blowing up a white latex glove just as two male doctors enter the room. "Look! Balloons," he says, waving the latex glove over Fly's face. The doctors barely glance in Ben's direction but he lets his makeshift balloon deflate and stuffs the limp glove in the back pocket of his jeans.

"This party is finished," says the older doctor, studying Fly's IV bags, not even glancing towards Digger and Ben. He stands close enough that Digger can smell the sour coffee on his breath. Fly still hasn't moved, seems no more aware of the doctors' presence than he was of his friends'. Digger sees now that one doctor is much younger, possibly an intern, and follows the older, watching over his shoulder. Both step in line to Fly's bedside chart. Rebuked, Digger and Ben step back, and Ben points his head to the door.

"We gotta stay for a bit," whispers Digger. "We haven't gotten a single word out of Fly."

Ben follows him away from the doctors and they slip towards the curtains of the other bed across the room. They hear the raspy breath of another patient they hadn't realized was there. Machines hum and beep, a ventilator rasps, and Ben and Digger watch the doctors hover over Fly.

The older doctor's silver hair is shorn so short his scalp shows through. "He's dehydrated," he says to his intern. "Self-inflicted, if you can believe that. The sugar caused the seizure, but he was low enough on fluids that he likely would have landed here anyway. We end up with at least one wrestler in here a year. We gave him a bolus of normal saline solution and now have him on 200 cc's an hour with twenty milli-equivalents of potassium. He should be ready to go by morning." He writes something on his chart and then, as if Fly can't hear him, he adds, "More muscles than brains. We're wondering if it'll take a dead wrestler to smarten the rest of them up."

Neither doctor addresses Fly directly and he looks up at them, with his prominent cheekbones and salt-flaked skin. He doesn't seem to care whether or not they take his silence as agreement regarding his stupidity. When the two men leave, Digger and Ben shuffle back to Fly's bedside. Digger notes a single liquid streak on Fly's salt-caked cheek and wonders if it's a tear.

"Gotta go, buddy," Ben steps forward so his hip is pressed against the bar on Fly's right side, gives the sleeve of Fly's hospital gown a tug. As an afterthought, he pulls a packet of lube out of his breast pocket and tosses it on Fly's bed. "Just in case the nurses get friendly," he says.

Digger leans over the bed, lowering himself into the familiar sour smell of dehydration. "You'll be okay, buddy. Remember: you don't break through the wall unless you hit it first." He cringes at his own stupid cliché and puts a hand on each of Fly's shoulders, squeezes.

He steps away but Fly reaches for his arm, the first movement he's made since they arrived.

"I had to try," Fly whispers. "Only an idiot would miss going to the Olympics because he didn't make weight."

But it looks like Fly is going to miss it because he did make weight. Digger circles Fly's wrist with his thumb and forefinger, "You did your best."

Like that ever made a difference.

Four

Sadie drives the icy streets from her grandmother's back to the U of C, where she has a five-hour shift at the athletic cage. Five hours of tossing towels, assigning lockers, and checking shoe tags when all she wants to do is sleep. Her arms are so fatigued they ache when she turns the car's steering wheel, her triceps feel heavy and sluggish, and her whole body begs to be submerged in the dark, blank comfort of sleep. She knows she could sleep all day if she let herself—she probably even needs it—but her athletic carding cheque is not enough to get her through the month.

Rookie swimmers on the varsity team used to ask her what classes she was taking. "Classes," she'd laugh. "I finished those years ago. I'm in a full-time swimming class." Now that she's a relic of the university and a name in Canadian swimming, no one asks her why she's still here anymore. She just is.

Her little copper car sputters and belches as she pulls into her spot at the Phys Ed building.

"We made it yet again, Copper Bullet." She pats the dusty dashboard. As a 1985 model, Copper Bullet objects to the six o'clock, forty-below mornings even more than Sadie does. He's been puttering her to and from the pool ever since she was sixteen, and considering her current financial situation, she doesn't imagine replacing him anytime soon. Because she still sleeps in her childhood bedroom at her parents' house, Copper Bullet is the closest thing she has to her own place.

She drags her heavy aching body out of the warm car—the heater is the one thing in Copper Bullet that still functions perfectly—and pushes the driver's seat forward. It creaks in protest and Sadie pats the car's frosted hood.

"Ah, Copper Bullet, I feel your pain."

She reaches into the back seat for her gym bag. There's another practice this afternoon, so she won't have much time after her shift. She'll hang her stuff to dry out while she's working, and maybe she'll be able to sneak in a quick nap on a locker-room bench or a gym mat. Or maybe not: she'd better get in a weight workout too. She digs around in the back seat for a cleanish T-shirt and pair of shorts, then grabs her shoes, a copy of Joseph Gold's *Read For Your Life*, and a pillow. Who's kidding whom, she thinks; she'll probably use the book as a pillow. Ever since finishing her degree, she's been carrying around ambitious books like this one but rarely cracks a spine.

She slams Copper's door. "Transportation. Gym locker. Library. Roommate." She scrapes "my champion" into the frost on the old car's back window and heads for the Phys Ed building.

After the excitement of the qualifiers this weekend, it's almost painful to be back in this routine: *swim, eat, work, eat, sleep, eat, weights, eat, swim, eat, sleep*. No fanfare, no celebration, no change, just more of the same. But she knows she'd better find a way to mute the pain and rise above the boredom, because she's got seven more months, seven months in which she not only has to do "more of the same," but has to find a way to do it faster.

"Hey, Sade. It's been slow today, should be an easy shift," says Russ, a varsity basketball player, handing her the keys and giving up his stool at the cage window. He looms over her and stares down at her wild hair. "Saw you in the paper this morning. Nice work! Off to Australia!" He swings a white towel over his shoulder, headed for a post-shift workout.

"Thanks, Russ."

"Thanks? How about a little enthusiasm? How about a big fat YEE-HAW!!"

Sadie smiles. "Oh, I'm thrilled to death, trust me. I definitely am. I'm just tired."

"Hmm, Sadie tired? That's something new." He pushes her shoulder affectionately and lopes towards the exit as the first sweaty customer approaches the cage. "New as sweat," she hears him finish as he rounds the corner.

The cage smells like sweaty towels, but she only notices when she throws another towel on the dirty clothes pile and a stinking whoof of air billows up to her face. She sits on the stool and folds her arms on the cool metal counter, props her chin on them, and tries to focus on reading Gold's introduction: "This book is for everyone who likes to read and everyone who wants to like to read. It is a book about the value of reading fiction, about the importance of story to your personal life, your coping skills, your mental health and your relations with other people. Reading is too important to . . ." Already, she can feel heavy sleep, shadowy dream figures pulling at her.

But a thud shakes her metal pillow.

"Don't work too hard, Sades."

It's Russ again—looking for a ball to shoot hoops. He bends over, leaning his long torso through the cage widow, pointing to his favourite ball hidden in the corner behind the floor hockey sticks.

Sadie pulls herself from the stool and bends down for the ball, not ready for the dizzying rush of blood to her head. She grabs the side of the counter to steady herself and holds her other hand across her eyes. "Man, I have to wake up." She shakes her head and gives her cheek a slap.

"I don't know why you do this lame job if you're so tired, Ms. Carded Athlete. What d'you need this for?"

Uncarded athletes always hassled Sadie for being carded, thought her life so much more glamorous and lucrative compared to theirs.

"Do you know how much I make off carding, Russ? Less than I'd make on welfare. How'm I gonna live off that? Not when I'm this hungry! Food alone demolishes my monthly carding cheque in less than two weeks."

Russ's eyes latch onto her midriff as if to find evidence of this gargantuan appetite. She notices him looking and blushes.

"You swimmers are a weird bunch, spending three-quarters of

your time underwater. Always tired and hungry. I swear you're all in some kinda gilled cult," Russ palms the ball appreciatively, "flopping around like beached pickerel all the time."

He practices his jump shot on the concrete wall above the cage window, exaggerating the neat follow-through of his shooting hand. Sadie notes the long muscles in his arms and down his sides, not as long as a swimmer's muscles but not as bulky as a wrestler's, a good middle size. She turns to work, grabs a basketful of hot towels from the dryer.

"Is it drugs or just sleep deprivation? Brainwashing? Too much chlorine?" Russ asks, smiling, not breaking the rhythm of his shots. "I bet it's an underwater sex thing. A twisted underwater sex cult." He grabs the ball with both hands, his huge palms swallowing it whole. "Can I join? You must need some guys in your sex cult, 'cause those swimmer guys are a bunch of homos."

Sadie throws a clean, warm towel over his head and laughs. "Go play your games somewhere else, Russ."

She walks to the back of the cage and starts to fold the clean towels, snapping them loudly to keep herself awake. She remembers a CBC documentary on narcolepsy. A woman being interviewed said she felt as if she were a puppet and every so often, without warning, the puppeteer simply let go of her strings. No matter where she was, she had to fall to the floor and sleep. *Narcolepsy?* thinks Sadie as she contemplates curling up for a nap in the cupboard of clean towels. *I feel like that every day.*

Five

*D*igger and Ben leave the University of Toronto hospital and slog through the slush back to the dorm. They're staying on campus because the trial matches were supposed to be held at the university gym. Were *supposed* to be is key—supposed to be, until CBC said they'd only televise if the wrestlers came to them. Now they're supposed to bus to downtown Toronto tomorrow to wrestle in a cramped studio at the CBC headquarters, just so CBC can pre-tape the matches and plug them into some dead TV spot on a Sunday afternoon three or four weeks from now.

That's what Digger gets for picking a low-profile sport. Maybe Digger should have stuck with hockey like his dad always said. As if he had a choice. As if people freely chose their sports, picked what their bodies would excel at. Maybe if he'd been born in Iran, or India, or Turkey—one of the countries that appreciates wrestling, that packs stadiums with sweaty, screaming fans—then he'd be a national hero instead of just another unknown amateur athlete.

But no, he's in Canada where he was born, wrestling because that's the particular sport his body type and temperament are suited to.

Earlier, when they'd left the weigh-in, it was a typical February in Toronto, grey and wet, the clouds hanging low to the ground, a ceiling too close to his head. Digger craves the Calgary sun, his hometown's open blue skies. Now as he and Ben leave the hospital, it's already dark.

Ben doesn't say a word all the way back to the dorm and neither does Digger. They wind their way through the people and the litter. Both hunker over, slouched as if carrying the sky's darkness. Their feet drag along the wet pavement.

Digger would like to be able to say they're both thinking of Fly, of their buddy's bad luck. But they're not. They're both thinking of tomorrow, of themselves.

They arrive at the residence high-rise, twenty-five floors of concrete, more greyness. In the elevator, Digger pushes 7 for the floor he and Fly have been assigned. Ben hesitates instead of pushing 9, where he's been put with one of the trainers.

"Want company or feel like bunking alone tonight?" He still hasn't raised his head, but studies the elevator's worn carpet. His drooping posture reminds Digger of the end-of-season sunflowers he's seen in his mom's garden.

"Sure. You take Fly's bed. I need someone to whip at crib anyway."

Fly's not going to be back tonight; that much is for sure, and nerves will keep both Ben and Digger from getting an early night's sleep before tomorrow's 9:00 AM warm-up anyway.

Ben looks at Digger and lifts the right side of his mouth in a half smile, swings his gym bag over his shoulder and follows.

The room is close and dank, a square of cement-block walls with a single bed on either side. Digger and Fly's sweat-soaked clothes lie in crumpled wet balls between the two beds. Digger swipes his hand across one bed, knocking a gym bag, a pair of wrestling shoes, and some magazines to the floor.

"All yours."

"Thanks, buddy."

Ben flops down on the bed, knowing from experience not to throw himself into it too hard. These beds have only the slightest spring. They've slept in enough Eastern Block dormitories not to count on spring.

"Not exactly the Four Seasons," Ben sighs, leaning his head back on a thin foam pillow, grayed with age.

Digger organizes his stuff for tomorrow: red singlet, blue singlet, favourite shoes, team sweats, towel—and throws the sweaty stuff (his and Fly's) in a green garbage bag brought just for this purpose. By the time he's collected all the damp gear, the bag's three-quarters full. He ties a tight knot in the top and throws it in the closet, closes the doors.

"Clean!" He waves a hand towards a chest of drawers, inviting Ben to unpack the workout bag he's dropped on the floor, but Ben stays prone on the bed.

"The countdown's on, Big Benny. Tomorrow this time, we'll know. One way or another, it's over." *For good* remains unspoken, but they both know: if they don't come out on top tomorrow, it's over *for good*. Digger's thirty-one and Ben is twenty-nine. Digger's had two knee surgeries, a broken ankle, and has pinched nerves in his neck that give him stingers almost every practice. Ben has a dislocating shoulder, a bum elbow, and a bad lower back. Their bodies have withstood too much abuse already. For now, neither thinks of what happens after, what comes next, but both know that tomorrow is their last chance to put the right ending on this story.

They don't even pretend they're going to play cards. The crib board stays tucked in the side pocket of Digger's gym bag. Ben lies on his back on one of the single beds, tossing a blue foam stress ball from one hand to the other. He stares intently at the ceiling, as if the key to victory is written there. Digger lies on the other bed, six feet from Ben, on his stomach, propped up on his elbows, ignoring a knot tightening between his neck and shoulder. He's grabbed a pad of paper and pen, planning to make some notes for an inspirational speech to give at next week's provincial champs to the kids' team he coaches, something to distract him from the weight of tomorrow's matches.

But all he's done is doodle Olympic symbols, five interlinked rings with the year 2000 sketched underneath. He presses his pen hard into the page, going over and over each ring, tracing and retracing the year 2000. His fingers cramp and the deep blue ink seeps through to the page below. This is an old ritual, but one he hasn't done since he was sixteen. Digger Olympic-doodled his way through most of elementary and high school. The logo covered his pencil cases, his notebooks, his binders. But back then it was the five rings, 1992, and GOLD in sure block caps. 1992 came and went, and so did 1996. So today he carves 2000 and tries to make the numbers look just as sure. He leaves off the GOLD though. *Maybe,* he thinks, *that was my problem in the past: looking too far ahead of myself. This weekend, I'll just worry about getting there.*

There's a rap on the door and their coach, Saul, pushes it open a crack, sticks his silver speckled head through. He was a strong, square middleweight when he wrestled, but he now has a medicine-ball-sized gut and his legs look too short to carry the load.

"Everything alright, guys? Feeling ready?"

He doesn't smile and his eyes are intent under furry black eyebrows. He taps a pen on the clipboard in his hand, then pushes it at the bridge of little round glasses perched on his broken nose and hooked on his cauliflowered ears, physical signs of his past life as a wrestler.

"Yeah, we're good," Digger's voice cracks into the silence.

"Ben?"

"Yep. Good," he clenches the stress ball in his right hand.

"'Kay then. It's nine o'clock. Get a good sleep. We'll be up at seven—get you around and moving before warm-up, get some good food in you. Tonight, relax and sleep. We've done the work. Tomorrow's just a matter of showing up at the mat." He looks at Ben, who appears about to squish the stress ball into his right fist. "But I mean *really* show up there, show up at your best. You guys have looked great at practice, looked fantastic all month. Let's see *that* Digs and Ben on the mat tomorrow."

He looks from Digger's eyes to Ben's, waits, but neither speaks.

"All right then," he gives the door two firm slaps with his palm. "Get some rest."

The door clicks shut and Digger closes his doodles, takes a deep breath.

"We're good to go, Benny. This is the fun part, bud, the place where we show our stuff." As he says these words, the knot in his traps loosens and he begins to believe. He runs through a list of his attributes: *I'm strong. I'm fit. I'm a smart wrestler. I'm an experienced wrestler. I'm a technical wrestler. And as a twelve-year veteran of the national team, I have more experience than anyone in Canada. Why would anyone beat me?* Those thoughts make him want to run the rez stairs. He swings to his feet and punch boxes Ben, who's sitting on the side of his bed, pulling his gear out of his bag, laying it out to dry for tomorrow.

Jab. Kick. Jab

"Wanna go, guy, wanna go?! Want some of this?"

Ben laughs.

"Save it for tomorrow, Digger," he throws the stress ball at Digger and gets up to strip down for bed.

He's right. An adrenalin rush is not what Digger needs now. He needs sleep. He picks up a bottle of water from the floor, takes a long deep drink.

Ben smiles at him, sticks his arm out, and they clap hands in a side five. Each takes his turn to run down the hallway to the rez washroom to pee and brush his teeth. Digger goes first and is tucked into bed waiting for Ben to flick the light switch off. Lights off, they both sink into their pillows and the only noise is water running in the pipes above, no tossing and turning, no talking, no snoring, not even any loud breathing. Still, it would be asking too much to expect either of them to sleep. Either way, Digger thinks, after September's Olympics, it will be time for a lot of Peter Pans to grow up.

Not this Peter Pan, he assures himself, lifting a hand into the streetlight shining through the window, making a shadow rabbit hop across the wall above the little room's doorframe. A shadow dog from Ben's side of the room jumps up to chase it.

Six

Marcus has scheduled a special distance practice for this afternoon. He's rented one lane for the hour before regular practice so he can focus on distance swimmers and do some pace work. Sadie and Bogdan worry about what Marcus will do with them. They tell each other the workout can't be *that* hard—not yet. They hope for technique work, a nice gentle reminder to keep elbows high, head flat, toes pointed in. They worry instead about impossible pace times, no rest, an hour of physical torture.

But when Marcus walks in, pen behind his ear and clipboard in hand, he doesn't smile. There's a rigidity in his shoulders and they know immediately that he's not here to brush up their technique. Sadie feels the same quickness in breath she fights off before a race. She watches Marcus closely, hating the vanity implied by his still lean muscles, detesting his heavy hair that looks too coarse to be anything but a wig, loathing his long sideburns (what is it? Still 1970 for God's sake?), hating especially the way he turns to write the workout on the whiteboard without greeting either of them.

Sadie and Bogdan exchange a look. This workout is going to suck. Sadie moves over to the wall, reaches up and presses her arms into the cool tiles, stretches her back. The pull along her spine wakes her body. The sleep crawls out of her limbs as she shakes her ankles and wrists. She flattens her right palm into the wall, fingers splayed, and reaches her left hand around her back to lift her left foot to her butt. She stretches out her left quad and then switches to her right side. She presses her forehead into the cool tiles. *Work time, Sade.* She pulls herself towards the pool's edge, imagining herself as Yeats' rough beast slouching towards Bethlehem.

"SAAAY-DEE, BOG-DAAAN, YOU'RE BOTH HERE. PERRR-FECT!!" Marcus's sudden smile implies he's their host rather than their executioner.

He turns his back to them again, his shoulders wide in his red Dinos golf shirt. His black marker continues to squeak across the whiteboard.

"We're doomed," Bogdan mutters too low for Marcus to hear.

Marcus steps away from the board and claps his hands, a lone sharp smack at the end of his sentence:

50 x 100 on 1:10

Sadie takes a deep breath and bends her head to her knees, relaxes into the stretch. Tears prickle the back of her eyes. She's tired. *50 x 100 on 1:10?* That's four lengths on one minute and ten seconds, repeated fifty times. *This is going to hurt.* Plus, they're just getting started. They have six months to build on this pain, to multiply this fatigue. Sadie swallows hard and raises her head, gives each leg a quick kick that jars her kneecaps, and pulls her tight plastic cap over her head. She looks at the oversized pace clock on the wall—four coloured hands circling, marking the minutes.

"Okay, guys, red hand at the top. Let's get started," says Marcus, the same way he does every practice, no trace of emotion, no sign this is a challenge, or a joke.

Sadie shrugs at Bogdan, who tightens his swimsuit string, pushing his hand down the sides of his suit, as if he has something to tuck in. This set will take them past the allotted hour and it's supposed to be a specialty practice, usually designated for technique work. They may still have to do the regular workout once they're done.

"Fuckin' hell," says Bogdan with one last fierce tug on his suit. He's careful to say it quietly enough that Marcus doesn't hear. "This is probably for your benefit, Ms. Olympian."

Marcus does overhear that one. "This, Bogdan," he says "is for everyone's benefit. We're a team and you have Nationals in six weeks." *Nationals don't mean shit in an Olympic year* is what he doesn't say. "You could sneak in for carding if you knock off some time," he adds, trying to lure Bogdan in with the promise of a little extra cash. Sadie looks away, knowing that in comparison with the Olympics, a shot at the pennies of carding means nothing.

The red hand hits the top and Sadie slams off the wall, arms overhead and shoulders pressed into her ears, pulling herself into herself. *The smaller I can make my body, the less energy I will expend, the faster I will go.* Her legs kick hard, propelling her through the water and finally to the surface. Her right arm rounds the water—an arm over a keg barrel—and pulls the water so it pulses by her body. Then the next arm and the next arm—each pull moving more water than the last.

One, two, three, breathe. One, two, three, breathe. She slides easily into the rhythm of her stroke, suddenly alert. She's five metres behind Bogdan and they circle steadily around the black line on the pool's bottom—up on one side, back on the other. Bogdan could go a bit faster, but he holds Sadie's pace and the pair forms a strong current, helping each other along. The worry of the challenge has faded and Sadie's now in each stroke. The even splashing of her own arms, her own feet, soothes her. Her breathing fills her ears. She sees the black T on the pool floor, a T that marks two metres to the wall. She takes one firm stroke towards the wall, then pulls both arms up towards her face, bends at the hips, knees to the chest, and flips her legs over, doing a half somersault, heels close to her butt. Her feet bounce evenly on the wall and she pushes hard, pulls her body back into a streamline, herself into herself. She doesn't think. She acts. Her body knows the movements. She repeats three more lengths and pulls into the wall, making sure to breathe towards the pace clock so she can check her time. 1:02. Eight seconds rest and forty-nine more hundreds to go.

"Sadie—watch yourself on the walls," Marcus shouts through his cupped hands. "No breathing. Three strokes in and three strokes out." Marcus writes something down on his clipboard. "Same for you, Bogdan. Anyone breathes into the walls, the hundred doesn't count."

Sadie takes deep, even breaths—if she gulps, she'll cramp—and she watches the red hand of the pace clock. Three, two, one: push and streamline. Each hundred blends into the next. She and Bogdan rarely speak, saving their energy, except the occasional, "Good work, keep it up," rasped out between breaths. "Halfway there! Twenty-five more!" Bogdan does most of the cheering, sullen and fake though it may be. Sadie's having a hard time catching her breath and needs those few seconds between hundreds to bring her heart rate down.

Marcus watches Sadie closely, his pen attacking his clipboard, as he shouts commands.

"High elbows, Sade. You're flinging your arms now that you're tired. Control the stroke. Good technique when you're tired means good technique in a race."

"The streamline's gotta be tighter. Pull your arms in so your biceps are pressed against the back of your head. I know it's hard work—swimming fast is hard work."

"Don't plant your feet on the wall. Bounce. Your legs should be pushing before your feet even hit the wall. It's a hot potato. Anticipate."

"You're lifting your feet out of the water. That won't move you anywhere. Keep all your kick under water."

"Control, Sadie. You're flailing again." His voice is smooth and strong. He is stating the obvious, his tone implies, and she must follow his directions.

Sadie nods, her chest heaving. She tries to do as he says, tries to fix her kick without losing her arms, to fix her arms without changing her breathing, to fix her breathing without screwing up her turns. She thinks of all this and she watches the red hand: Three, two, one, go! Three, two, one, go! She forces out the occasional, "Good work, Bo. Keep it up." But her whispered cheers mix with her heavy breathing and she doesn't know if anyone even hears them. Once she gets past the middle mark, past the twenty-fifth hundred, *you're making it, you're making it* becomes her swimming rhythm.

Marcus leaves the deck on the twenty-ninth hundred and doesn't come back until the thirty-second. Sadie sees him called to the pool manager's office and watches through the glass window as he talks on the phone. Bogdan and Sadie keep going on the pace time, enjoy the five seconds of silence after each hundred, give up on their weak cheers.

"This is fucking bullshit," sputters Bogdan, making a horking noise deep in his throat and spitting forcefully into the next lane.

Marcus is back too soon. "Your head is too high in the water, Sadie. Press your forehead down. Even when you breathe, I only want to see half your face out of the water."

Sadie knows this, knows that the water will dip down around her mouth, creating a tiny hole from which she can inhale air. She doesn't have to lift her mouth out of the water to breathe. She presses her head down and keeps swimming.

"Last five. Let's see them faster. I want them all negative split—the second fifty faster than the first."

They don't waste the breath to respond, just push off and go—faster turns and harder kick. Once again, they find faster when they thought there was no faster left. Even Bogdan doesn't say a word.

An echoing *thud thud thud* fills Sadie's ears. Even though she's soaked with cool water, her neck sweats when she lifts it from the pool. Her face feels blood red.

She pulls into the wall on number fifty and breathes towards the clock. 1:05. YES. Bogdan holds a finger over one nostril and snorts the contents of the other into the poolside gutter, then pushes off again, floating on his back towards the other end. Sadie holds onto the edge and lets her whole body fall under the water's surface. Cool water caresses her head. She pulls off her cap and lets the relief wash through her hair. Her arms scream with muscle fatigue and she lets her grasp fall from the pool ledge, lets her body sink further into the cool.

"Good job, Sadie," Marcus says when she comes up for air. He extends his hand for a shake, an unusual gesture for him.

"Hey, your mom called," he says casually, scratching a sideburn and studying his clipboard.

31

Sadie feels her forehead wrinkle, and somewhere behind her exhaustion realizes she should register alarm. No one calls during practice.

"Something's happened to your grandmother. You're supposed to meet your family at Foothills Hospital after practice. Two hundred metres easy and you can go. That's it for today." He stops and looks over his clipboard as if to make sure. "Yep, see you tomorrow morning."

My grandma? Sadie wants to say. *What is it? What do you mean another two hundred and then go?*

But she doesn't. She knows she's lucky to get this much information from him, knows she's lucky he took the message at all. *No calls during swimming* is the rule, and there's no such thing as an exception. A successful athlete, Marcus would say, must block out the rest of the world, must concentrate on the task at hand. There will always be crises, there will always be emergencies; the athlete who is going to succeed under pressure must learn to draw into the body, to perform despite *any* distraction.

Sadie does her two-hundred-metre swim-down very slowly, each stroke exact, each turn precise and graceful, then pulls herself heavily, awkwardly, from the pool and drips her body to the showers, to the change room, to Copper Bullet, and to the Foothills Hospital in the blowing snow.

Seven

*I*nside the CBC studio, there's a single wrestling mat. Tables and chairs crowd each of its four sides: VIP spectator seats run along the south and west sides, the judges' tables along the east side, and cameras and lighting across the north side. The studio is pink, and Digger can't get the weird colour out of his head. He's about to wrestle some of the biggest matches of his life and the place is pink. Every wall is the colour of cotton candy, and six feet off the floor along the walls runs a foot-thick border in a jello pink.

"Ah, frosted rose. Absolutely lovely," he says to Ben in a high-pitched voice, biting the inside of his cheeks.

The seats are not the high-school bleachers wrestling fans are used to. Instead, there are rows of plush maroon armchairs, like the seating at an upscale movie theatre or an opera house. The place doesn't even smell like a wrestling meet. Not a hint of foam mats stale with male sweat. Here it smells like new plastic, like freshly unwrapped furniture.

From the third row up, all the seats are empty. The cameramen have corralled all the "fans"—family, friends, and other wrestlers—into the front rows, so the place will look full on the TV.

Saul warns Digger that the camera lights will be hot.

"Great, because I don't sweat enough already," says Digger, rolling his eyes.

Saul stands with his short legs spread wide and his hands on

33

his hips. He too stares in disgust at the pink walls. "Well, if anyone wants to score on you, he'd better do it within the first thirty seconds or you'll be too slippery to get a hold of."

But Digger knows the downside is that the referees might keep stopping his matches to towel off his arms, legs, chest, back. The breaks will give his opponent a chance to rest—an impediment to Digger's standard wear-down technique. Stamina is his biggest asset. He needs to be able to use it. Guys with fast-twitch fibre muscles prefer matches with short, intense bursts of energy; Digger is all slow-twitch fibre—strong but slow—and likes his matches long and steady.

Mitch Filson, an ex-Olympian, sits at the camera table while a technician mikes him. He'll be the commentator for the TV, but no one in this building will hear what he says. No one in this audience needs a commentator. Anyone who would bother to come watch wrestling will understand what's happening. The CBC personnel will be the only ones who don't, and they won't want to know. They'll joke about two men rolling around on the floor together.

A quick look around this glammed-up competition space and Digger wishes he were back in University of Calgary's sweatbox. Somewhere more real.

Ben gawks too. "Pink, man! Pink? You've gotta be kiddin' me."

"Yeah, let's find a warm-up room. This cotton-candy pink is giving me cavities."

"Okay, guys," Saul steps in. "But make sure you're comfortable with this room. Like it or not, this is where you're wrestling the Olympic qualifiers. It'll be no time for a toothache." He points them downstairs to a more subdued wrestling room, one with real wrestling mats that smell like sweat, the way they're supposed to.

As they sit with their backs against the wall, lacing up their boots, Fly walks in, bag of barbeque chips in hand.

"Still eatin' shit!" Digger laughs, jumps up, and slaps him on the back.

"You AWOL, dude? Or'd they give you a get-out-of-jail-free card?" Ben finishes lacing his boot and leaps to his feet.

"They let me out," he says, shoving another salty chip in his mouth, "with a warning not to wrestle. They said if they see me back there tonight, they're leaving me on the doorstep to die." He laughs, but Digger knows that not wrestling is killing him. "Well, I'll leave you guys to do what you gotta do. Just wanted you to know I'm here." Another round of high-fives and Fly and his barbeque chips are gone.

Ben and Digger find themselves a space among the other wrestlers grunting and contorting on the warm-up mats. They warm up in sweat shorts and old, ratty T-shirts. Each wears his favourite "lucky" shirt, Ben his Team Canada shirt from the year he made the National Team for Commonwealths, and Digger an old Brock University shirt, from his undergrad days in Ontario. The Brock shirt is so faded the logo has all but disappeared, and the white material is so transparent that the colour of Digger's nipples shows through. The shirt is Digger's lucky charm, but it wouldn't even make a good dishrag. The ripped seam down the right side shows off Digger's lats and abs.

Other pairs of wrestlers just like them litter the mats, each duo claiming an eight-foot squared section of mat and performing a kind of choreographed grunting dance.

Digger shoots for Ben's leg and Ben gives it up easily, lets Digger follow through. Up and over, they neatly swing to the floor, Digger on top and Ben face down underneath.

"Smooth single leg, Digs. Perfect," Saul calls from the sidelines.

Digger wraps both arms around Ben's middle and rolls, pulling Ben with him. Digger arches as his own back faces the mat and he pulls Ben over top. They end where they began—Ben face down on the mat, Digger laying on top—but that'd be two points Digger for exposing his opponent's back to the mat.

"The dreaded Digger gut wrench," says Ben from the bottom.

Both jump to their feet and this time Digger lets Ben take a leg. They move, reach, and roll, sometimes stopping when they roll too close to another pair of grapplers. Soon they have a good sweat going and both lift their shirts to wipe the stinging sweat from their eyes. Only once does Digger stop to massage a stinger shooting down his neck.

"That's good, guys. Now scrimmage a bit. Get your heart rates up," says Saul after twenty minutes. Saul plays the encouraging coach role today only—for the Olympic Trials—saving his usual abrasive insults for the return to Calgary.

Digger and Ben start going hard now, pushing at each other's bodies, grabbing each other's wrists, shooting for each other's legs. Digger listens to the sound of Ben's feet—quick and full of energy—and his breathing—growing rapid but not heavy. Neither gives up a point now. Another ten minutes and Saul calls Digger aside.

Digger follows Saul down a hall scattered with wresters, some stretching, others galloping, some simply standing with eyes closed and foreheads pressed against the wall. The sharp smell of sweat makes Digger's eyes water. Saul walks without words until he finds a secluded spot and leans his back against the wall. Digger stops across from Saul, leaning against the facing wall. The narrow hallway leaves little room; their knees almost touch. Neither smiles, and Saul holds Digger's eyes for a long time, saying nothing. Digger refuses to drop his gaze.

"You're ready, Digger."

"Yep," he forces out, hoping he sounds convinced.

"You have to remember—it's just another match. Don't put too much pressure on yourself. You've wrestled Harrison dozens of times. You know how to beat him. You're the better wrestler. Just go out there and show it." Saul finishes and sets his mouth in a straight line.

Digger stares at Saul's cauliflower ears, the hardened cartilage, the misshapen bulges, the swollen-over passages to the inner ears. "Easy as that," Digger half smiles, trying not to think of the two previous Olympic qualifiers that were supposed to be just as easy.

Today's qualifier is a ladder structure, with Digger placed on top by virtue of his first-place finish at the last Senior Nationals. Everyone else has to battle it out to see who gets to wrestle him for first place.

Harrison is second, so unless one of the ladder-climbers beats him, maybe Spencer the big dumb kid from Lakehead in Thunder Bay, which is unlikely, the battle for the eighty-five kilogram Olympic spot will be between Digger and Harrison, old rivals who have met at the National Championship finals the last three years in a row. Digger always beats him at Nationals. Olympic Trials, though, they've not been Digger's meet.

"You know Harrison's style," says Saul. "He's lazy but dangerously explosive. Don't underestimate him and don't let him use his tricks. He'll sit back and let you do all the work. When you're tired, he'll catch you for a couple of points and then play defense until the end of the match. You have to wrestle smarter than that. Make him do some work."

Harrison's passive style is awkward for Digger, a workhorse who likes to go full out right from the start. Harrison has a low centre of gravity and flexible hips he's hard to take down and turn, tricky to score on. But fast enough to sneak in a flashy move once Digger's worn himself out.

"Don't try to rack up the points. Remember you only have to be up by one to win. Show some patience. Don't always try to score. Sometimes you just wait."

Digger nods, trying to let the advice sink into his body, attempting to understand it physically. Intellectually, he knows that it's good advice, but it's not the way his body wrestles. Once he's on the mat, patience will be the last thing that comes naturally. His body wants to go, to fight, to score, to sweat. He *thinks* at practice, not in a match. In matches, he wrestles on instinct alone.

He breathes slowly and evenly, trying to instruct his body on the virtues of patience: this time he'll wait Harrison out.

"Okay, then," Saul bats him lightly on the head with his clipboard. "We're good to go. Your match will be near the end. I want you to stay down here. Relax. Do some visualizations. You don't need to watch the other matches and get all worked up." Saul's heavy hand rests on Digger's shoulder. "See you out there."

Digger stays in the hallway for a minute, turns to rest his

forehead against the cool concrete wall, tries to slow his breathing. He knows he can't rid himself of nerves and the best thing to do is control the symptoms. *If you can hide the body's signs of nervousness, you can convince yourself you're not nervous.* He takes three more deep breaths and walks slowly back to the warm-up room.

Eight

The doctor—a nondescript man she wouldn't recognize if she saw him on the street in ten minutes—meets Sadie at the intensive care unit. Eva had a heart attack in the afternoon while Sadie was working at the cage. No one told her, because they didn't want to interrupt her afternoon practice. They chose, instead, to call Marcus and have him send Sadie over once practice was finished. The doctor assures Sadie that Eva is now resting comfortably.

"Will she be okay?" Sadie asks him.

"She's eighty-two years old. Okay becomes a relative word."

"Is she dying?"

He looks into her face now and whatever he sees there—grief, fear, loathing—impels him to say more. "She's not well and has not been well for some time," he sighs and rubs the back of his neck. "Her heart is weak. Her lungs are filled with phlegm. There's a low-grade infection. Her blood sugar is high, her blood too thin. She hasn't been taking her medication properly. There are signs her kidneys are starting to go. If she gets out of here, she won't be able to go back on her own. She will need full-time care."

Sadie lets this deluge hit her. "But she cooked for me. This morning."

"Mmm. It seems she has been doing a lot of things she shouldn't do." He pauses and Sadie studies his face for the first time. She sees that his eyes are red, and his dark hair could use a good combing.

"A lot of seniors fight the loss of their independence," he continues. "With your grandma, I believe this attack marks the official defeat in that battle."

He tilts his head towards Eva's curtained bed. Sadie notices that his eyes are hazel, the ends of his hair curl slightly around his ears and need trimming. "What you can do is be with her," he says. "She'll appreciate your company when she wakes."

He nods and looks as if he might even reach out to Sadie's shoulder, but he turns and hurries away, gesturing to a nurse down the hallway.

Sadie sits by Eva's bed and stares at the three metal bars encasing Eva's mattress, scared to look at her face. When she does raise her eyes to her grandmother's, she sees that the skin around Eva's eyes is a grayish blue. Her mouth hangs lax. She's not wearing her teeth. She looks 102 instead of 82 like she did this morning at breakfast. Sadie reaches for her hand and feels the cold bones. Were her fingers always this bony? There seems to be no flesh at all. Eva doesn't open her eyes and Sadie watches the screen monitor above her head, trying to divine where her grandmother is right now. The heart rate reads 138. Is that high for her? Now it dips to 66. Is that too low? Too erratic? Should she get someone? She wonders what the flat blue line means. It's followed by a canary-yellow question mark. The lollipop-green line is the most mesmerizing. It juts erratically up and down—one time looking like a medieval castle, the next time like the Rocky Mountains. If she stares long enough, the lines and colours are beautiful. She forgets what she's looking at.

Eva's arms look the worst. They're dead already. *Skin like leather.* But it's not like leather. It's skin like no skin, skin like decayed skin, skin that has been taped together with clear plastic, red and purple blood and flesh showing through. The flesh falls loose from her bones, barely clinging, and the skin looks like the dried-up paper on a roll of garlic sausage, ready to peel off. In some places, the skin folds, doubles and triples over itself, yellowed. Sadie almost believes she could get her fingernails underneath the skin and peel it off layer by layer to expose the greasy meat below.

"Sadie?" a weak parched whisper rises from the pillow.

"Gran!" Sadie quickly wipes her eyes on her shoulder, the stiff cold material against her face reminding her that she's still wearing her parka. "Are you trying to scare us all to death? If you wanted me to come visit tonight, you just had to ask!"

"Water . . ."

Not getting the usual smiling *harrumph*, Sadie doesn't know what else to say.

She fumbles with the blue plastic jug on Eva's bedside table. As the water pours into the plastic cup, she remembers she hasn't had a drink since practice. Her mouth is dry and sour. Her gut feels rotted. She wants to raise the whole jug to her mouth, guzzle the entire litre into her stomach. Instead, she unwraps a straw, inserts it into a cup of water, bends the straw at its fold, and holds it to Eva's lips. Sadie palms the back of Eva's head, feels its heat as she lifts her head towards the cup. Eva can't easily get her lips around the straw and Sadie jabs her in the cheek twice before getting the straw into Eva's mouth. Finally, Eva takes two long draws of water, then falls back on the pillow, eyes closed, veins showing on her lids.

"Oh Sadie," she shakes her head back and forth, "I never wanted to get this old."

"Grandma! You're not that old. You were buzzing around the kitchen just this morning. You'll be fine. You're tougher than that!" Sadie takes pride in her own toughness, uses that pride to rise above her body's pain.

But Eva's ear has fallen to her right shoulder and the muscles around her mouth hang loose. Sadie kisses the papery cheek, knowing her grandmother would be embarrassed to be in public without her teeth for so long, and steps into the hallway, grabs a Diet Coke from the vending machine, and jogs through the cold to her old car in the parkade.

Nine

*D*igger finds a quiet corner in the warm-up room behind some rolled-up mats, the ones CBC must've decided weren't good enough for television, and lies on the ground, his legs pressed up against the wall. His eyes are closed and he knows he must look as if he's sleeping, but he's not. He's playing his upcoming match over and over—seeing each second of the five-minute bout playing out just as he wants it to: He waits for Harrison to make a move and open himself up, get off balance; Digger scores early, catching him in an inside trip and slamming him to the ground, then plays the defensive game. No showboating. He only has to win by one. Each time, he comes out ahead—just by one or two points, but always ahead. One time, just for fun, he pins Harrison's back to the mat and wins in the first twenty seconds, but the rest of the times, he pictures himself wrestling cautiously, wisely—waiting for the right moment, forcing Harrison to do something, to put himself in a risky position, just as Saul has told him to.

The room is strangely quiet. He hears rustling and the occasional thump as a pair of wrestlers hits the floor, but not the hooting and hollering, the loud laughter, the occasional swearing that's usually in the warm-up room. No one here smiles or even meets each other's eyes.

A hazy sleep tugs at Digger, so he jumps up and quickly jogs around the outside of the warm-up mats. First a regular jog. Then once with high knees. Once kicking his heels to his butt. Once swinging his legs straight out and leaning forward to touch his toes.

In the corner, a TV plays the pink matches from upstairs. A few guys stand around watching, nervously gnawing on their fingers. Ben's one of them—face focused on the screen—and as Digger jogs by, he slaps him on the butt.

"G'luck, buddy." Then over his shoulder, "Not that luck'll have anything to do with it." Ben must be up soon, because he's placed third at his weight and has to climb the ladder. But Digger can't think about him.

Last trials, Digger watched everybody, cheered for everybody, took his own win for granted. He regretted being a team player when Harrison beat him 3–2 and took his spot in the Atlanta Olympics.

Digger stops facing the wall and lifts his arms over his head, presses his palms into the cement tiles, stretching out his shoulders, bends down to a fountain and takes a long deep drink, then slides down to the floor to stretch his legs. His eyes fall on the TV screen and he can just make out his mom and dad in the second row of the bleachers. His dad's wide frame is clear in any crowd. At five foot eleven and three hundred pounds, he fills his seat and crowds into his wife's. Digger's mom sits like a young girl, with her knees pulled to her chest. Even at this distance, Digger can tell they're nervous, deliberately looking away from each other. His dad stares towards the door instead of the mat. One hand lies across his face and Digger knows he's gnawing on his thumb as he used to do at every major tournament. Digger's mom will pull on his arm, make him stop, but minutes later the thumb will be back in his mouth.

Digger hasn't talked to them since they arrived in Toronto, hasn't even thought of them, actually. Normally, he'd be running out between matches to chit-chat, see how their hotel is, how they slept, where they went for breakfast. He would've gone for dinner with them last night at the hotel, where his dad would've ordered the biggest slab of red meat on the menu and drunk a full bottle of red wine. His mother would've acted like a stranger, unsure of what to say to this hulking wrestler she saw only once a year now. Digger would've been left to make conversation, asking about weather in Hazleton, the latest school board politics, how her garden's looking. But this weekend, he's letting them take care of themselves.

Really, he's surprised they came. They used to be at every meet and every fundraiser—never missed an opportunity to travel with him or to place a write-up in the local newspaper. His mom would write the articles, filled with boasts, and sign them with Saul's name (better that such boasting come from the coach than the parents). Both Digger's parents were stupid with excitement for the last two Olympics—you'd think they were competing themselves. In 1992 his mom had already taken eight months of Spanish lessons but lost her chance to put them to use when he didn't even qualify for Barcelona. *No Pain, No Spain*, they tell you. *Plenty of Pain, No Spain anyway*, they don't. In 1996 his mom reserved five-star lodging—a big splurge for two schoolteachers—and had to sell the reservation on the Internet when Digger didn't make it. Not much was said, but he knew his dad wished there'd been fewer lead-up articles in the *Hazleton Free Press*, knew they quickly tired of explaining why Digger wouldn't be going after all. As Digger approached thirty, they came less and less. As a Phys Ed teacher, Digger's dad was forced to feign interest in the athletic achievements of other people's kids. Doped out on antidepressants, he could manage it. Throw in some booze and he wasn't so successful. In the end, one too many students complained about booze on the gym teacher's breath and he was forced into early retirement. Digger's mom put on her blinders—ignoring people's comments—and continued to teach, while her husband continued to drink. Eventually, both retired and parked a little trailer in Arizona, where they passed most of the winter. But here they are, having flown in from the South to watch his third try. *Third time lucky*, he hopes.

He pops up and does some jumping jacks. *Forget about the last times. Focus on this time.* He looks for the door. Fresh air is what he needs.

When there's only one match left until Digger's, Saul comes to collect him. Saul doesn't say anything, just puts his thumb and forefinger around the back of Digger's neck and squeezes, then makes a fist with his other hand and hits the bottom of it on top of Digger's fist. There's nothing left to say.

Too quickly, Digger's in his corner, stripping down to his singlet. The fans in the bleachers run together, a smudge of colours. He doesn't try to pick anyone out, face or voice, just ignores the far-off mess of noise.

Digger can see that Saul is talking to him. Saul's lips are moving. But his words slide away before connecting with Digger's brain. Digger jumps up and down, slaps his thighs hard to wake up his quads and hamstrings. Saul's hand hits Digger's back between the shoulder blades and pushes him towards the centre of the mat.

Digger's heart beats quick and loud—with excitement, not nerves, he tells himself. The ref goes through the usual ritual: runs his hands down Digger's arms and then his opponent's, checking that they're not too slippery, that their fingernails aren't too long. Harrison—short and stocky—stands across from Digger. Good. Harrison must've beat the big Lakehead kid in the semi-final. The Lakehead kid would've thrown off Digger's visualization. He has plans for Harrison.

Digger wears red, Harrison blue.

The ref holds his hand between the wrestlers, indicating that they must shake hands. Harrison steps forward first, then Digger, and they touch hands quickly without meeting eyes. Digger's sweating already and his hand feels slippery against Harrison's dry palm. Digger raises both hands to his own face, three hard slaps to his cheeks to get him going, three bunny-hops backwards. Another ritual. Then he moves to the centre, and the ref blows his whistle for the match to start. This is it: five minutes to determine whether Digger is ever going to be an Olympian. Or not.

He lowers himself into his stance—knees bent, arms forward, feet shoulder-width apart, a solid base for balance. *I'm givin' ya nothing* runs through his head. *Today you're working for it, lazy bastard.*

Digger's own voice is all he can hear, though he knows others must be yelling—Saul, Fly, his dad all shouting for him. One word echoes in Digger's mind—*Patience*.

Two legs, a torso, two arms: that's all he sees. At first he's not really trying to score at all—not trying to force Harrison off balance and gain control—just trying to tire him out. Harrison's rushing at him, hands flying at Digger's head, his wrists, his legs. Digger batters him off, staying low and blocking Harrison's hands with a forearm, holding Harrison's wrist tight, pushing his head hard into Harrison's forehead, reaching for a hold of his other arm. Harrison's breath sounds slow and shallow, his grip heavy and strong on Digger's arm, his feet a light patter on the mat. There's a lot of match left. Digger reaches for Harrison's leg, could get a point by lifting and forcing Harrison to the mat, but is careful not to overreach, doesn't want to teeter himself off balance. Main thing now is to maintain a solid, safe position. Hips underneath him. Harrison scrambles, his legs slippery with sweat. Digger can't reach the leg and has to remember not to topple himself off centre, open himself up for Harrison to score. Digger keeps pressing forward into Harrison's space, cue words (*dance, move, breath*) bouncing in his head as he presses a shoulder into Harrison's gut, stretches his right hand for a grip on Harrison's thigh. He won't force something that's not there. That's how Harrison'll sneak his point, waiting for Digger to stumble off balance exhausted, and then explode, forcing him to the mat. Still, Harrison's been fighting off Digger's heavy hands for a full minute and he's tired too. Digger listens again. Harrison breathes in deep, laboured rasps now. Good. And he stinks of sweat, but no points have been scored. Legs tire first, so Digger keeps his eyes on Harrison's knees: straightened legs will mean fatigue has set in.

Digger wants a point and gets a good grip on Harrison's wrist, squeezes and pulls, trying to climb the arm like a rope and get control of half Harrison's body. But Harrison's on the run—pushing his free hand against Digger's chest, pulling his upper body back—and he hops out of bounds. The ref blows his whistle. *Ha! A warning for running away, chickenshit.*

"Caution, Blue. You gotta wrestle." The ref looks to Digger for direction—Digger can decide if he wants Harrison up or down—and Digger points to the ground.

Harrison gets down on all fours, his explosiveness less of a threat when he's not standing. Digger gets behind him and places his hands on the small of Harrison's back, heart beating fast. Harrison's singlet sticks to his body, wet through with sweat. If he's tired already, this is a good chance to turn him for two points. *Score early, Digs, score early.*

The whistle blows and they both lunge forward, Harrison trying to squirm out of Digger's hold while Digger squeezes both arms tight around Harrison's waist. Digger's gotta turn Harrison's back to the mat for some points. Digger's face pours sweat, slippery against Harrison's back. His forearms press against Harrison's soaked singlet. Harrison's knees fall forward and the two men land flat on the ground. Digger drives his legs into the mat; his arms throb, but he keeps them tight around Harrison and tries for a gut wrench. Harrison twists and squirms, digging fingers into Digger's forearms, peeling Digger's hands off his torso as quickly as Digger can get them on. Digger breathes loud and heavy now, but so does Harrison. Both drenched, their bodies slide against each other. All Digger's effort is focused on trying to clasp his arms around Harrison's torso. *Fat fuck, I can barely reach.*

Digger's chin digs into Harrison's back, feeling the vertebrae hard against his face. *Might as well make this as uncomfortable as possible.* He watches the ref out of the corner of his eye. Is he going to blow the whistle for inaction? *Tick-tock. I'm not turning him. Time's running.* Digger's rib cage heaves with breath but he tells himself, *If I'm this tired, Harrison must be ready to collapse.* Digger slides down to Harrison's legs, digs his chin into Harrison's ass, and tries to lace up the ankles—twisting one over the other, squeeze and roll, force him on his back that way. *Shit—not working*—Harrison's strong limbs press hard into the mat with all his force. He won't budge. Digger slides back up Harrison, forces the palm of his hand hard into Harrison's lower back so he can't escape.

The whistle goes. "Inaction. Wrestlers stand."

It's my match, Digger thinks, slapping himself hard on the forehead with the word *my*.

They stand. The whistle bleats.

Digger doesn't make an immediate move, just leans forward in his stance and watches Harrison—slows things down to think for a second, checks Harrison's hands and hips. He's a diamond of legs and hands: the second he tilts off balance, Digger will attack. But Harrison doesn't try anything either, just moves around and fakes shots towards Digger's legs. *Lazy fucker.*

The next fake, Harrison reaches too far, gets his hips off-centre. Digger reacts immediately, grabs hold of both Harrison's arms—pulls them hard towards the ground so Harrison teeters forward—and swings his leg fast, catching Harrison's heel and trying for a quick foot sweep.

Shit! Harrison's too fast. Digger's swung off balance with the swing of his foot. Harrison catches Digger around the waist, scoots behind, pushing his head into Digger's back. They go sprawling out of bounds. Digger almost falls to the ground and Harrison's behind him, arms around Digger's waist from behind. Digger knows Harrison'll be staring at the ref, trying to look like he's in control for a point. *Cheap theatrics.*

"One Blue."

An iffy call. Digger looks to the ref, then to Saul. "We were out of bounds," Digger shouts, spraying sweat and spit in Saul's direction.

Saul moves both hands in a downward motion. Telling Digger to cool it, let it go. *Focus on my own match, not the referee.* Digger's down one to zero.

He can imagine his mom pulling her knees tighter into her chest and his dad pushing the palms of his hands into his head. Pink walls close in around him. *Block it out, block it out*, he chants to himself, walking back to the centre circle. *Breathe.*

He lifts a hand to wipe the sweat dripping from his nose, itching his face. His eyes sting. He tries wiping his forearm across them, but his arm is just as soaked. Harrison's stalling now—standing knees

48

bent, facing Digger, cupping a hand behind Digger's head every few seconds, pulling down on his neck, so it looks like he's trying something, but not pushing for anything that will put him at risk of losing balance, being scored on. Digger knows Harrison's best bet is to hold Digger off and win with his one point. But Digger keeps the pressure on: he shoots at Harrison's right leg, but Harrison is too fast. Digger grabs Harrison's right arm just below the elbow, but they're both slippery now—his hand slides off. He can't reach too far, can't give Harrison any chances. *If he gets up any more points, I'm fucked.* Digger dives for both legs and Harrison does two quick steps backwards. Out of bounds. Both slap to the mat with a wet thud. *Tweet.* Digger rolls to his back and stares up at the ceiling: pink. He springs to his feet.

"Blue, you're backing up. Caution."

Digger nods. Perfect—Harrison's not getting away with his shit. The refs are being good about calling the cautions. For a change. Without looking at Saul, Digger signals the ref to put Blue down. Harrison standing makes Digger uncomfortable.

Harrison's on all fours and Digger's behind him, struggling again for the gut wrench. Digger's cheek slides against Harrison's drenched back and his face lifts and falls in time with Harrison's breathing. That breathing's all Digger hears. He can feel Harrison getting tired—his muscles lax and sluggish so that his grip's weakened and his hands feel lighter, an old woman slapping at mosquitoes—and Digger gets his arms around Harrison easily, clasps his right hand around his left wrist and pulls into Harrison's gut, but both wrestlers are slippery now. It's like wrestling a seal dunked in oil. Digger tries to roll him to the right, digging his chin into Harrison's spine and using the full force of both legs to push. Harrison grunts but it's as though his shins and hands are glued to the mat; he doesn't budge. Digger leans, pulling with all his force to the left. No better. Right again. *Tweet.*

"Inaction. Stand."

Digger shakes his arms and sweat splatters to the mat. He slaps himself once in the face as the whistle tweets to wrestle. Harrison's blurry through the sweat now, but Digger dives at him again. The whistle tweets again and Digger slams a foot hard into the foam mat. Half-time and he's down.

Saul throws a white towel at Digger and then uses it to wipe sweat off Digger's arms, chest, and back. He talks low and steady, close to Digger's ear.

"Calm down, Digger." He presses the towel against Digger's chest, reminding him to control his breathing. "What was that weak dive at the end? You're lucky you didn't end up on your ass." He keeps his voice soft, whispering.

Digger doesn't say anything, tries to slow his breathing and lets Saul spin him around to wipe off the sweat pouring down his back.

Saul drops the towel and grabs Digger's fingers, shakes his arms, sending ripples to his shoulders. The ripples remind Digger of the stinging pain in his traps. "It's okay," Saul continues. "He's getting tired."

I'm not?

The ref blows for the wrestlers to return to centre.

Saul pats Digger's lower back. "Hey, Digs, you can't gut wrench him. Quit trying. Go for the ankle lace or something."

Can't gut wrench him? Whose fucking side are you on?

The whistle cuts the air thick with heat, and Digger and Harrison jostle for position against each other, their hands scrambling to grab hold of each other's wrists, as they butt heads, foreheads pushed tight together. Digger dully registers the pain across his scalp but ignores it, swiping his right foot at Harrison's left. He almost hooks Harrison's ankle, but Harrison quickly jumps away. They stumble but both wobble upright. *Almost got him.*

Well into the second half now and Digger's still down; a lump of "what if . . ." weighs heavily in his stomach. *Dive for his right leg.*

Digger knows he's thinking too much. After a perfect match, he won't remember who did what. He'll have to ask who won. Today, he thinks every move. He catches Harrison's left calf with both hands, lifts it up and up, just above ninety degrees. All he's gotta do is push, give Harrison's one standing leg a swipe of the foot, get Harrison down and over. But Harrison hops back, even with Digger's grip on his foot. Both fall, but just out of bounds. They're on their sides, neither on top. No dominant position, no point. Digger's face hits the mat hard and a sharp pain pinches his trapezoid. His teeth crack together and he swallows hard. If he spits blood on the mat, the ref will stop the match and men in plastic gloves will swarm the mat, mopping and spraying disinfectant. Digger can't afford a break now. His head aches, his eyes sting, and his vision blurs with sweat, but he notices that Harrison breathes even harder, his feet move slower. As soon as the whistle goes, Digger's shoulder hits Harrison in the gut, he's bent over and pushing, chin digging into Harrison's rib cage. Digger needs some points soon or he'll never go to the Olympics. Pink everywhere. How's he supposed to wrestle in pink?

He clasps his hands together around Harrison's waist—a good hold but not a good position, more on the side rather than solidly behind Harrison. Harrison grabs Digger's head and shoulder, balancing himself, but his hands feel light on Digger's neck, not the two-hundred-pound slabs they were four minutes ago. Digger pushes, but still Harrison miraculously manages to stay on his feet and hop out of bounds.

"Another caution, Blue!"

Digger looks at the clock. Forty-five seconds left. He points down to the mat, gasping for breath. Harrison takes his time getting there, trying to sneak a rest. In other years, the asshole would've found a way to undo his shoes—used it as an excuse to take a break. Cheap trick. Now all wrestlers have to tape their shoelaces before the match.

The whistle bleats and Digger lunges forward. His arms are around Harrison's thighs before the two men hit the ground.

Can't gut wrench him? goes through Digger's head. He thinks about trying for the ankles. Harrison squirms wildly, striving for the safe zone at the edge of the mat. *Can't gut wrench him?*

The hell I can't—this prick's going over. Because this time I'm going to Sydney.

He crawls his arms up Harrison's torso, breathes deep, grinds his teeth together, and digs his chin into Harrison's spine. Harrison's face is pressed hard into the mat. Digger jams the hard part of his right hand—the bone along the thumb and heel—just above Harrison's rib cage. Forcing his hands into Harrison's ribs with all of his strength, he lets his breath out in a grunt, squeezing and squeezing. His legs dig into the mat; his thigh muscles throb. He presses and he presses, can feel the air going out of Harrison, can feel Harrison's body becoming part of his own, deflating into Digger—there's as much resistance in him as a bed sheet; he'll turn when Digger does. Still, Digger doesn't loosen his grip; he squeezes tighter, feeling the blood throbbing in his own forehead.

They both let out a deep wailing yowl as Digger rolls him up and over, Harrison's hips popping up in the air as Digger exposes his back to the mat for two points. Harrison's chest heaves for air now—Digger feels his back rising and falling as he easily holds him for five seconds, keeping his arms tight around Harrison's waist, one of Harrison's arms still trapped down his side in Digger's grip. Harrison squirms weakly, trying to shake out of Digger's grip. Digger watches the ref. Five, four, three, two, one. The ref holds up a thumb for Digger's point and Digger quickly pulls his fist back into Harrison's rib cage, pushes his legs hard into the mat, driving, driving—Digger's eyes squeeze shut, his chin hurts forcing itself into Harrison's spine, the hard part of his right hand rams itself into Harrison's ribs, he's barely aware of Harrison as a person squirming for escape. If Digger can roll him over again, that'll be another point. Digger's legs give one last explosive push into the foam mats—and they roll as one, Digger maintaining control as he exposes Harrison's back to the mat.

Five to one for Red! Only fifteen seconds left. Harrison has wiggled out of Digger's arms, but is still splayed flat on his stomach, face pressed into the mat. Digger lies on top for a while, too tired to initiate another move. *Tweet.*

"Inaction. Wrestlers stand."

Digger claps his hands together—once and down low. He wants to raise both hands in the air and cheer, but he's learned to save celebrations for the final whistle. They grapple standing, facing each other, moving slowly, heads bent together, hands touching. Digger won't shoot for Harrison's legs this time—the only way Harrison could win now would be to catch Digger and get him on his back. Digger just holds Harrison's hand and waits, thinking ten, nine, eight, seven . . .

Tweet. Match over. Digger lets go of Harrison's hand and raises one hand in the air. His eyes scan the seats for the place he'd spotted his mom and dad on the TV monitor. They're already moving towards him. Harrison kicks the mat once, but then reaches to shake Digger's hand. The ref holds them each by the hand and pulls them to centre to raise Digger's arm in victory. Sweat still pours into Digger's eyes and down the back of his neck, stinging and itching. *Thank God.* Digger jogs the four steps back to Saul, smiling in his corner.

"Thought you said I couldn't gut wrench him?" Digger says through the sweat pouring over his face, tasting the salt.

Saul laughs and pulls Digger's head under his armpit, rubbing his knuckles against Digger's wet bristle of hair.

Ben and Fly rush to the mat. Grabbing Digger's shoulders, they pull him from Saul, grasping his heavy, sweaty hands, waving them in the air. His parents stand behind Fly and Ben, his dad ferociously shaking Saul's hand—too ferociously? Digger prays he's not drunk—and his mom looking towards Digger and clapping.

Thank God, I'm going. Digger tastes metallic blood and feels as though his teeth are floating. He runs his tongue around the inside of his mouth and spits. Is this the taste of relief? He can see euphoria—can see it on his coach's face, can see it in his friends, in his parents—but all he can think is *Thank God. Thank God. Thank God.*

Six beer mugs rise with a clang. "To Digger!" Five voices compete with the pub's noise. The group, tightly sandwiched into a booth, waits for the appetizers: potato skins, nachos, deep-fried calamari, and five-cheese dip. Fat, fat, and more fat. Digger can feel Fly's thigh pressing into his right side, Ben's elbow into his left, and his dad's knees from across the table. His dad concludes the cheer with, "Off to the Olympics!"—the phrase that has so long eluded him. He's been using the word in every sentence since the match finished: *My son at the Olympics; guess we'll have to book our tickets to the Olympics; not just anyone has real family in the Olympics; Helen's gotta call the Hazleton paper, tell 'em Digger's really going to the Olympics.*

"Finally," Digger says, grinning and shifting his hips to make himself more space.

"Never mind the 'finally'," says his mom, Helen, both her elbows on the table, no room for them at her sides. "You're going . . . and we—Denis and I both—are very proud of you." Digger wonders if she's pinching his dad under the table, because he nods solemnly.

"You bet we are!" hollers Fly. "Diggedy dog! Goin' to The Show!" Fly appears to have forgotten his own failure.

"Going to the Freak Show," Ben mutters.

Digger leans back and feels his arms stick to the pseudo-leather of the booth, feels Ben pull away from him on his left. Ben lost five to four in his final match and hasn't said much since. He's wearing his usual purple velour shirt with the giant collar and brown corduroy pants that flare at the ankle. Before the trials, he'd been yammering about growing a mustache, claimed he could start a trend, but so far he's still clean-shaven. Tonight, his loud appearance signifies more fun than his mood delivers.

The waitress approaches the table, carrying a big round tray at shoulder height. She slams down a giant spread of chicken wings—extra spicy—and two orders of potato skins sweating melted mozzarella.

"Here's something to get you going," she says, tucking a long wisp of stringy hair behind her ear and biting at a steel ring pierced through her lower lip. "You guys look starvin'." Her eyes light on each of the wrestlers and she pulls at her pants that have slid down past two jutting hip bones.

"Are we ever!" says Fly with a chicken wing already halfway in his mouth. "And you should know—we're not just your ordinary hungry boys. When's the last time you served an Olympian?" He sucks the already bare bone in his hand.

She puts her hands on her hip bones—her pants slid down

again—and faces Fly, sucking her lip piercing into her mouth.

"Not me," Fly quickly corrects her. "This here stud." He pronounces stud with two syllables, stu-ud, and pats Digger on the shoulder. "Just qualified today, demolishing all competition, walking to easy victory." No one contradicts Fly. Instead, they all smile.

"Yep, going to the Olympics," adds Digger's dad, "and I can't help but notice that we're completely surrounded by no beer." His eyes sweep the table, indicating the empty glasses as his wife's elbow catches him in the ribs in time with her hissed "DEN-IS!"

The waitress pulls a pad of paper out of the back pocket of her jeans and a pen from behind her ear, makes a quick note. "Well— I'll talk to the manager—I'd say this victory calls for a free pitcher, anyway." And with a flick of her hair, she turns and wiggles her nonexistent ass back to the bar.

"A pitcher of beer? I was hoping she'd give ya a congratulations kiss. A hug at the very least." Fly bounces in his seat, a small mound of chicken bones piling in front of him. Everyone watches Fly pop an entire wing into his mouth then spit the bone out clean.

"That girl?" asks Denis, wrinkling his whole face in disgust. "Too skinny! An *Olympian* needs to marry a big strong girl. Big strong wife means big strong kids."

Digger feels himself sink in his seat. He's heard this speech before. "Right. And big kids mean . . . ?" He knows the answer, of course. A shot at future Olympians. He wonders how his mom feels about this particular obsession of her husband's. She's not exactly huge. Though she was a good athlete—a varsity tennis player when she met her future husband, a national team rugby player. And look at them; they'd made a big kid. And an Olympian.

Fly's already answering, "You don't have to worry about Digger, Denis. Digger loves big girls. Always drooling over the rowers and the swimmers. He wants a girl who hasta turn sideways to fit her shoulders through doorways. He wants her triceps bigger than her—"

"Won't be the same in Sydney without you, Fly." Digger decides to change the subject. "Without either of you," he adds, glancing at Ben.

"Ah, my chances were outside anyway," says Fly, "even if I'd been smart enough to cut weight right. Good enough that my best buddy's going."

"Yeah, bring us back a T-shirt," says Ben into his beer.

"Your chances were outside too, Benny. Liven up," says Fly bravely, considering Ben is twice his size and not in a good mood.

Digger studies his mother's scrunched features and wonders what she makes of this exchange. She spent the last ten years of her career as a kindergarten teacher and always seemed ill at ease with adults. Put her in a room of five-year-olds, though, and she was laughing, clapping, singing, all bent down on one knee, meeting every child on his or her own level. She always seemed happiest playing with kids.

Ben glowers into his empty beer mug. "Outside, hey?" he says with surprising violence. "Someone shoulda told me that six months ago. I coulda found better ways to spend my time." The waitress returns, plopping two pitchers on the table with such force that beer spills out over the tops and splashes the table. Digger's dad heartily grabs the pitcher and refills his own glass, swigging merrily before filling the others. Digger's just glad his dad's not completely relapsing to his rugby days and drinking straight from the pitcher.

Saul leans forward so Ben and Digger hear his words loud and clear over the noise of the pub. "You all wrestled tough," he says, pronouncing each word slowly and carefully. "You put in a good showing, Ben. You can be proud."

"Yeah, well, I'll have to be proud while watching the Olympics on TV." Ben rotates his beer mug in his hands—round and round and round. Digger's mom slides her beer mug away from her on the wet table and excuses herself to go the washroom. Limbs lock and tie together as she climbs over her husband and around Saul, bumping knees with Ben and Digger.

"If your match ended half a minute earlier, you'd be watching on TV with me, Digger," says Ben. "I'm the other guy—the guy with the bad luck."

No one says anything and Digger listens to his dad slurping beer.

Ben studies the table, finally seems embarrassed by the silence. "Sorry, Digs. I don't mean to ruin your party. I'm happy for you, I am." He lifts his beer mug, "To Digger."

Digger's dad is quick to meet it. "Going to *the Olympics*." Except this time it sounds like *'lymkicks*.

"Ruin his good time?" blurts Fly. "As if!" Fly hasn't turned down the volume on his voice at all. "Didja see him rag doll Harrison all over the mat? Roll him this way, roll him that way, roll him whatever way Digs wantsta roll him."

"Yeah, and to think I didn't believe you could gut wrench him," Saul winks at Digger's dad, who's signalling the waitress for more beer.

Digger feels his face muscles loosen into a smile. "Were you mind-gaming me, coach? A thirty-year-old veteran of the National Team and you're playing mind games?"

"Worked, didn't it?" Saul reaches out to shake Digger's hand yet again, but when Digger meets it, Saul pulls his hand back and softly bats Digger across the cheek. Digger's mom has returned and Saul stands to let her into the booth. "I'm off to bed, my boys. Too old for this late-night beer drinking, Mr. Digger, Mrs. Digger," he nods at both of Digger's parents. "Some good work you did here—not a bad kid at all." He looks to his three veteran wrestlers, "Now you guys don't need to stay out all night. Your real work is just about to begin, Digger. Get some sleep." He strolls off, hands deep in his sweat pant pockets as the waitress approaches with two full pitchers of beer.

"Denis, your medication," Helen whispers sharply.

"Forget my m'cashun," Denis slurs. "We're talkin' the 'lymkicks." He puts both hands in the air. "Woo! The 'lymkicks! Woo woo!" He sways back and forth like the lone tree in a prairie windstorm.

Digger feels his neck sweat in shame. "Here we go again," he groans to his friends, "Sorry."

"Fuck it, Digs," Fly says. "Let's hit the Brunswick. With any luck there'll be a Best Ass contest and the women's varsity swim team will be stripped down to their thongs like last time." He jumps from the booth.

Suddenly, cheap recycled draft in plastic glasses sounds delicious.

Digger slinks out of the booth behind Fly. "You got it, mom?" he asks, casting a guilty backwards glance in her direction, watching her pry the beer glass from her husband's grip.

She pronounces each word crisply, "I always have it, son."

At that, Digger and Fly stride out of the pub with Ben shadowing after them.

Ten

Sadie drives into the main entrance of the Foothills Hospital. A brown brick hospital set in rolling brown hills. It's been a dry winter and white snow barely dusts the ground. Brown dominates the landscape: brown grass, brown trees, brown cars. Sadie thinks how much more hopeful she would feel if things looked whiter, cleaner. Or if it were summer and the hospital was nestled in the comfort of green hills. Instead it's a building for the dying, nestled in dead-grass hills. She drives by the Grace Women's Health Centre where her mom works, spending most of her time dealing with infertility, miscarriages, and stillbirths. She pulls Copper Bullet into the closest parking lot to the main building, and the cold wind stings her face as she runs to the hospital's front doors.

In the building's hallways, urgent beeping surrounds her and nurses and doctors bustle quickly in either direction, bumping and jostling against her. She stands, stunned, knowing she's in the way. It's all so clumsy and busy after the two hours she's just spent underwater. She picks a direction and forces her way through the tumult of bodies and sounds, weaving and ducking the chaos, longing for the deafening water.

Once Sadie gets to the little room, she cuts up Eva's roast beef into squares, hands her each piece on a fork. Eva chews. "Mmm. Not much flavour but it's good and tender. A bit more salt maybe. But good." She smiles. The Jorgenson appetite's the last thing to go.

"Want some pear?"

When Eva nods, Sadie takes the little spoon and breaks half a canned pear into bite-sized chunks.

"Wanna chocolate?"

Eva smiles. Chocolate's not allowed. Eva's blood sugar is already too high. Sadie grabs a Lindt chocolate ball out of the bedside drawer. A perfect orb wrapped in red and silver foil. She pulls on the foil ends, watches the globe unravel, and hands the chocolate to Eva.

Eva holds it between her forefinger and thumb, sets it on her tongue, lies back into her pillow with her eyes closed.

"Mmm." Her eyes are shut but her smile is wide.

"Good?" Sadie asks, crushing the shiny foil and stuffing it under wads of Kleenex at the bottom of the trash, where the nurses won't find it.

"Ah, Sadie." Eva's mouth looks lax and sad again with the meal over. "Doctor says my kidneys are going."

Sadie kicks the plastic garbage can under the side table.

"It just takes so long, dying does, so long."

"Don't talk like that, Grandma."

"It's okay. I've had a long life. A good life. Enjoyed my grand-children. But this old bone cage of mine has done all it can for me."

Sadie smiles at Eva's use of bone cage, knows she remembers the phrase from Sadie's rehashing of an English 101 lecture on *Beowulf.*

"I'm going to win a medal for you, Grandma. At the Olympics." Sadie says this out of nowhere; it feels like the only thing she has to offer.

Eva opens her eyes and pushes her hands into the bed by her hips, trying to shift her buttocks so she can get a better look at Sadie. This effort is more than Sadie has seen her expend since that last breakfast she cooked in her little apartment. Sadie hates the sight of Eva straining her weak arms, black and blue from IV needles.

"A medal?" Eva asks. It sounds so much less impressive in her mouth. "Just let it make you happy, girl." She closes her eyes and lets her head fall back on the pillow.

While Eva sleeps, her mouth falling open so that Sadie can see her tongue coated with bits of chocolate, Sadie thinks about the morning's practice. Marcus gave his standard "SAAAYYYDEEE, YOU'RE HERE" greeting, and she turned away, saying nothing. He didn't ask about her grandmother, and Sadie knew the omission was deliberate: the two hours were not about grandmothers. The two hours were about swimming.

This morning had been a pretty standard practice: twelve thousand metres, eight thousand of them at elevated heart rate. Sadie was in a distance lane with Bogdan and Katie, a younger swimmer who might have a chance at national team in three or four years.

Sadie didn't say much to anyone, just got in and swam back and forth, counting the same cracks and wads of gum on the pool floor, noting a particularly large clump of hair in the deep-end drain. Marcus didn't say much either—not until Sadie was twenty-five hundred metres into the practice. Then she glided into the wall and Marcus barked, "Sadie. Out."

Marcus never called anyone out of practice. Sadie jumped out, feeling a nervous tingle in her bladder. Even her body's fluid wanted to escape. She stared at his triceps, wondered how many hours in the weight room it took to keep them so defined long after his swimming career had ended.

"What's the problem, Sadie?"

"No problem." She didn't trust herself with words, could already feel a liquid burn behind her eyes.

"It's clear there's a problem. I've watched you swim enough hours for enough years to know when there's a problem."

"Sorry." She looked towards the pool, eager just to have her head under water.

"Apologize to yourself. That's who you'll be letting down." Marcus put his hand on her forehead and pushed up her face so her eyes met his. "Look, I know your grandmother is sick. But we're short on time here. There's no place for slackers at the Olympics. No slackers and no excuses. You gotta push everything else out of your mind."

Force my own sick grandmother out of my mind? Suddenly, Sadie was angry, the heat of her anger bringing beads of sweat to her upper lip. "All right." She said the words quickly, almost as one syllable, and strode towards the pool, knowing she had to get back in before she said something to piss Marcus off. Then she'd never get out of here. Get back in the pool and get the set finished.

"All right then. Back in," Marcus waved, dismissing her. "Start up with the rest of the lane."

Sadie fought the water, pushing it, pounding it, thrashing against it. She grunted at the walls, swore at the pool's bottom. At the end of practice, she climbed out of the water, felt her face burning red.

"Well, that was certainly faster. But not exactly what you'd call finesse swimming," Marcus commented from the pool's edge. "Try to resolve this by next practice." Marcus patted her shoulder, but Sadie brushed his hand away. In the dressing room, she yanked on her clothes. With T-shirt and sweatpants sticking to her still damp body, she jumped in Copper Bullet and ground his gears straight back to the hospital.

The first days of Eva's stay in the hospital, Sadie quickly falls into a routine. Routines are what she's good at. (Eat) Morning practice (eat), to the hospital (eat), afternoon weights (eat), back to the hospital (eat), evening practice (eat), shift at the cage (eat), back to hospital for a quick good night (eat). Cycle it the next day and the day after that. It doesn't take long for Sadie to realize that Eva is dying. Just not fast enough. Not fast enough for Eva, not fast enough for Sadie.

"Some people fall asleep and just don't wake up," Eva says weakly that afternoon. "Others suffer."

Sadie focuses again on the folds of skin along Eva's forearm. In some places the skin folds and sticks in the air as if Sadie could grasp it and pull it away from the bone, hearing the tear of Velcro.

Sadie holds Eva's shaking hand. Yesterday morning, when Eva had more energy, she told Sadie, "I vibrate. It must be the weakness. Everything's so heavy. My body. Heavy."

Today she's not talking. She lies back, eyes closed, and moans. A long, unconscious, painful sound. Sadie holds Eva's shaking hand

and stares intently at her face—at the broken blood vessels freckling her cheeks—and asks, "What hurts, Grandma? Tell me what hurts." Eva moans. "Grandma, tell me, what hurts?"

If I could just know, Sadie thinks, *maybe I could take on some of her pain.* But Sadie knows everything hurts—Eva's heels, her ankles, her hips, her back, her bum, her stomach, her lungs, her heart, her urethra chafing around the catheter, her veins bristling with IV needles—it all hurts. When Eva opens her eyes, they're filled with a murky fluid. The whites are the colour that day-old tea leaves on the inside of a mug. Sadie holds Eva's vibrating hand and listens to her moan and wishes she would die.

Guilt drips through her.

She keeps sneaking Eva gourmet chocolates that coat her mouth's insides and then stuffing the wrappers in the bottom of the trash so the nurses won't scold her or kick her out. Eva smiles at their cooperation in deception.

Eva's blood sugar is high, but Sadie decides that's the least of her worries.

"Chocolate's not going to kill her," Sadie tells Russ one night at the cage, but then adds, "Or maybe it will, but there are worse ways to go."

Still, a few days later, when Eva's hands start twitching more violently, Sadie suffers. *Did I do this to her*, she wonders, *is it the chocolate?*

Sometimes her dad is there, standing near the doorway, leaning against the wall and looking as though he's holding his breath, as if his mom's dying is an inconvenience to him. "Oh, good you're here—I'll go and let you two visit," he always says. As Sadie walks past him, he whispers, almost growls, "I hate hospitals!" As if anyone likes them. As if death, old age, and sickness were invented as a personal affront to him alone.

Her mother is there more often, before or after her shift, wearing her uniform that looks more like pajamas, loose pants and a long shirt with bright squares of colour. The white dresses suited her so much better. She questions the nurses, checks the charts, refills the water jug—all business, before squeezing Eva's shoulder and striding back to the Grace Women's Health Centre.

Eva has quit wearing her teeth, and the collapse of her cheeks makes her face pointy, unfamiliar. Her bobby pins are gone and greasy hair sticks to her forehead, her cheekbones. While a nurse props Eva's pillows, Eva's gown falls off her shoulder, displaying the top of a bare breast. The nurse reaches over to fix her, while Sadie looks on, hands clasped in her lap.

"You're falling to pieces, sweetie," the nurse says gently.

Sadie has never heard anyone call her grandmother sweetie.

"I don't care anymore," says Eva. She doesn't even open her eyes, doesn't feign a smile.

"You're flashing some skin, Grandma! Did you learn that from your soaps?" Sadie forces an energetic lilt into her voice. Eva doesn't laugh. Maybe she doesn't hear. One side of her mouth slants down. Is it a stroke? From the chocolate? That will happen if her blood sugar gets too high, her blood too thick to run through her veins.

Sadie goes to the bathroom and runs a rough face cloth under the cold water, wrings it out and returns to hold it against her grandmother's forehead. Eva issues a barely audible moan. Sadie thinks of Marcus ordering her to resolve her issues—he seems so small and far away. She considers skipping today's swimming practice altogether as she slowly smoothes the greasy hair out of her grandmother's face, tucks it behind her ears.

Eleven

*D*igger sinks as deep as possible into his plane seat, pulls a sweatshirt over his pounding head. Draft beer. He should know better. That's it, though: the last whoop-up until after the Olympics. No more drinking. Fly fidgets in the seat next to him, tossing from one side to the other, readjusting his pillow, moaning, none of which makes Digger any more comfortable. The flight attendants push a cart up the aisle, and the smell of heated plastic makes Digger gag.

"Never again. I feel like shit."

"You feel like shit? At least you had something to celebrate. I feel like shit *and* like a loser who messed up making weight at the Olympic Trials."

True: Digger has no right to complain.

"Need some pain killers?" Digger reaches into his flight bag and grabs a vial of pills, dumps an assortment into his palm. Big, small, medium, green, yellow, blue, flat, round. "What d'ya feel like?"

"What are these ones?" Fly grabs the biggest.

"Percocet? No. Muscle relaxant? Or maybe anti-inflammatory. Let's see . . . those ones I got after my knee surgery. Yeah, anti-inflammatory. That'll do nothing. Take one of these. With some food or you'll be barfing all over my shoes."

"All righty, Dr. Digger." Fly washes the Percocet back and pulls his jacket over his head, settles in for the long flight to Calgary. "All righty, Dr. Tom," he mumbles from under the jacket before falling to sleep.

Digger looks out the window but the plane's right in a cloud and there's nothing to see. He tries to remember the last time anyone called him his name. Thomas Stapleton. The natural assumption—and the one most people make—is that his nickname is related to his wrestling career, to his work ethic. People think it comes from the sport cliché: "dig deep, dig hard," finding a way to make it through that last fifteen minutes of a grueling practice, to come out on top in that five minute overtime when neither wrestler has anything left.

It's true—Digger is that kind of a digger. But that's not where his name comes from. He's had the name since long before he ever set foot on a wrestling mat.

"He's had it since he was a baby," his dad slurred at the post-trials party in 1992, just after Digger missed qualifying for Barcelona. "He dug at his nose like a coal miner, that kid. We couldn't keep his fingers outta his nose. Dig dig dig. Right away we knew he was a digger."

Digger thought for sure he'd take a good razzing for that. *Thanks, Dad.* But the guys never mentioned it. Somehow, he got to remain Digger the Work Horse.

Digger sometimes wonders if the guys would've razzed him about the true source of his nickname if he had made the Barcelona Olympics. Maybe they figured the Digger legend had taken enough of a beating that weekend with his failure at the trials and that he couldn't handle being demoted to "Digger the Nose Picker" in the same year.

Digger twists in his seat, trying not to wake a snoring Fly. Fly sweats stale beer. Last night on the way back to rez, long after Ben had slunk off, Digger and Fly were both stumbling and Fly started into some slurring lament. "Fly who eats shit and bothers people and Digger who never gives up, who works 'til he gets what's coming to him. Ever find it hard to live up to that name, bud? Ever just wake up and think, *Geez, I wish my name was just Fly?*"

Digger swatted him away, changed the topic. It wasn't the time to talk about Fly's Olympic Trials fiasco, and Digger wasn't in the mood for a maudlin complaint. Now, staring out the window, nothing to see but the outline of his own reflection, Digger thinks of the work ahead of him in the next seven months and wonders if he would rather be called Fly. Does it wear him down to show up day after day at practice and have every coach and every wrestler expect that he'll excel, that he'll push until he hurts and then push some more?

No. Sleep's heavy pull slides his head towards the window, damp and cool against his cheek. No. Athletes are experts in mind control. Digger would be nowhere without thought-blocking. He's vigilant against those distracting thoughts, those random ideas that could interfere with his dream. He simply doesn't let them in. Blocks them. Just says no. Turns his focus to visions of his success, visions of himself atop podiums, visions of himself bearing gold.

He runs his tongue over his dry teeth. Cracked, he thinks, remembering his dentist's warning. Countless tiny fracture lines covering all his teeth. Wear a mouthguard or you'll lose them, had been his dentist's advice. A mouthguard? Forget it. He'd worry about his teeth when he retired.

As Digger falls off to sleep, he sees himself in Sydney on the middle podium (a Cuban to his right, an American to his left), the Canadian flag rising high above the rest and everyone in the country clapping. For him. Everyone seeing him as Champion. Cracked teeth, broken nose, swollen ears, slight nerve damage to his neck— but *Olympic Champion.*

Twelve

Sadie sits on deck, stretching before practice. The concrete feels warm against her legs and the air heavy and comforting, the silence interrupted only by the shuffling of a few early swimmers dumping their gym bags on the bleachers before stretching out on the warm deck. Water drips from the ice bags at her shoulders and runs down her arms. Sadie attempts to summon the energy to start her pre-practice routine—stretching, sit-ups, and push-ups—when she sees Bogdan looking at her. As usual, he wears nothing with a dinosaur on it. "Calgary Dinos" is his pet peeve. Who ever heard of a fast swimming dinosaur? Bad team names in general irk him. He liked to use Elk Valley Dolphins as an example. The Elk Valley is in the southeastern corner of British Columbia, nestled in the Canadian Rockies. Dolphins? Why not the Elk Valley Bull Trout—the Bullies? Or Elk Valley Cutthroat—the Cutties? Name your team after A) something that could swim; and B) something indigenous. That's all Bogdan was after, he claimed, a little logic.

He's still staring at her and not smiling. Bogdan smile before practice? Unlikely! His lean muscles always have a tense, angry look about them. She expects him to offer some unsolicited advice—*if your shoulders hurt, don't just ice: unless you're doing rotator cuff exercises, they'll hurt anyway; make sure you hold each stretch for twenty seconds, then push further; you've been flailing lately, keep your elbows high tonight.* Something like that. Bogdan loves to tell everyone what to do. Sadie raises a side of her mouth and nods. "Hey, Bo."

"You swimming tonight or just floating up and down the pool again? Dragging off my wake?"

She looks for a smile, hopes he's joking. She expects unsolicited instruction from him, but never outright hostility.

He moves in on her pause. "Maybe you can afford a holiday now that you've secured your spot at the Olympics, but I still have to work. I need to get carded this year."

Sadie can't answer, a heavy "but" stuck in her throat. She swallows hard. Bogdan walks away, pulls a cap over his head, and dips his goggles in the water. She watches him spit into the lenses and rub each with a forefinger. She lowers her head to her knees, too tired to object, too tired to say, "My grandmother is sick, you asshole." Too tired to say, "I'm carded because I made the carding cut-off time. You're not because you didn't." The muscles in her face, around her mouth, too exhausted to form the words. She closes her eyes and breathes in the chlorine smell of her own skin.

A hand touches the back of her head. She blinks hard, then looks up. It's Marcus. He's sneaked up on her without his usual: "SAYYY-DEEEE. YOU'RE HERE. PERRR-FECT."

"You okay, Sadie?" A blue T-shirt strains tight across his chest and he smells as though he's come straight from the weight room.

"Yep. Great."

"No, I mean it. Are you OHHH-KAYYY?" He pronounces each letter as though it has special significance and drops to a squat in front of her, pressing his hands against her cheeks and turning her face to meet his. Sadie feels the force of tears gathering in her skull, coughs at the liquid in her throat. She raises the back of her hand to her nose and moves her head two quick shakes no. No, she's not OHHH-KAYYY. She feels too fatigued to fight this liquid burn but knows she can't let these tears go, doesn't have the time. She holds her breath and squeezes them back.

"Sadie, I know this has been an emotional week for you. Qualifying for the Games, coming right back into hard work, dealing with your grandmother." He runs his fingers through his thick hair, combing it back in place after his workout. "But you gotta ask yourself, you have to decide: do you want it or not? No one else can decide that for you." Words she's heard so many times. Marcus should make himself a tape recording.

He lets go of her face, rests his hand on her knee.

She nods, feels the hitch in her throat loosen.

"It's not up to me, Sadie. I can't make world champions. World champions make themselves."

World champions? Marcus never talks about rankings, only about time, about personal bests. *World champion.*

"Your grandmother's illness is unfortunate."

Unfortunate?

"But there will always be something. You have to focus on what you can control."

Sadie rotates her neck and feels her traps loosen. She takes three deep breaths and forces herself to meet Marcus's eyes.

"Do you need a practice off to make up your mind?"

"No."

"This is the last time I'll offer. After this, you're in."

"I'm in."

"PERRR-FECT." He gives her a full smile, and she notes a silver cap on one of his molars. Sadie's not sure she's ever seen Marcus's molars before. "Hit the water, then." He pats his clipboard on her head before moving towards the whiteboard at the foot of the pool.

Sadie eases herself into the cold water—past her hips, past her belly button, over her breasts—and does her three somersaults. Feet over head, feet over head, feet over head. She reads the first set on the board and, without looking at Bogdan, gets in line.

"Red top, guys. Hold your technique together. Think about pacing. Always negative splits: second half faster than the first half."

Sadie thinks of nothing but her own arms and legs, the force they exert on the water. Her pulls are so deep and so hard that she decreases her stroke-count-per-length by two full strokes. Pushing off the wall, she loves the feel of the water rushing by her, her hands one on top of the other, stretched high above her head, her biceps pushed hard against her ears. *World champion.* She pulls into the wall right on Bogdan's feet.

"Bogdan," Marcus yells, "you better pick it up or let Sadie go in front of you." Bogdan says nothing but leaves no room for Sadie to move in front of him. On the next length, his feet pull ahead, out of Sadie's reach.

Marcus says nothing the rest of practice; neither do Sadie nor Bogdan. It's a quiet practice but a good one: 11,500 metres and Sadie holds a practice personal best for the 40 x 200 on 2:30. At the end, Bogdan lifts his shoulders out of the water and reaches out his hand. "Much better, Sadie." He doesn't say sorry. She looks down to his hips just under water, at his faded blue swimsuit instead of his eyes, but slaps her fingers across his in a gesture of pseudo-forgiveness.

"Aww, Sades, don't be like that," he says, tackling her around the shoulders and pushing her under water, holding her at the bottom of the pool and tickling her underarms. She fights back, bending his fingers and pinching his legs, and they both come up laughing and coughing.

"Okay okay," Sadie sputters, "but you pull that tough guy shit before practice again and I'm gonna drown you for real."

As Sadie turns from Bogdan and pulls her body out of the pool, Marcus reaches for her hand and gives it a tug. "Welcome back."

In the showers, the hot, strong pulse of water massaging her shoulder and back muscles, Sadie feels good. *World champion.* Some might think it impossible, but she's going to be there, be at the Olympics. That already puts her among the world's best. Making the step to the world's best . . . well, maybe. Bogdan's right—she's been slacking—but she has time left before the Olympics. Maybe. She could step it up. Focus. She knows she could improve her turns—that gives her a few seconds right there. She can reduce her practice pace times, push herself harder. She loves to train, loves the narrowing of life, the tight schedules. Gliding through her days with a series of checkmarks: workouts done, weights lifted, times made, goals achieved. She scoops a handful of suds from her hair and blows them into the air. Why not? Someone has to win. She raises her face to the stream of hot water, opens her mouth, and gulps deeply.

At her locker, she pulls on her sweats and turns to zip up her gym bag when Katie startles her out of her own thoughts.

"Sadie, I brought you something." She hands Sadie a clear Tupperware container filled with chocolate chip cookies. "Just to say congrats. On the Olympics . . . and I'm sorry . . . about your grandma." Her dark, small eyes hold Sadie's. She's forced her chlorinated hair into two long braids and has a Dinos toque pulled low down over her forehead.

Sadie reaches for the container, surprised at her own sudden quick blinking. She's so damn emotional lately. "Thanks, Katie. That's really . . . sweet," she says. As teammates, they spend enough time together, go through enough hardships, to be like family, but they're also competitors. Katie will one day take Sadie's spot just as Sadie once took Lucinda's spot. Sadie remembers being like Katie, thrilled at being in the fast lane, swimming behind Lucinda Fryer—the fastest distance swimmer in the country—and being completely baffled by Lucinda's hostility. "I appreciate it; I really do, Katie."

"No problem." Katie smiles shyly, slips both hands under her toque, scratches her wet scalp, and then pushes the toque down closer to her eyes. "I just . . . well, you're a motivation, you know, and . . . well, thanks." Katie's face looks hot with embarrassment. Her head drops and she turns to leave.

Sadie reprimands herself. *Cut the kid some slack*, she thinks, *She's not out to steal your spot. Not this year, anyway. Even Lucinda loosened up. Eventually.* "Katie!"

Katie turns back to her.

"Really, I mean it, thanks." Sadie steps towards her, but stops just short of opening her arms in an embrace.

Before leaving campus, Sadie stops at the cage to share Katie's cookies with Russ. They stand side by side leaning against the counter and popping cookies into their mouths.

"Katie?" Russ asks. "She's the cute short swimmer with the braids and the dimples, right? Always in a toque?"

Sadie nods yes.

"Mmm, well, the cookies are yummy too. You got yourself an admirer."

Sadie laughs. "Just someone considerate," she says. "How about that? An athlete who thinks about someone other than herself for a second."

Russ rests his hand on the small of Sadie's back. "I'm thinking about someone other than myself right now."

His fingers stretch across her lower back, warm and heavy. She thinks of his hand swallowing the whole basketball. She knows his advance is meant in jest. Well, half in jest. *Maybe*, Sadie thinks, *maybe*. She puts her hand on his, lets it rest for a second before lifting his arm and letting his hand fall with a thud to the counter. *Too easy*. And basketball players are even worse than hockey players, though not as bad as wrestlers. And at least he's not a swimmer—too incestuous. Still, *No more*.

"Nice try, Russ." She feeds him one last cookie, her back still warm. "You'd have better luck with Katie. Me, I've been around this building too long."

"Don't tell me you're signing off jocks?"

"Right now, I'm signing off everybody. For awhile. But thanks for the offer, bud." She hands him another cookie and zips up her parka.

"Guess you're too famous for me," he says, pulling a campus paper from under the cash register. The headline reads, "Six Athletes to Represent University of Calgary at the 2000 Sydney Games." There's her, a wrestler, a couple volleyball players, and two runners. A coloured picture of Sadie dominates the page—her head squeezed into a red plastic cap. One goggled eye shows above the waterline and her mouth opens wide, her tongue a purple slab. She looks like a mutant sea creature. She quickly scans the page, her eyes jumping to the other picture—the wrestler, Thomas Stapleton, in an obscene position, bent over with his head buried in the crotch of another wrestler, face turned away from the camera. She wouldn't know it was Stapleton at all but for the tag line: *Stapleton Shoots Deep*. The tag line and the legs. She's noticed those legs in the weight room before—sharp line of definition running from below his shorts to his knee, quads bulging over his kneecaps. She shoves the paper back at Russ, pointing at the wrestler. "Check out those gams. Too bad I've quit jocks." She zips her jacket right up to her chin and slings her gym bag over her shoulder.

As she heads to the exit, Russ yells after her, "Hey! If you change your mind about jocks, remember I offered first. Don't forget your best cage buddy!"

Sadie holds a thumb in the air, then disappears around the corner and hums to herself the entire drive from the pool. She notices a few white flecks on the windshield and flicks on her squeaky wipers. The sky is trying to snow and she hopes for a big dump of white powder, something to clean the brown world Calgary has become this winter. She pulls into the tiny cul-de-sac where her parents live. The lights are off. She slides Copper Bullet into the far right of the carport, leaving room for her parents' van, a hangover from the early morning carpools to swim practice. Walking by the tall birch tree on the front lawn, dead branches reaching upwards, she wonders if her father will cut it down before it rots and falls over.

Inside, she listens for the hum of CBC radio from the kitchen, but the house is quiet and dark. Usually, she'd find them playing crib at the kitchen table—her mom with a strawberry tea and her dad with a Guinness, one Guinness that would last him the whole night, growing warm long before he finished it. Tonight, they're probably at the hospital. She grabs a quick handful of raisins and a granola bar from the kitchen, and heads straight for her bedroom. She flops across her bed, her muscles too exhausted to hold her upright any longer. She doesn't sleep, though, just lies on the duvet, thinking of what Marcus said after practice. Her still-damp hair makes her scalp itch against the pillow and the smell of chlorine suffocates her. Swimsuits hang on doorknobs and wet towels over the bed frame. Years ago, she Scotch-taped a poster of Alex Baumann and Victor Davis to the wall, medals hanging around their necks and a "Let's Get Crackin'" slogan beneath their feet. The tape has yellowed—just as her adolescent crush on the eighties Olympians has faded.

Next to the poster hangs a plaque: "Reach For The Stars: Even If You Fail, You'll Land On The Moon." Her high school coach was a big proponent of that theory: "If you reach your goals," he used to say, "you've set them too low."

That plaque, too, has been hanging in the same spot since she was thirteen. That one, though, does seem appropriate, not that she wants to admit this to herself. Not with the Olympics six months away, her desire for a medal growing and aching inside her. She doesn't want to think about that goal being something she was never meant to reach. Having goals an arm-stretch away made sense when she was thirteen at the beginning of her swimming career, always checking another time standard off that endless list. She closes her eyes and pulls her feather pillow over her head. She's too close to the end of her career to dwell on the idea of unattainable goals. Nothing but disappointment from here.

She slides under her down duvet and feels the sheets scrunched to the foot of the bed. Oh well, she tugs the duvet around herself, building her own cocoon; she'll make the bed properly tomorrow. God, who thinks of making a bed before 5:30 AM practice? Too tired.

What's been wrong with her lately? She's sick of her own whining and reminds herself that she loves to swim, loves the power of pulling herself through the water, pounding her legs off the wall, loves the silence of water filling her ears, the meditative repetition of stroke after stroke, length after length, hour after hour.

Of course, there's more to her. There must be, mustn't there? But with four hours a day in the pool since she was twelve, she hasn't had time to discover what that more might be. That will have to come later. She has a degree; eventually she'll have to get a job—a career, even— but for now, she is too consumed with the essentials of swimming, eating, and sleeping. There's no energy left for self-exploration. At twenty-six, a niggling question has entered the back of her mind: what happens when it's over? What happens when she can no longer race? *Not now*, she tells herself. *Six months to the Olympics. Six months.* She falls asleep to visions of herself with her arms thrown straight in the air and her feet firmly planted on the middle podium, a cool, heavy medal weighing against her chest.

It could be one hour later or six hours later, she has no idea, when she's woken by a soft rapping on her door. She's still in her sweatpants and Dino parka. She raises her hands to her face and rubs her eyes. Her skin is hot and she wonders if it's time for morning practice.

"Sadie? You sleeping?" Her mom sticks her head into the room and flicks on the light. Her shoulders fill the doorway, wide shoulders her and Sadie's only similarity. Not only can her mother not swim, but she's afraid of water. Won't even go on a boat.

Sadie throws her feet over the side of the bed. "Am I late? Did I miss practice?" She jumps up, stumbles over the sheets tangled around her feet.

"No. No. It's only 11 PM. Relax. God, Sadie, you're still wearing your jacket. Did you have some dinner?" Sadie feels she's about to be scolded, scrambles the covers off the floor into some imitation of a made bed. Her mother is Dorothy on her birth certificate but Dot to everyone who knows her—as practical as the period at the end of a sentence.

"Mom, I can take care of myself. I just fell asleep. That's all." Sadie lets her weight back down on the bed and takes off her jacket. The smell of her mother's vanilla perfume tickles her nostrils, makes her want to sneeze. Her eyes come into focus on her mother's face, makeup smudged a little around her eyes, making her look tired. Sadie notices strands of white along the hairline of her dyed red hair.

"Sadie, we just got back from the hospital."

"Yeah? How's Gran?" Sadie yawns. She's waking up and is happy she has a full night of sleep ahead of her before morning practice. She notices her mother has not yet taken off her coat and is covered neck to ankles in heavy white fur—a tower of white. This luxury is a last remnant of a more self-indulgent life, a life before swimming fees, when her mother spent money on herself instead of on her daughter's swim coaches. The jacket has yellowed at the cuffs, but her mother insists it's warm and still wears it all winter long.

The coat hangs open. Sadie can see the tight red V-neck shirt underneath, skin hanging in wrinkled folds at her throat's hollow. "I meant to go tonight but just fell dead asleep after practice."

"She's . . . Grandma's . . ."

Sadie looks up. "She's not worse, is she?"

"Sadie, yes. Grandma passed away this evening." After only the slightest pause, she corrects herself, "Died." As a nurse, she refuses to kid herself or others. Sickness is a fact of life. Death: a fact of life. Sadie's mom's words come faster, each one placed tightly on top of the next. "She wasn't awake again since this afternoon. We would've called you to come down if we thought you could talk to her one last time. She was on so many painkillers . . . she was incoherent anyway. Morphined to the max. No sense you being there for that."

Sadie pulls her jacket on and stumbles towards the door in a half jog.

"There's nowhere to go, Sadie," says her mother in her best Head Nurse voice. She grabs Sadie by the elbow as she brushes past the cool fur of the white coat. "It's over. Sit."

Sadie falls back towards the bed and sits. No one disobeys her mother when she puts on her Head Nurse's voice.

"We'll start taking care of details tomorrow," she says, pulling off her heavy coat and folding it across her forearm. "There's nothing to do now."

Sadie studies the loose skin at her mother's throat as her mind struggles to contain the finality of this news. She feels like she should say something, but can't think of what. She looks past her mom and sees her dad in the kitchen, his large frame bent, elbows propped on the counter holding him up. Old friends call him "Bill the Barge," his university football nickname, and he's still humongous, even toppled over like this. Since university, he's grown a small belly, symptom of his addiction to his mother's cinnamon buns soaked in melted butter. *How typical of him to send his wife with the news*, thinks Sadie before looking at him more closely. His eyes are red, but Sadie wants to ask if he's sad no one will bake for him anymore, no one will make his favourite Sunday dinner.

How could they not have called her?

He pushes his hands on the kitchen counter, lifting himself upright, and half smiles at Sadie. He moves slowly to his wife's side in the doorway, lays his hands on her shoulders as if to hold himself up. "She was comfortable," he says.

Sadie sits frozen on her bed, no words coming to her.

"She just slid away in her sleep," he continues, perfectly willing to soften his daughter's grief, not afraid of platitudes like his wife. But his words also come quickly, too close together. "She was happy that you spent so much time at the hospital. It meant a lot. She really . . . she loved you." Love is not a word Sadie has heard her dad use before. She feels tears running down her face but still she can't move, can't speak.

"We've talked to Marcus," her dad says. Her dad's always the one who's cared about swimming, who got up at five in the morning when she was a kid, fried her two eggs, pulled her from bed, and drove her to the pool. "We called him from the hospital. He said to take a couple practices off. You can use the rest." He lifts his hands off his wife's shoulders, holds them together, palm-to-palm in a sort of prayer, studies his forearms as if he's only just noticed how huge they are.

His words come from far away, and they barely reach her. She feels them slide off her body and land in a puddle at her feet. She should be angry that her parents called Marcus before they called her, but she only wants to sleep, to curl up under her poster of Alex Baumann reaching for the stars and sleep and sleep and sleep. As if it's happening to someone else, she feels her body lifted by thick football arms and covered with a soft duvet. Someone brushes lips to her forehead, then the room is blissfully dark, and Sadie sleeps.

Thirteen

Saul stands against the wall of the gym, one arm resting against his belly, the other held up to his ear. As Digger approaches him, he sees that Saul is pushing a key into his ear, rotating it in the canal. A habitual practice of his.

"Hey Digs," Saul says, pulling the key from his ear and smelling it. "Wife says the ears are starting to smell. Rotting."

"Surgery?" suggests Digger. Some wrestlers, once done competing, get reconstructive surgery, scrape away the scar tissue, open up the ears.

"You kidding me? These are my war medals. Evidence of service done."

"I guess. If you can still hear all right." Digger inadvertently holds a hand up to his puffy ears, pinching, testing for tenderness, digs inside one, then smells his finger.

"Hear? What do I wanna hear you dolts for?" asks Saul, giving Digger's back a swat with the sweaty towel he's just picked up off the wrestling mats. "I'm better off if my ears swell right shut. Besides, if I can get this key into just the right spot—Ahhhh, heaven! The perfect eargasm."

Saul walks towards the gym's exit, picking up towels and water bottles along the way. Sweaty teenagers try to get his attention—*coach, hey coach, coach.* Saul's rule: when practice is over, he's off duty.

"What do I need? A bloody Closed sign to hang around my

neck? I'm not here to wipe your noses and hold your hands. I'm here to teach you how to wrestle. I just did that. Now move along." He makes theatrical sweeping gestures with his arms and used towels.

As the teenagers shove out, a new group pours in: eight- to twelve-year-olds—all skinny arms and skinny legs. Two dozen bony kneecaps.

"You gonna take these kids on your own today, Digger?"

"No prob." Digger plays along. He always takes these kids on his own—Saul having no interest in anyone under legal driving age—but each time, Saul asks him anyway, and keeps his own name as official coach, these kids part of *his* job description.

Today the kids are shy with Digger, sneaking glances, acting like smitten teenage girls. Rather than racing out on the mats and filling the room with the sound of their falling bodies and cracking voices, they stick close to the wall, eyes tied tightly to their own shoes. Digger walks towards the group, aims for Josh—the biggest, loudest kid and the group's leader—and makes a joking sweep at his leg.

"I'm in the mood to wrestle. Any takers?" The boys keep staring at their shoes, so he grabs Josh by one leg and one arm and swings him up over his head, laughing, "Looks like it's all you today, big guy." With Josh resting across the back of his shoulders, Digger looks at the other kids. They all stand back. When he tries to make eye contact, they look at the floor and giggle. He kneels, setting Josh's feet on the ground. Josh scuttles and reattaches himself to the group.

"What's the matter with you guys? Usually I'm your own personal jungle gym. Today you're all acting like I'm Britney Spears and if you have to talk to me you're gonna pee your pants."

Three of the younger boys actually have their legs crossed tight, as if they might pee.

"What's up?"

His words sound hollow in the silent gym. He hears the whoosh of a furnace kicking in as the boys continue to study their own feet.

"Good lord! Someone speak up!" His voice echoes in the quiet gym. "This is getting weird."

Digger catches a movement from the corner of his eye. It's Nazir, the smallest and most hyper of the kids, the one Digger has a hard time keeping on the ground. Whenever someone asks, "Where's Nazir?" all eyes go to the ceiling. Now Nazir comes slowly towards Digger, dragging a gym bag almost as big as himself. When he's at Digger's feet, practically stepping on Digger's toes, he rummages through the bag. Digger can feel nerves radiating off the boy's lean body, can almost hear his heartbeat. Nazir stands up and Digger sees he's pulled a ball cap and a pen from his bag. "It's just that we want your autograph. Josh was s'posta ask, but he's chicken."

Now, Josh too has thawed, leaps towards Digger with a pen. Suddenly, all the boys rush towards him, waving pens. Pens and ball caps and posters and wrestling shoes and old meet programs. Loud voices crash against Digger, as the boys grapple to be first in the line.

Digger feels a laugh rising up from his core. One of his first coaching rules is never laugh at a kid, no matter how funny—if the kid is serious, do not laugh. Today he bursts out laughing—can't help it.

"Autographs? Last week, I couldn't even get you to listen to me and this week I'm a hero?"

Nazir's words shoot out fast, aimed straight at Digger. "But we all saw your match on the TV. The big screen over at Josh's. Your match and your interview. You killed that guy! Now you'll be in the Olympics. You'll probably kill all them guys too."

"Whoa. Whoa. Whoa. Thank you, I guess. But, guys . . ." he searches for words. True, this is the Olympics, true it's what he's always been aiming for, but . . . but but but. "Just because something's on TV doesn't make it more real. I've won lots of matches." Their eyes all turn up to him; staggered by the raw admiration, he forgets his point for a moment but then pushes on. "And I've lost a lot of matches. And I'll continue to win and lose matches." He stops, momentarily confused, his head spinning.

"So you don't care about the Olympics?" Josh has pushed to the front of the group, and jumps into Digger's opening.

"Of course I care about the Olympics. It's the only thing I've wanted since I was your age. But qualifying for the Olympics this weekend doesn't make me a new person, doesn't make me a better person. It's not even my greatest accomplishment." He takes a deep breath, wonders if he's making any sense to these kids, wonders if he's making any sense to himself. He's got them dumbfounded at least; no one jumps into his pause this time. "There are world championships every year," he says. "I've been in those. Plenty of times. In 1998, I got third." Here, noise bubbles up.

"Bronze medal, sweet!"

"Wicked!"

"Awesome!"

He holds his hands up to quiet them. "Now, every four years they call the world championships 'The Olympics,' put all the sports together, and show it on TV . . . that doesn't make it better or more significant than the other years."

Doesn't it? Digger wonders. "You guys, put all your pens away— this is a wrestling club, not a fan club, so let's wrestle."

There's a flourish of pens as the boys quickly shove them deep in their gym bags, eyes still trained on him.

"Circle up," says Digger with one piercing clap of his hands. The boys scramble into a perfect circle around him. "'Kay then. Today we'll work on gut wrenches. Volunteer for demonstrating?" Before Digger has time to pick a wrestler, Josh leaps over two other boys and kneels before him. Through the entire demonstration, not one boy speaks, not even a whisper. Even Nazir remains on the ground and listening. In fact, the whole practice goes that way—boys diving over others to volunteer, watching Digger intensely during every demonstration, driving themselves to get each move precisely right, asking for clarification whenever they don't understand a move *exactly*.

Digger leaves the gym stunned, not sure whether to be flattered by their attention or offended that it took this one meet for him to capture that respect.

Fourteen

Sadie releases herself into that first deep, dark hole of sleep and decides not to come out. She misses her first morning practice in a decade, sleeps dreamlessly straight through it, the rest of the morning, and most of the afternoon. Around three PM, she peers at her clock through barely open, sleep-crusted eyes and decides that she won't be making evening practice either, then rolls over, pulling her duvet high up around her ears. She feels vaguely surprised that it's so easy.

She's reminded of her favourite Yeats poem:

> *Turning and turning in the widening gyre*
> *The falcon cannot hear the falconer;*
> *Things fall apart; the centre cannot hold.*

Her brain thick with sleep, the idea of Marcus as a falconer strikes her as quite profound. This far from Marcus, she wonders how he ever had such a hold over her. The thought sleepily occurs to her that she may never get out of bed, never return to the pool, again. As she has always suspected, the first practice was the hardest to miss and after that one slip, the whole foundation of her training discipline would come crashing down, falling apart around her. The slacker in her would take over. Yes, the pool, always her centre, has lost its hold.

What, she wonders, has held the whole thing together this long?

I have an intense burning desire to be a champion. That was the phrase she learned at National Youth Team swim camps. *I have an intense burning desire to be a champion.* They repeated the mantra over and over—a room full of fourteen-year-olds chanting the words in unison. *I have an intense burning desire to be a champion.*

After Eva's death, Sadie only has an intense burning desire for the comfortable mindlessness of sleep, and the phrase *intense burning* now reminds her of bladder infections. She remembers Jenga, the game she used to play with Eva, where sticks are piled high and players remove one at a time, trying to leave the structure standing. The first one to knock the pile over loses. Her structure was plenty high, the odds had grown higher and higher, then the death of her grandmother was the one stick she pulled at that brought the whole thing crashing down. She feels guilty even at her sadness. Who's she sad for? Eva pronounced herself ready to die. Sadie's sadness must be selfish. Like her dad, perhaps she's only worried where her next stack of pancakes would come from, her next post-workout feast of hot cinnamon buns soaked in melted butter.

Or maybe her sadness wasn't selfish but a tribute to a life well lived. But if Eva's life was an example of how to live, what was Sadie doing with her life?

She thinks of all those other fourteen-year-old swimmers, the ones with whom she endlessly repeated *intense burning desire*, the ones with whom she shared *The Olympic Dream*, even while having no idea what it meant for the shape of their lives. A few of them are still in the game—Bogdan, some girls she races against from Toronto, a butterflyer from Vancouver—but most are not. Only the best are left. At least "best" is the term Sadie has always used. Maybe it's "most stubborn" or "most single-minded" or "most willing to put the rest of life on hold." She stayed because like a train on a track, it was easier to stay than derail, easier to keep piling sticks on this structure than start building a new one. She swam because swimming was what she knew. True, she also believed she could attain a little fame, have people know her name.

Swimming fame never impressed Eva. Maybe Sadie wanted the

gold medal for that—the media attention to show Eva: *Look, Grandma, I'm that good.* Let Eva boast at bingo about her granddaughter on TV. But surely it was more than that. It had to be. Didn't it?

"To succeed at the highest level," Sadie's childhood coach had told her, "an athlete needs talent, work ethic, *and* luck."

And Sadie knows this to be true. She knows, even on her worst days, that she has the perfect combination which has brought her this far. She just doesn't know if she has the energy left to go farther.

On her better days, on the many days that she needs swimming and still believes in Olympic glory, she doesn't think she has put anything on hold, she can't think of a single sacrifice. So she's twenty-six without a career, without a boyfriend, without having anything nearing a start on a family, and with a rusted-out car and her parents' spare bedroom for a home. She made her decision long ago—swimming fast is what's important to her.

Tomorrow. Yes, tomorrow again it will be important. She squishes her eyes closed and crawls deeper into the covers. She dozes sporadically and each time she wakes, she thinks of her grandma's small apartment with its hidden stashes of chocolate, its smell of fresh baking, then, remembering, she pulls the blankets higher.

During the three days before the funeral, she conducts her life largely from the confines of her bed. Its warm darkness envelops her, holds her. From her cave of blankets, she hears what goes on beyond her little realm—muffled condolences, flower deliveries, meetings with the pastor—but she has no desire to participate in any of it. A few times she feels that old panic, that overwhelming anxiety, and jumps out of bed, grabs a running shoe or a swimsuit, thinking she must go lift weights or swim. But immediately she finds she's faint with the effort and that closing her eyes and pulling the covers far over her head lets her ride out those waves of anxiety, ride them straight back into deep sleep.

On the second afternoon she hears Lucinda, her ex-teammate/competitor, in the kitchen. She slides off the bed and crouches on the floor, leaning against her bedroom door. Lucky Lucy was her nickname in 1996 when she suddenly improved light years, slashing her eight-hundred metre free time, claiming a competitive spot on the Canadian national scene just in time for the Atlanta Olympics. Loony Lucy became her nickname afterwards, when—bitter at a mediocre Olympic performance—she began to speak out against the Games themselves.

Sadie makes no move to leave her room, to greet Lucinda, to thank her for coming. She only wants to listen, sleep-creased face pressed against the door.

"I think she's being a big baby," Dot says over the teakettle's whistle, "locked up in that room. Bill's always treated her like a hero. A sporting legend under our very roof." She leaves no space for Lucinda to respond, keeps talking as she clinks cups together and bangs them on the counter. "'Leave her be, Dot,' he tells me. 'It's too close to her Olympics to go upsetting her. Let her do what she needs.'" She says these words in a big dumb voice, one an actor would use for a cartoon St. Bernard. "Her Olympics? Your mother just died, I say, and you're worried about the bloody Olympics?" Sadie hears her mother's voice move farther away and a clunk of dishes pounding the kitchen table. "Of course, I don't really say that. Wouldn't dare poke a pin in his fantasy of Sadie Jorgenson and her Olympics."

Lucinda starts to say something, but Dot interrupts her again.

"Listen to me. I'm sorry. You've swum at the Olympics. I don't mean to devalue that achievement. Really, I don't. It's just—this house has been a swimming house for way too long. And Sadie—she's twenty-six years old, for God's sake—"

Sadie leaves the door and crawls back into her bed. She doesn't want to hear any more.

Her dad must win the fight, because no one bothers her during the next two days. No one asks her to bake squares for the funeral reception, to put her English degree to work and help write a eulogy, to welcome sympathetic visitors. No one tells her to come grieve with the rest of the family. She doesn't know why, but she is allowed to segregate herself.

On the morning of the funeral, Sadie kicks the duvet to the foot of the bed, rolls herself off its edge, stretches, and stands before her closet, searching for something to wear. She rarely wears anything other than sweats or maybe, for dinner at a restaurant, jeans. But she finds, in the back of her closet, a black dress she wore at her last varsity athletic banquet. With a dark cardigan, it will do.

No one comes to wake her for the funeral. She only knows of the date from overheard kitchen conversations. She's surprised her mother hasn't come to drag her from the bed with a lecture on strength and practicality.

She sits back on her bed, clutching the black dress in her hand, and wishes someone would tell her what to do, *make* her do what she needs to do. She eyes her crumpled duvet. She dreads walking into the kitchen in full daylight, facing her mom and dad after she has avoided them for days, only leaving her room to sneak food from the fridge or use the washroom during the night or when she knew no one else was around.

Now, what will they expect of her? Will her mother expect her to be strong, even noble? To smile and shake hands with her friends? To make a small speech? Will her dad want to see guilt at the three days of missed practices? Will he expect her to fly back into the pool, energized and ready to race? Will he want them to weep together over Eva's death?

She wonders briefly if Marcus will be at the funeral, if he is even speaking to her. It was just a week ago that she promised to step up her training, get back on track, and now she has spent three full days in bed.

She stands again and stretches; her arms feel skinny, her head light, and she avoids looking in the mirror. She hasn't been eating enough. She can't stay cloistered in her own bedroom. She tosses the dress onto a chair and pulls on a pair of torn sweatpants, grabs a towel, and steps into the kitchen. Her parents look up from their coffees at the same moment, both startled, as if they've forgotten her presence, forgotten that she dwells among them. The room has the abrasive smell of burnt coffee.

"Want some eggs, Sade?" Her father pushes himself out of his chair and lumbers towards the stove.

Sadie's mother doesn't leave her time to answer, but points to the paper spread out on the table before her: "Grandma's obituary is in today. They did a nice job with it."

Nice job? What difference does it make?

Her mother stands and offers her chair. She's already dressed in an A-line black dress that makes her waist look tiny. Oil bubbles in a pan on the stove and her dad pulls a carton of eggs from the fridge. Sadie plops into her mother's chair to read the obituary, but a stale smell billows from the neck of her sweatshirt. The odour of sweaty sheets and sour breath makes chlorine seem a pleasant alternative.

"Let me just shower first. I'll get ready for the funeral and then come read it with you."

Her dad switches off the stove element. Sadie flees from the room without waiting for comment from her mother.

Bogdan, Katie, and Marcus sit together tightly in the back row of the church. Out of their swimsuits, strangled by ties or stuffed into nylons, they look like strangers to Sadie. As her eyes pass over them, she's reminded of the old swimmer's joke: "Sorry, I didn't recognize you with your clothes on." But then she remembers that she too—squeezed into a black dress that cuts into her armpits and pulls across her back—looks like someone she wouldn't care to know.

Only the chlorine sheen of Bogdan's bleached hair gives away the group's connection to Sadie. Jammed into these formal clothes, they almost look like real adults, but their hair is chemically stripped so badly it springs straw-like from their heads. As Sadie settles into the front pew, she notices that her own signature scent of chlorine has dissipated. Normally when she sits, a whoosh of her own hot smell of bleach rushes up to envelop her. This time, all she smells is the baby powder aroma of deodorant, and she feels a moment of overwhelming panic, a burning need to pee. She fixes her gaze on Eva's coffin. The lid is open and Sadie can see half of Eva's cheek, her nose, and her chest. She can just make out part of the mouth sewn into a grim line, an expression Eva never wore while alive. Sadie wishes

Eva was wearing her floral dressing gown, stained with coffee and pancake mix—something to make that corpse resemble the real Eva. Sadie cannot reconcile the grey stillness with the busy grandmother she remembers. That stillness causes the opposite reaction in Sadie, a violent, riotous bubbling inside herself. She tries to breathe slowly and deeply—in two three four, out two three four, in . . . then out—tries to quiet the tumult of her insides, to stop the cool sweat that breaks out on her upper lip, on the back of her neck. The sweat wets her dress around her armpits and along her neckline. In short quick gulps, she swallows the liquid that pools in her throat.

Just in time she races from the front pew, out the side family door, all too aware of her father staring and her mother bent over, smoothing her nylons. She doesn't make it to the bathroom but kneels over a waste bin in the hallway, vomiting the eggs her dad insisted she eat before they leave. Greasy pieces of rubbery egg white splatter the garbage can, and Sadie continues to heave long after she's emptied her stomach. Coughing, she wipes the saliva off her lips with the back of her hand and staggers to the bathroom. Splashing cold water on her face, she notices the comforts of a washroom made for mourners—a cushy velvet couch in the corner, vanilla candles burning on the side tables, Kleenex boxes on every counter. Her stomach still turns and belches and she runs for the closest of the three stalls, kneels over a toilet bowl. No more food comes up, but she continues to gag and spit. Once there's nothing left to spit, she falls to sitting. Sadie spends the rest of the service sitting on a cool tile floor, her faced pressed against the wall of the bathroom stall, and the back of her throat burning acid.

She emerges for the post-service reception, smoothing her now damp, sweaty hair back into an elastic. Her mouth tastes sour and her dress sticks to her back. She waves briefly at her parents, seated at a central table, Lucinda bent over them whispering condolences, but she can't join them, too aware of her own behaviour as inappropriate, as freakish. Instead she skulks way into a far corner of the room where Bogdan, Katie, and Marcus sit at a round table next to an elaborate arrangement of lilies.

Katie looks different without her toque on—more like a girl. Pretty, even. She drinks from a hard plastic glass filled with bright pink fluid and holds a napkin piled high with four or five squares: chocolate, peanut butter, marshmallow, raspberry jam.

Bodgan chews rapidly, his cheeks full of food, but looks up at Sadie as she approaches. "Y'okay?" he asks, showing something chocolate inside his mouth.

"Yeah," she plumps into a chair. "God, you guys stink of chlorine!" Her stomach clenches with guilt at her own smile, the muscles around her mouth stiff and unexercised.

"Ah, so you do remember the smell," Marcus says but, seeing Sadie's smile disappear, quickly adds, "I'm not here to lecture you. You take as much time as you need. But getting back to the pool might be good for you, getting back to what you know."

Suddenly, Sadie's body aches for the water.

Fifteen

"Showtime! Bring on the Digumentary!" Fly lies on his stomach, closest to the TV, jumbo package of licorice between his elbows, one long red piece dangling from his lower lip. He, Ben, and Digger have met at Digger's basement suite to watch a CBC profile called "Quest for Gold"—a special segment all about Digger.

"They should call it your 'Quest for Blondes,'" says Fly. "Think of the chicks that'll be there. Keep an eye on the pole vaulters. YUUUM-MYYY." He takes a fierce bite of licorice, and Digger thinks, *That's another reason we call him Fly: the constant buzzing.* "And I hear the synchronized swimmers have some special tricks for the hot tub," Fly says, smacking his licorice. "Those gals can hold their breath forever! Now that, my friends, is talent! You may have to conduct some Olympic events of your own, Digger."

Digger and Ben lounge out on the faded couch behind Fly, Digger's head at one end, Ben's at the other, their toes bumping in the middle. Even though it's midday, little sun makes it into the suite, and Ben has to flip on the overhead light to read his *Sports Illustrated*, alternating his attention between an article on professional football players and the TV. The ledge of the dugout window is filled with plants: a spider, a jade, and an aloe vera his mom brought on her last visit. All look a little droopy and brown around the tips and edges. Fly repeatedly suggests that Digger stick to cacti.

"Shh! Shhh! It's starting," says Fly, the only one who's been talking.

On the TV, a thin white woman with a tidy bob streaked blonde and red stands on Bondi Beach, a slight breeze blowing her hair around her neck, and specks of surfers riding the whitecapped waves behind her.

"Wouldn't it be nice," she says to the camera, "to stroll along Bondi Beach, dipping your feet in the surf, waiting for the afternoon's session of Olympic Beach Volleyball?"

A girl with hair like maize walks in front of the camera wearing a white bikini next to her toffee-coloured skin.

"Diggedy Dog!" says Fly. "See that—that's what I'm talking about." He pushes an entire piece of licorice into his mouth, rolls up the cellophane bag, and tosses it over his shoulder.

"This is the last weekend of our contest," continues the calm host with her high eyebrows, "and your last chance to win two free tickets—"

"C'mon c'mon c'mon," says Fly. "Fast forward, honey!"

Olympic music flares and the scene shifts to a mix of feet scuttling across a wrestling mat.

"Hey man, those are your feet, Digger!" Fly cheers.

"The black shoes are mine," says Ben, looking up from his magazine.

"Wrestling is a challenging sport," they hear the host explain with the camera back on her face. "One that combines the contact of rugby with the speed of soccer."

"You got it. Wrestling rules," Fly pronounces through a mouth full of chewed-up licorice.

"First up, let's meet Calgary's Tom Stapleton—"

"Tom Stapleton? Who the hell's that?" Ben nudges Digger with his foot.

"—a seven-time National Wrestling Champion, Tom trains with the best here at University of Calgary."

"That's right. We's the best," Fly pushes his hands above his head in a "raise the roof" pose.

"A lot of great athletes have come out of the little room down here they call the sweatbox." The view switches back to the wrestling room; two wrestlers roll by, the backs of their T-shirts sweat-soaked. Saul's voice booms incomprehensible in the background. "It's a sport that demands incredible stamina, strength, and speed—*and*," she adds as if surprised, her eyebrows flying even higher into her bangs, "the champion must have the ability to think fast." Suddenly, Digger's sweaty, beaten face fills the screen.

Ben laughs, "Expect that mug to think fast?"

"It's got a remarkable history," the on-screen Digger says between heavy breaths, the microphone almost up his nose, "It's one of the oldest sports known to man. I think it's a great sport," he stops, lifting up his T-shirt and using it to wipe his face. "People hear the word 'wrestling' and they think the big, so-called 'professional wrestlers.' The strong guys," he continues, having caught his breath. But now the camera flashes away from him and to a picture of Hulk Hogan wearing tights and throwing another tight-clad fat guy from the ropes.

On the couch in Digger's basement, Digger and Ben groan in unison.

"In reality our sport is nothing like that at all," Digger's voice continues. "There's lots of technical aspects—it's not just these big strong guys people think of." The camera flashes to Digger rolling Ben around the mat, both of them looking very much like those big strong guys people think of.

"Although it's not that popular a sport in Canada and the United States, it's the national sport of more countries than any other sport in the world. Athletes participate in wrestling in more countries than any other sport in the world."

"You tell 'em, Digs!" says Ben from deep in the couch.

"I started wrestling at a young age," the TV Digger continues, "when I was only eight years old." The face of young Digger fills the screen. He's proudly wearing a brown homemade singlet, chest arched forward to stretch its straps, a medal hanging around his neck. Digger barely recognizes himself—his nose small and straight, his coarse brown hair longer and jutting out in a plethora of rooster tails.

Fly erupts in laughter. "Freeze frame, man! I *need* a copy of that."

"My parents both had athletic backgrounds," the TV Digger continues nonplussed, while the real Digger has one eye half-pushed into the couch cushions and a hand on the other eye. Young versions of his parents parade across the screen, his mom in a fresh white tennis skirt, racket swung over her shoulder, her chin and chest jutted out, her dark ponytail sweeping between her shoulder blades.

"Meeeooowww! Now that's YUM-MY!"

Digger pulls a cushion out from behind his head and tosses it at Fly.

Then there's his dad in a white and red tracksuit, lined up with the rest of the national rugby team, all of them sporting thick mustaches, Digger's dad looking alarmingly like Digger himself.

"All right, Mr. Digger! That's what you need for The Show, Digs, a mustache." Fly has opened a new bag of candy and holds a piece of licorice above his upper lip in demonstration.

"My parents were key figures in getting me involved in sports," Digger says seriously into the camera. "They've always been my biggest fans. But my dad sometimes gets annoying, with all the advice he gives me." He adds this last bit as if it's occurred to him he may sound too clichéd, too cheesy. On the screen, Digger, his parents, Fly, and Ben eat corn on the cob and laugh at some joke that seems to have originated from the head of the table, where Digger's dad sits wearing a chef's bib and handing out second helpings of fat T-bone steaks. Ben and Fly self-consciously turn their laughing faces away from the camera.

From the couch, Digger laughs, "That was it, guys. Your chance to be stars."

"Right now," the TV Digger says, with an apparently endless resource of things to say about himself, "I'm living on my own—but you wouldn't know it with these two clowns always here." The word 'clowns' comes out with a smile. The TV fills with Digger's basement apartment, dying plants in the window, and he sinks deeper into his faded couch. Fly and Ben are onscreen again, this time in Digger's basement suite and playing to the camera.

"You ever see the show *The Odd Couple*?" Digger asks the host, the dimple in Digger's right cheek showing. "'Cause that's kinda how it is around here. Every once in awhile I get a big pile of laundry in my room and Fly says, 'It's laundry time.'"

"You're good at that," Fly laughs onscreen, taking another bite of the submarine sandwich sitting on the coffee table in front of them. "The homemaker stuff."

"He thinks he's got me figured," Digger smiles, as if flirting with the host. Or with Fly. "Thinks I fall for his flattery. But I actually do it because," and here Digger looks shyly at his feet, "because I like having him around—"

"Awww, shucks, Digsy," the real Ben says, tapping Digger with his foot. "You're too sweet! Actually, you two'd make a cute couple."

Fly shushes him.

"—because he's a fun . . . fun . . ." Digger studies the coffee table before him as if looking for another word, ". . . fun guy."

Fly laughs aloud, nodding his head exaggeratedly and again raising his arms above his head. "That's me: a fun fun fun guy."

The camera flashes back to the sweatbox, filled with grappling duos. Digger explains in the voice-over, "We're sparring here. We've created an intense training environment. No one wants to give anything up here." The camera flashes close on Digger, his face dripping sweat and his hair stuck to his forehead. "There's a lot of pride in this room. For the next forty-five minutes, we'll wrestle live and beat the hell out of each other." The screen flashes to an image of him on his knees and sweating, holding tight to an opponent's thighs.

Then Saul appears onscreen, standing outside under a blue sky, the Phys Ed building behind him. "Tom is a very very hard-working, committed individual," says Saul. "He covers a lot of the bases that are required for a wrestler to be successful. He lets very few things distract him." Saul stops talking but the camera is still on his face, waiting for more. "Those are the reasons he's had tremendous success." He lifts his key to his ear.

"Oh no! Eargasm!" Fly and Digger yell in unison.

Now there's a big gym filled with kids. Digger stands in the middle of a circle, demonstrating a move with Josh as his partner. Nazir sits quietly, legs crossed, watching. "One of the things he does is spend a lot of time with kids," Saul says.

"You're a hero, Digger," sulks Ben from the couch. "If you ever get a girl over here, play the kid part. Girls love that stuff." Ben turns back to his magazine.

Now Digger's running on a track. "I have an intense burning desire to be successful—"

"Intense burning desire?" Fly laughs.

"—And I mean: I wanna win. I'm prepared as I can be, but I gotta . . . I just gotta . . . I'm so focused and I wanna win so badly that sometimes in a real important match I'll pull through and win just because I want it more than the other guy."

Suddenly Saul fills the screen, nodding his head. "He's definitely a medal contender. We expect big things of him, but even more important than that, he expects big things of himself." Again the camera stays on his face. Saul's eyebrows pull together, and he looks into the distance, as if hoping a cue card is pinned to one of the clouds.

Digger's voice is back: "If it's an equal match, I think the one with the biggest heart is going to win . . . because there comes a time in the match where you just gotta dig down deep. Deep. And there's nothing left. And . . . and, uh . . . if you got the heart for it, you're going to be successful in the sport."

The scene shifts and Digger sits alone on the mats in the wrestling room, his arms resting across his big knees, as he looks deep into the camera. "There's really no secret to success. People want you to tell them the secret. But it's the same as with everything: hard work."

"Shiii-ite!" erupts Fly from the floor. "You call that a secret, man! That's the best you can give me?"

Saul is back, having apparently found the cue card on that cloud. "Guys like Dig—I mean Tom—keep us coaches in wrestling a lot longer. If I could have a whole team of him, my job would be easy."

Digger laughs, speaking to the TV, "Say that to my face, you tough bastard. Just once, I'd love to hear it!"

The onscreen Digger wears a suit, sitting stiff-backed on a stool in a CBC interview studio, camera inches from his face. "Wrestling makes me happy," he says. "I'm doing something I love and I'm getting by—"

"Just barely!" Digger interrupts and grabs a piece of Fly's licorice.

The onscreen Digger looks like his back hurts. He rubs his palms across the knees of his pants. "I don't do it for the money. There's none of that in the sport. I don't do it for the fame, the prestige, the glory. I do it because it's something I enjoy. And if I do it, I'll prove to myself I set a goal, I worked hard, I achieved it . . . and I wasn't lying to myself all these years."

"Lying to yourself like the rest of us shmucks," says Ben from the far end of the couch. After a silence, he pushes out a rough, metallic laugh.

Onscreen, Digger runs into the sun. He plods along a dirt trail through the foothills, the blue sky huge.

"Man, are you a Clydesdale! Move those monstrous gams!" Fly mocks the TV.

You can hear the running Digger breathing heavily, labouring, but another Digger speaks whimsically in a voice-over, "I've learned a lot of lessons in sport and when I'm done, they're going to help me in life."

The Olympic music comes on and the five minutes end. "Join us next week when we profile another Calgary Olympian—swimmer Sadie Jorgenson."

On the TV commercial, little brown faces litter the screen, skinny and sunken compared to Digger's, and a sturdy, pleading voice announces, "Five-year-old Melanie lives in a shack and has no

97

fresh water. At night she goes to bed on a hard floor with an empty stomach. Melanie drastically needs nutritious—"

Fly clicks the mute button. "A star is born!"

Digger pulls himself out of the crevices of his couch and rises to turn the TV off. He can't meet his friends' eyes. He feels exposed, as if they have just caught him masturbating.

Sixteen

*A*s well as jumping back into the pool, Sadie also jumps into bed with Russ. The two types of body ache are so similar and Sadie treats herself to both. After her first practice back, a practice that is more thrash than finesse, more muscle than technique, she stops at the cage.

"Greetings, fellow towel folder!"

"Hey hey, my swimmer girl's returned." Russ drops the ball he's been bouncing against the wall and faces Sadie, his wide smile warming her. "Welcome back, babe." He reaches his long arms out in an embrace and she presses her chest against his, wills him to pull her in tighter. His chin rests on her head and his hands stray down to the curve of her waist.

"Sorry about your grandmother." He squeezes his palms against her hips.

She lifts her head, deliberately letting her brow brush his stubbled chin before letting go of the embrace, tickling her fingers down his forearm, gently holding his fingertips. "Thanks, Russ."

"Hey," he says, holding her pinky between his thumb and forefinger, pulling as she steps back, "my shift is almost over. Wanna grab a coffee?"

"Yes, I do."

By the time Sadie and Russ reach Copper Bullet, neither has mentioned a coffee or gone through the pretense of selecting a café.

Sadie clears a spot for him in the passenger seat, pushing away sports bras and running shoes, flutter boards and pull buoys. "Sorry. This isn't just a car. It's also my apartment."

"In that case," Russ's eyes scan the length of the vehicle, "we'd better go to my place."

Sadie forces herself to forget the nauseous embarrassment she's felt in the wake of previous encounters with jocks, knowing that each episode meant nothing, yet everyone in the building knew about it. She focuses on the hardness of his forearms, on his astonishing length from shoulder to wrist, and imagines those arms wrapped around her and around her and around her. She scrutinizes his massive basketball player's hands and thinks of how small and protected, how fully contained, she'll feel inside of them.

"To your place." She flirtatiously flicks her hair as if this is something they do all the time, as if it isn't something she's spent the last year trying to avoid. Russ's knees are pulled tightly into his chest and his head presses hard against the roof of her tiny car. *He really doesn't fit,* she thinks. But then she ignores this too.

As she grinds Copper Bullet's gears through Calgary's frozen streets, taking peeks at Russ's long beefy fingers, Sadie decides it'd be best to turn off her brain altogether and listen to the pleasant buzz crawling up her body. She needs this. Deserves it.

Russ's heavy hand rests on the back of her neck as his other hand points her into a parking spot behind a three-storey walk-up apartment building minutes from the university. A large cluster of identical buildings spreads out around it, and Sadie isn't sure she could find her way back to this one if she wanted to.

Athletes call the buildings "The Projects" because the apartments are filled with poor jocks—mostly carded athletes with the government paying their rent. Russ isn't carded, which means his roommate probably is. Sadie struggles to remember who Russ rooms with, prays she'll be saved the humiliation of someone she knows (or, God forbid, has slept with).

Russ holds her hand in his gargantuan mitt that makes her feel petite and leads her up the three flights of stairs. The dimly lit halls smell of mold and Sadie holds a sleeve to her nose, breathes through her mouth.

"To the penthouse," Russ smiles and then, noticing her pace slow, he stops and lifts the fingers of her right hand to his chest. A light touch, a gentle touch, a touch that brings all the blood rushing to her skin, wakes every nerve ending. She is surprised that such a big hand can carry such little weight, yet provoke such tremendous response.

"Y'okay with this, Sade?"

She is.

Thankfully, the lights are off when they enter the apartment. The greasy smell of ground beef hangs in the air. Sadie hopes that this means the roommate has eaten dinner and gone out.

Without turning the lights on, Russ pulls her close to him right there in the front hall. Her head only reaches to the curve between his neck and shoulder, and his body seems to fold around her. Enjoying the novelty of feeling small, Sadie finds it so easy to let him lead her into his bedroom, push her onto his bed, so easy to leave all the decisions, all the initiatives, to him, pure pleasure to lie back and let his hands steer.

And the sex is good. Russ performs like a star, hitting every position she has ever heard of and a few she hasn't. It is a test of stamina, strength, flexibility, and endurance. Eventually, Sadie loses track of her own orgasms, though she is sure Russ has not. At any moment, she expects judges to emerge from the closet holding placards high above their heads—*Oh, it looks like 9.8s across the board, folks.*

"Thank God your roommate's out," Sadie whispers, surprised and embarrassed by her own shrieks and screams.

"Shhh!" she laughs. "Stop it. You're making me too loud."

"Hmmm, seems to me that you like it," Russ says, sliding a finger just where he knows he'll make her even louder. As she starts moaning again, he whispers in her ear, teasing, "Stop means go? You're confusing me."

But he doesn't seem at all confused.

Later, while Russ sleeps on his back, mouth falling open, Sadie eases her bra out from under his head, finds her pants under his bed, and quietly reassembles herself. Once dressed, she pauses before leaving, gently squeezes his big toe. She got what she came for.

It's too bad, though, she thinks as she eases the door closed, sneaking a final look at his smooth face, every muscle relaxed. *He looks so harmless asleep.*

Seventeen

"**D**igger! If you're going to go for it, you gotta take it! You hesitate, you lose." Saul stops barely long enough to take a breath and then his voice fills the room again, loud over the scuffling of bodies. "If I see you backing up again, Digger, you can back right out the door, back up straight on home!" Saul's hands are on his hips, whistle around his neck, his eyebrows scrunched so low his eyes almost disappear underneath them.

Digger pulls himself off the mat and crouches back in position to do another takedown with Ben—Ben's slower than him; Digger should be handling him easily. He nods towards Saul to show that he's heard; the nod is no different than if his mom had yelled after him to get milk—nod, *yep mom, consider it done*. Saul's harshness has no effect on Digger. In fact, he barely notices. It's just part of what makes the sweatbox "the sweatbox." It wouldn't fit if Saul said, "Excuse me, Digger, I couldn't help but notice that you took a step back when Ben attempted that last shot. If you don't mind, I'd prefer you to please try to be more aggressive. Thank you."

Saul's coaching tips arrive wrapped in insults and tied with a threat.

The sweatbox lives up to its name today, the thick blue wrestling mats slippery from the sweat pouring off the twelve pairs of scrimmaging men. Each pair wrestles in a standing position until one wrestler scores a takedown, and then they stand and go again.

The room's too small for everyone to ground wrestle. Each pair of wrestlers has an imaginary six-foot-squared space and bumps other wrestlers along the edges. No one talks, but constant noise—grunts, curses, squeals, yelps, snorts—fills the room.

So far, Ben has taken Digger down three out of four go's. Digger walks back to the centre of their imaginary square, hitting himself hard on his forehead with the heel of his hand. "Jesus, Digger, get it together!" he says to himself with his eyes closed.

He lowers himself into his stance—knees bent, hands reaching out towards Ben—and without words they lunge at each other again. They're jostling for position, Digger bent over with a hand clasped behind Ben's knee, when Fly and his partner come screaming into Digger. Fly charges his red-headed opponent and the redhead hits Digger straight in the lower back. He and Ben crash to the ground.

Digger leaps up, kicking Ben in the head as he steps over him, lunging towards Fly. "Fuck, you guys! Watch where you're going."

Both lighter wrestlers mumble *sorry*, scurrying back to their own space for another takedown.

"Be sorry all you want. If that head comes into my space again, it's going up your ass."

He lowers his body into its stance—arms bent, hands forward, torso leaned over slightly, and legs braced—facing Ben and aiming for his knees. Ben rubs his ear where Digger's foot smashed it, then bends into his stance. Digger grabs Ben's thigh easily, but the leg slides out of his hand just as easily. Sweat greases their limbs.

"You gotta take it, Digger. No one's gonna give you anything in Sydney. Take it!" Saul watches only them, and his voice raises easily above the thuds, grunts, and curses echoing in the small room.

Digger wipes the sweat from his eyes, blinking from its sting, and shoots again, this time aiming for an ankle. He gets the ankle, but his own foot hits a puddle of sweat and his leg slides out from under him. He sprawls on the floor, falling to his back, and Ben lands across his chest. Digger manages to arch so his shoulders don't touch the mat. Still, taking an opponent straight from his feet to his back means three points for Ben.

"Holy Christ, Digger. Which one of you is going to the Olympics? Which one?"

This time Digger does not nod at Saul. He stands, rubs his forearm across his wet face, makes a snorting noise in the back of his throat, and bends into his stance, arms forward, ready to go again.

Ben mumbles under his breath, "Thanks for the reminder, coach," and moves to shoot for a knee. Before his hand reaches Digger's leg, Fly and the redhead come stumbling from the right. They're not moving fast, but Fly's body bumps Digger's arm and the pair falls at his feet. Digger lifts his own foot and brings it down hard on the ground, just missing Fly's ribs, then he kicks him in the ass with his other foot.

"Last fucking warning." His nostrils flare and Ben grabs the sleeve of his shirt, pulls him away. Without meeting Fly's eyes, Digger moves back to the centre of his own imaginary square and again lowers himself into position, ready to attack Ben's torso.

Saul looks on but says nothing. Everyone wrestles, wrenching limbs, torquing torsos, slamming bodies.

Digger shoots hard, his hand clasping the back of Ben's upper leg, his shoulder hitting Ben hard in the abdomen. *Uhhnnn.* The painful sound of a man's wind leaving his body catches Digger in the ear. He takes Ben down easily and wrenches him once over on the ground, hard.

"Better, Digger, better." Saul has stepped back and leans against the wall, nodding.

"Standing wrestling only, Digs," Ben says, quietly rubbing his ribs. He addresses his comment more to the floor than to his opponent. Digger's face muscles are clenched, his eyes narrow—a mood his friends know well.

Digger stands back in position, waiting for Ben, when Fly's body falls, hitting him sharp in the back of the knees. Digger's knees buckle slightly but he recovers quickly, turning with lynx speed. Fly has already stood, arms out, hands open in apology. Digger charges— head into Fly's belly, arms circling his torso—and runs Fly full speed *smash* into the cement wall.

"You could've taken my knee out, you moron!" yells Digger. "My fuckin' knee! I have Olympics in six months and your stupidity is going to cost me a knee?" Each word comes faster and more frantic than the last. Spit flies from his mouth, his eyebrows low over his eyes.

"Do you think you're the only one in the room?" shouts Digger, inches from Fly's face. "Do you think I have time to be watching for you? Do you think I have time—" He feels the muscles in his cheeks, around his eyes, relax. He feels like he might cry, like his whole body will melt and he'll lose himself. He can see that the prospect of his tears frightens his teammates even more than his anger. Fly gingerly reaches towards Digger's shoulder. But Digger's muscles tense again and his fist rushes at Fly from the right, *thud,* the sickening sound of knuckles meeting skull.

Fly's right hand instinctively balls into a fist, his left moves protectively to his own already swollen cheek. But Digger has turned his back and strides to the door, leaving the sweatbox.

TWEET. Saul blows his whistle. "Alright everybody, stay in your own space. Watch your boundaries. Everyone back in position."

Fly still leans against the wall, hand cupping his cheek. "Stay in your own space? How 'bout if Digger keeps his fist in his own fucking space?"

Saul blows his whistle again. "You're all right, Fly." Single clap of his hands. "Let's wrestle."

And everyone wrestles.

Eighteen

*T*he furnace clicks on, nudging Sadie awake before her alarm clock blares. Her dad has set the automatic thermostat to warm the house just before she has to get out of bed. The low rumbling from the basement of the house is the first sound Sadie hears.

Her body feels glued deep into the warm mattress. She wishes the mattress would swallow her. Her eyes burn with grit when she tries to open them. She can't push her legs, her torso, out from the warm blankets and off the soft mattress. Her brain's job is to propel the unwilling body, but today her brain feels as though it's made of cold oatmeal mush. Sleepily, she wonders if her encounter with Russ has made her more willing to give into her body's urges. Give into one, give into them all. She presses snooze, closes her eyes, and decides she'll make up the extra half-hour at the end of practice.

When she walks on deck, Bogdan and Katie swim busily in the far lane, moving circles around the black line in sync. Marcus stands at the foot of the pool, keeping an eye on all the lanes, their unseen falconer. Except this gyre never widens, always the same tight circle around the same black line. Sadie hears a continual light splashing, the sound of moving water, and the occasional thud of a kickboard against the deck, but really it's all so quiet. She thought the noise of training would be louder, thought there would be more evidence of all the work going on under the pool surface. When she's the one swimming, her breath, the water, her heartbeat all mixed and pounding in her ears feel loud.

After an extra half-hour of sleep, Sadie's body jitters with energy, as if she's drunk six cups of black coffee. Her skin prickles with jealousy at the train of swimmers making its way up and down the pool at increasingly rapid speeds without her, and she hopes that Marcus won't hold her up with a lecture. But he merely glances at his watch and then leans his head towards the proper lane, as if he doesn't want to disturb the quiet, the soft melodic splashing of water. She hurries past him, slips into the shallow end, catching her breath at the cold, and joins her lane, where Katie makes room for Sadie to go ahead of her, but after Bogdan. The next hour and a half passes without a single non-swimming thought entering her head. She's all muscle and speed.

After practice, women from the early morning kinesiology class crowd the shower room, but Katie makes space in her shower cubicle for Sadie to share her stream of warm water. They stand to either side of the stream, taking turns rinsing themselves, washing shampoo out of their hair, and running cool water through their chlorine-eaten practice suits. The noise of women's laughter and gossip bounces off the walls. Katie and Sadie add to the noise, shouting to be heard over the other voices and the running water.

"Did Marcus give you a hard time about being late this morning?" Katie's arms are raised above her shoulders as she massages shampoo into her own scalp.

"No, he didn't say a word." Sadie points to the bottle of shampoo and Katie tosses it to her. "Maybe he's still cutting me some slack because of my grandma." She squeezes a bottle hard, squirting pink candy-coloured liquid into the palm of her hand, and wonders why they make shampoo in colours that look good enough to eat. "Not that I want to be accused of playing the dead grandmother card," she adds. "Bogdan's already been giving me enough grief. He thinks I've been slacking."

"Ah, Bogdan. Charming guy, for sure. He ever smile or say anything nice?" Katie has just moved up into the fast distance lane.

A few weeks ago, Bogdan and Sadie were her idols. Now they're her peers. Sadie realizes that Katie expected a warmer reception than Bogdan's given her. The next thought—*or than I've given her*—she pushes away, trying to forget how she'd barely said hello to Katie on her first practice in the fast lane, just let her eyes slide over her and mumbled, "Word of advice: stay away from Big Chief Yellow Cloud. He'll piss on your leg."

"Bo's alright." Sadie rubs the back of her wrist across her eye to catch shampoo dribbling down her face. "He's just a little intense." She holds her face up to the water for a second. "Aren't we all?" She smiles, offering this question as an apology for her own initial coolness towards Katie. "And he really thought he'd be in Sydney. That's his problem with me right now."

They take turns rinsing the shampoo out of their hair.

"You still got some there," Katie touches Sadie's hairline just behind her ear.

"Thanks. I'm such a spaz. Shampoo in my eyes. Shampoo in my ears. Shampoo in my hair. Half the time my bangs are filled with it and I don't notice until I see them in the rearview mirror."

Katie laughs. "Typical swimmer! In her own little oblivious bubble. Awesome underwater pull but struggles with the simple day-to-day tasks. Clumsy too?"

Now it's Sadie's turn to laugh. "Clumsy? My God, yes! My high-school basketball coach used to call me Gills. Said I had no business being on land. I don't even know why he put me on the team. Just so he could laugh at me, I—" She stops talking, noticing the surprised look on Katie's face. "What?"

"Get this—my high-school nickname was Gills. Same reason—no land legs. I couldn't walk into a classroom without banging into a desk. The home ec teacher banned me from emptying the dishwasher because I broke too many dishes."

They laugh.

"Two fish out of water!"

"Oh well, I like it better under water anyway."

Sadie nods and rinses a glob of shampoo off her toe.

As they push open the heavy exit door of the change room, Sadie wonders if Russ will be working at the cage. She feels a nauseous tightening of her stomach at the thought. This'll be the first time she's seen him since she nudged her bra out from under his sleeping head, and she's not sure she's ready to meet him in the fluorescent light of the cage. She doesn't have time for the energy suck that boys and sex always end up being. And she knows she'll hate the new way he looks at her, as if he can see through her clothes.

She hears his voice before she sees his face. "If it isn't the swimming sex cult," he says. "Out on a day pass, ladies?" She's afraid to look in the voice's direction, scared the flirt is aimed at Katie rather than at her.

When she does look, she sees that it's indiscriminate. Aimed at whichever one of them wants to be caught. He's leaning up against the counter inside the cage, waiting for them to come chat.

"Sade."

"Russ." She sets her gym bag on the metal shelf outside the cage, digs through it for a toonie to buy a drink, curses her heart for beating faster. This is something she noticed long ago. Encounters with men are like races: her body responds the same to them all, can't distinguish between significant and not. Even if she's swimming a hundred-metre free at a fun meet, once she steps behind the blocks, her breath gets short, her heart beats faster, and she has to pee. Her body reacts as if every race is the Olympic Trials.

"Hey, you left this at my house last night when you snuck out." He reaches under the counter and pulls out a red Dinos swimming toque.

"Thanks, Russ. Real discreet." She pulls the toque down low over her eyebrows, blushing at Katie's sidelong glance, then buries her face back into her gym bag.

"Ah, right, shhh!" He holds an index finger to his lips. "I feel so used, so abused," he continues, looking at Katie now and extending his hand. "I'm Russ. Sadie's never introduced us. She keeps all her cutest friends for herself."

Katie rubs her wool toque hard, scratching her wet hair underneath, looks to Sadie, but then shakes his hand. He goes back to folding towels without releasing the girls from his gaze. "Hard practice?"

"Hard-ish," Sadie lifts her face from her gym bag, toonie in hand.

"You must be tired. You had a late night."

"Tired-ish."

"That's two ishes in a row."

"I'm in a very ish mood today," she says.

He turns his eyes to Katie. "She was a lot more friendly yesterday when she started making her casual advances on me."

Advances? His language makes Sadie think of military attack, enemy warfare, casualties. She bends down to tie her laces, falling beneath his scrutiny and the conversation.

"Hey, I had some of your homemade cookies last week," Russ says to Katie. "They were dee-lish." Sadie imagines Russ's eyes devouring Katie's body with the last two syllables.

"Thanks." Katie's not offering him much, and Sadie wonders if she's not attracted or she thinks him out of bounds.

"So you're the up-and-comer distance swimmer? Sadie's eventual replacement? The new young hot thing?" His words are hot with lust in a kind of parody of flirtation.

Sadie stands up. "Real delicate, Russ. I'm outta here. Need a ride, Katie?"

Russ holds a white towel before him, "What? What'd I do?" He shapes his mouth into a wide O of innocence.

Katie follows Sadie out of the main Phys Ed building doors into the centre of campus, the cold Calgary air making their eyes water, and Sadie forces a smile before pulling her Dinos parka collar up around her face. "Don't worry about it, Katie. If you want him, you can have him. We just hooked up once—it meant nothing."

Sadie reminds herself that she knows better than to have expected differently—that she got what she wanted—and wraps her parka-clad arms around her body, hugging herself warm. Imagines herself a tower of red.

Nineteen

*D*igger takes a detour past the upstairs fitness room, the one where the general student population works out. Cardio machines line the front windows, and girls wearing ball caps and bra tops step vigorously, their headphones plugged in and their ponytails bouncing. Free weights clutter the back half of the room. There, the men outnumber the women. The costume of choice: gray sweat shorts and a sleeveless T-shirt. The exercises of choice: bench press and curls, the "Wasaga Beach Workout." *Biceps and pecs, baby.* Most of the students are still tanned from their February break beach holidays.

Digger's February break was spent in Korea.

"To be the world's best, train with the world's best," Saul announced, handing him a plane ticket.

Digger travelled there with the seven other members of this year's national team. They lived in dormitories, ate Korean cafeteria food, and trained six hours a day. The Koreans, Digger decided, need a little perspective. Their idea of a *light* workout includes a cold, rainy run straight up Mount Gwanak-san. At first, he envied the Korean wrestlers. They were national heroes, known by every school kid, every grandfather, fully supported and paid to do nothing but wrestle. Each member of the Korean team wore a twenty-four carat gold watch engraved with the Olympic year and his name, courtesy of the Korean government. The Canadians were lucky to get a sweatsuit out of their government.

By the end of his two weeks in Asia, though, Digger realized that maybe he didn't make eighty thousand dollars a year to wrestle, but he also didn't have to live with his team in a dormitory ten months a year, and his coach didn't get to hit him over the head with a stick when he screwed up at practice. The married wrestlers gave up living with their wives and kids to be on the team and be treated like mindless packages of muscle tissue and fast-twitch fibres. The wrestlers never complained, never talked back. And for fun they ran up mountains carrying a backpack full of rocks.

Now, Digger watches through the front window of the fitness centre as a male student, shaved bald and wearing a Senōr Frogs T-shirt, spots another student, wearing a purple spandex bra top and a ponytail, at the squat rack. A pink terry cloth sweatband sits on her forehead just under her bangs, though she doesn't appear to be sweating. The bald guy steps behind her at the bar, a hand gripped on each side of hers. They smile and brush against each other. Small freckles splatter the girl's nose, and her cheeks fold into deep dimples when she smiles. The Senōr Frogs guy says something close to her ear as she bends her knees to lift. Laughing, the girl lets her body fall away from the bar into her spotter. Digger tries to remember the last time he laughed during a workout.

He heads downstairs to the less glamorous and less crowded varsity weight room. An underground cement hole, a square of concrete smelling of metal and sweat. No one's smiling down here, especially not in an Olympic year. No fancy step machines down here, just a couple of bikes in one corner and rowing machines in the other. Mostly free weights clutter the room. Usually, he'll find at least a couple of speed skaters here lifting weights, women with legs each the size of Fly, doing squat after squat with 280 pounds resting on a bar across the backs of their necks and shoulders.

It's two o'clock in the afternoon, and Digger just woke up from a post-practice nap. Since he's not on the Korean national team, he should have a job, should sling towels in the cage or beer in the campus bar. But training sucks all his energy. He bounced as a doorman at The Drink for a few months, but just got rundown and then sick, straining to balance practice and sleep and work. Now he does his workouts and gets his sleep and uses his carding cheque to pay for his trashy basement apartment, and when needed, he accepts occasional "loans" from his retired parents. Humiliating at his age, but a means to an end. Just one more year. An advance on his inheritance, Denis calls the loans, to lessen everyone's embarrassment.

Digger's afternoon sleep left his eyes caked with gunk and he rubs at them with the heels of his hands. He raises his hands above his head, stretching the sleep out of his spine, knowing he needs to get a good weight workout in before the four o'clock grappling session.

There are a couple of other guys in the weight room—runners, they look like, with their scrawny shoulders—but no one he knows by name. Not Olympians or he would've read about them in the *Calgary Sun*. The clinking leg press weights echo in the empty room. Digger lowers his body into a corner on the opposite side of the room, stretches his feet in front of him, and strains to push his head towards his knees. The mat he's sitting on smells of moldy rags and sour sweat, and he's glad he can't get his head too close to it, his hamstrings knotting well before his forehead reaches his kneecaps. Hoping the runners don't notice his pathetic attempts at a stretch, he draws a deep breath and slowly exhales, counting to three and struggling to push his upper body closer to the stinking mat.

Ben and Fly had offered to come work out with him today, but he blew them off, knowing their silliness, their worn jokes, would distract him rather than help him. They have National Championships left this year, but in an Olympic year, no one cares about a national meet. The best athletes' training schedules gear up and taper down with one objective—optimal performance at the Olympics. Ben and Fly are sliding into holiday mode, showing up late to practice with beer on their breath. They'd fit in better at the upstairs gym. And Digger doesn't want to risk losing his temper with Fly again.

Last time, Fly came to him, right handed extended, two fingers stretched into a V, "Peace, bro?"

Digger knew himself lucky to have a friend who understood him so well, who didn't give much credence to that other Digger, the one slamming his foot into the floor and attacking his own best friend.

His legs already strong, Digger avoids his favourite exercise of squats and plops his body onto the chest press bench. Gripping his fingers tightly around the cold metal bar, he sighs. *Money in the bank*, he tells himself, just putting some strength away for when he might need it.

He runs his tongue over fuzzy teeth, and looks to each end of the bar. Two hundred and fifty pounds. He releases the bar and wipes his hands across his hairy thighs. Normally he'd lift more, but without a spotter this'll do. He thinks of the freckle-nosed girl with the bald guy upstairs and places his hands shoulder-width apart on the cool bar. Ignoring the knot between his shoulder blades, he takes three slow deep breaths and the metallic sweaty smell of the weight room fills his nostrils. Energy surges through his arms. He can count on that—no matter how tired he is, no matter how much his mind fights the workout, once he's directly faced with a challenge, his body rises to it.

Digger lies on the corner mat doing sit-ups, more for vanity than for wrestling, when he sees the big blonde swimmer girl walk in. He's seen her around and knows her name is Sadie Jorgenson, knows from the big article in the newspaper that she's going to Sydney in September. They've never spoken before, though. She comes over and takes a mat from the pile beside him, gives him the vague nod you give to someone you recognize but don't know, and moves ten feet away, laying her mat down next to the wall. She leans against the wall, reaching her arms high up it, pushing down with her head and upper body, sticking out her firm butt clad in red sweat shorts, SWIMMING emblazoned in bold yellow letters across the ass. Next she lifts her arms above her head, grabs an elbow and pulls it to the opposite ear. After performing this stretch a few times on each shoulder, she leaves her mat and moves into the weight area.

Digger pretends he has more sit-ups to do, lies back on the mat, and tries to think of something to say to her.

Here for a workout? Duh! Of course, she is. Too obvious.

How's the training going? Nah, too familiar.

Hey, congratulations on qualifying. Nope, too late.

Hi, I'm Digger. Uh-huh, and . . .

Mind fixed on this dilemma, Digger feels a foot nudging his hip and looks up to the wide shoulders and blonde head looming above him.

"Wake-up call," she smiles. "No sleeping in the weight room. Though I can sure say I know the feeling. I couldn't decide whether to wake you up or tell you to shove over and make room." She sits down next to him and extends her hand. "We've never actually met. I'm Sadie."

Digger meets her hand, his eyes fixed on her wide, solid shoulders.

Twenty

Sadie enters the weight room in the late afternoon and is met by the familiar wall of stale air—a mix of sweat and metal tickling her nostrils. Looking around, she's glad to see she won't have to stand in line for the weights today, no hoards of stinky athletes fighting over the bench press. In fact, the room's nearly empty—a couple of runners on the treadmill and a wrestler stretching over in the corner.

It's the first time since Eva's death that Sadie's been down to the weight room. She's ready now, ready to step up the training program, ready to put her body through the pain it will have to know if she's to succeed in Sydney. She's tired of the recent fits and starts in her program. Her body has grown less predictable than her sputtering old car: one morning it starts on time, the next it doesn't. She can't afford to be sputtering through this last leg.

She grabs a mat in the corner opposite the wrestler and throws it on the ground next to the closest wall. She stretches her shoulders, pressing her palms into the wall, and then stands straight, stretching her arms high above her head. She grabs her right elbow and stretches it to her left shoulder, feels a pleasant pull through her lat, and considers the paradox of the athletic life: listen to your body but don't listen to your body. Marcus insists that she know the difference between shoulder pain and shoulder ache, know when to swim through it but have the smarts to stop if she's edging dangerously close to injury. She must know if she's low

117

on protein—a mistake that could stop her body from rebuilding muscle after a draining swim. She must be aware of the difference between a muscle's need for increased calories and the body's craving for unnecessary fat, sugar, salt. Listen carefully to all this, Marcus tells her, but ignore the body's daily fatigue, its urgent pleas for more rest. At this morning's practice, he saw her fingering the persistent deep ache in her left shoulder and asked his standard question, "Is it pain or just a feeling?"

A subtle distinction—does it hurt or does it just . . . feel? Sadie knew the results of her answer, though. *Pain* meant stop. *Feel* meant keep swimming. "I just feel it," she answered, pushing off the wall, stroking hard. She'd spent too much time out of the water lately, couldn't afford pain.

After another quick shoulder stretch, pulling her left elbow behind her head, she lowers herself onto a weight bench, feels the back of her legs stick to the Naugahyde. She sees herself in the mirror and is struck by her size. She's huge. *With shoulders like that,* she thinks, *how could I be anything but a swimmer?* The fingers of her left hand grab her right shoulder, testing for pain, digging deep and pressing into the tendons. They let out sharp stabs to the touch but are not aching—she can easily lift her arms above her head. Tendonitis—swimmer's shoulder—is the curse of swimmers. The tendons simply wear out from overuse. Then the muscles give off a constant throbbing ache, a migraine of the shoulder. And every pull of the water is a steak knife straight to the shoulder's innards. Jab then twist. Remembering that debilitating pain, Sadie resolves to go easy on the bench press today.

As her eyes move away from the mirror, her hand still massaging her shoulder, they fall upon the wrestler in the corner. He lies on a mat, eyes closed like a boy on the beach, raising his face to the sun's warmth. She imagines herself curling into the space between his arm and his body, sharing his warmth, his comfort. Oh brother, she rebukes herself, didn't she just learn this lesson from Russ? Relearn it? No jocks. No guys at all.

Thomas Stapleton. His knees are bent towards the roof now and

118

she lets her eyes run the length of his legs—quads, hamstrings, calves. Great legs. She wishes he were stretching instead of just lying there. Watching him stretch always proves to be a great source of comedy. The famous inflexible wrestler. She admired that he beat his body to excel in a sport he wasn't built for. Big-shouldered swimmers—plenty of those. Inflexible wrestlers—not so many. Yet, he'll be in Sydney in the fall. There're only a handful of them on campus. They all know who the others are. She wonders if he too grapples with nerves, if he's scared he'll bomb, letting down all of Calgary, all of Canada—if he worries who he'll be when it's over.

Sure doesn't seem like it. He still hasn't opened his eyes and he looks utterly relaxed, so at ease with his role as Olympian. She doubts he sleeps through morning practice, resists doing weights, gets distracted by flings with towel folders. He knows, his sleeping features seem to say, how to handle the pressure of this last leg. She needs to tap into that attitude. She pushes herself off her bench, her legs making a sucking noise as they unstick themselves, and trots to his corner. *It is*, she's decided, *time to introduce herself to Tom Stapleton.*

Twenty-One

"*F*act Number One," says Fly, holding up his right index finger. "There's a girl—an Olympian—huge shoulders just like you love 'em. Fact Number Two: you think she's cute. So, said girl comes, no help from you, and lies down right next to your lame ass, says, effectively, 'Hi—here I am.' So far so good, right?" Fly's holding court at Baron's Court, the coffee shop in the campus Phys Ed building.

Digger barely nods, playing the straight man in Fly's show.

Fly continues. "Okay. So. This is where you lose me. Why is it that you're not on a date with this girl as we speak? 'I'm Digger. I'm scared of girls.'" Fly holds both hands with fingers splayed across his face, his mouth a big round O. "So you run away. Look, Digs. I can't hold your hand all the time. I can't walk you through every step. How about: 'Nice to meet you. Why don't we go for a coffee?' How about: 'I happen to be going to a movie tonight, would j'ya wanna come?'" Fly pauses, giving Digger a chance to respond.

Digger shrugs. "I dunno. I'm busy right now. I've gotta focus." He studies his long fat fingers, tears at a hangnail on his thumb. "I don't really have time for that stuff." He shrugs again but won't look Fly in the eyes.

"'I'm kinda busy right now'," Fly imitates him in a high-pitched squeal. "Good lord, Digs. We're not asking you to marry her. We're talking about a date here. Olympians do still have time to drink coffee, don't they?"

Ben wears the sullen look that has become his standard expression and lifts a Styrofoam cup of steaming coffee to his lips, slurps deeply. "This stuff's shit. I don't know why we come here instead of the new Starbucks by the library."

"For the view, my friend, for the view." Fly gestures over his shoulder to the gym bunnies making their way from the change room to the gym and back again. "But let's not let Digger off the hook so easily. It's no time to be changing the subject." He stops to eye a tiny woman in spandex shorts, then takes a big bite of the greasy grilled cheese sandwich in front of him. "Did you get her number at least?"

"Her number." Digger's eyes are still riveted on his hangnails. He shrugs and sighs. "No. But she's around all the time. I'll see her at the cage." He adds the last part quickly, not leaving space for Fly to jump in.

Ben has tilted his cup to get the last dregs of burnt coffee. Now he's ripping the Styrofoam cup into nickel-sized pieces, piling them neatly on the table before him. Fly and Digger watch him for awhile, shaking their heads at the tower of Styrofoam nickels.

"Okay. I'll get her number next time I see her," says Digger. "I'll ask her out for a coffee. I'll take her to a movie. Will that make you happy?"

But Fly has stopped listening. His eyes are fixed on a spot above Digger's head. Digger is about to turn and look when he feels a tap on his shoulder and twists his head to see the broad shoulders and curly blonde head looming above him.

"Oh! Sadie. Hi." His tongue feels stapled to the floor of his mouth.

"Hey," she smiles. "Sounds like your date calendar is full of coffees and movies. Busy guy like you got time for a weight workout? I'm heading down there now and could use a spotter. If you have time." She runs her hands along the wide bars that partition Baron's Court and waits for an answer.

Ben scoops up his pile of Styrofoam bits and rises to carry them to the garbage can, cupping both hands as if he's carrying water. The look on his face makes Digger think of the high-pitched squeaking sound Styrofoam makes when you bite it with your teeth.

Fly kicks Digger under the table. "Go already," he says and then turns his face up to Sadie. "That works perfectly. I thought I was going to have to do weights with him. Looks like I'm outta here." He stands and swings his gym bag over his shoulder. "Have fun, kids." They watch his back as he jogs past the cage and out the doors.

Ben shuffles back to the table, staring into his empty palms. "Yeah, I gotta go too." He pulls on a heavy jacket, though it's spring and should be warming up. "See ya, Digs." Without saying anything to Sadie, he buries his nose in the red jacket and scurries away.

"Sure then. Weights," says Digger. He moves his head to gesture towards the back of a disappearing Ben. "Don't mind him. He's a little off lately. Since the trials."

"Expecting to make it?" Sadie picks up Digger's gym bag and swings it over her own shoulder.

"Nah. I mean, his chances were sorta outside anyway. But I guess he didn't think so. None of us thinks so." He reaches for his bag from Sadie, but she shakes her head. "He's a little depressed, but he'll be okay," says Digger. "He's got bounce."

"You ready or you need to change?" Sadie asks as they head out of the Court. Both wear sweats already.

"I can wear this. You?"

"Yeah, this is good. Let's go." She pushes open a heavy door and leads him down the narrow dusty-smelling staircase to the weight room.

Sadie stumbles over a barbell in the entranceway of the pitch-black weight room, but catches herself as Digger flicks on the light. She flings his heavy bag from her shoulder onto the floor, and they automatically head to the far corner with the floor mats and sit down to stretch. On the floor, Sadie inchworms her way out of her sweat pants and Digger sees that underneath she's wearing the red shorts with SWIMMING across the butt. She stretches out her legs and reaches her hands over her toes, pulling her head to her knees. Digger notices that her shins and calves are covered in fur, thick brown-blonde fur. He can't resist reaching out to pet one. "Holy shit!" he says. "Look at these things. I can barely make out the skin underneath!"

Sadie swats his hand away. "Aren't you the sweet talker?" She reaches down and pets the other leg. "I know. I look like an ape. But I kinda like them like this. Warm anyways. Regardless, that's how they're staying until Sydney, 'til the big shave down."

"Shave down? You're kidding! Swimmers really do that? I thought that was just a male pornographic fantasy: the whole women's swim team naked and covered with shaving cream, running razors all over each other's bodies."

"Nope, we really do it." She jumps to her feet, stretches an arm behind her back. "People wonder how can a little hair really create resistance, but it's more than that." She leans over and rubs her hairy leg. "Partly it's psychological. The buildup of shave down. But never discount the psychological, never say 'it's *just* psychological'." She reaches a hand out to him where he sits on the floor.

He grabs her hand and jumps to his feet, decides he should change the subject. "So—upper or lower body day?"

Sadie pulls a hair elastic from around her wrist and ties her hair on the top of her head. "A bit of both today—some squats, some bench. I've been slacking lately—just getting going on weights again."

"Slacking? Now?" Digger looks confused, as if maybe he's gotten her mixed up with someone who's not going to the Olympics in a few months.

Eva's heavy body in its hospital green nightgown pops into Sadie's head, but she forces it out. She rubs her hands across the back of her shorts and steps towards the squat rack, steps under the bar so its cool metal rests on the back of her neck.

Thinking of the couple he watched in the upstairs gym last week, Digger steps in behind to spot her. The bar is already loaded with weight, and Sadie lifts her arms to grip it, hands shoulder-width apart, fingers splayed.

"Holy shit, you have huge hands!"

Sadie steps out from under the bar, puts her hand in front of her face, looks at it. "Mmm, not exactly what you'd call pretty, hey?" Her arm drops to her side and she ducks back under the bar, lifts her hands back into position. "All the better to pull water with, my dear." She takes three deep exaggerated breaths, forces the air in and out—*uhhh-hooo, uhhh-hooo, uhhh-hooo*—and pushes her weight into the bar, lifting with a great grunt.

Digger stands close behind her. "I just meant your fingers are long," he says. "Piano player's fingers, my mom used to say."

"*Eeeehnnn.*" She uses all her might to force the bar back up and onto the rack after her eleventh rep. "God, I hate weights," she says, rubbing the back of her neck, then lifting her T-shirt to wipe the sweat off her face. "The only way I'd play piano is if they held lessons under water. That's where I've spent most of my time . . . since I was four years old, anyway." She shakes her arms loosely at her sides. "Okay—three more sets." And she's back under the bar.

Digger holds up his hand so she can see it reflected in the mirror before her. "Big hands too," he points out. "My mom always told me I could be a piano player." He turns his palms towards his face and studies them. "A little beefy for piano, I think. And now . . . too many broken fingers." He opens and closes his fist so she can see it in the mirror. He wants her to see the effort each movement requires, the lack of mobility. "Not exactly Mr. Nimble Fingers either," he offers and steps in close to Sadie so his chest brushes her back, his thighs almost touch her buttocks. He places his grip just outside of hers and raises his body with hers, helping her lift the bar from the rack. He notes that the warm waft of air that hits him as she moves smells of chlorine, not sweat. For the rest of her workout, he stays close. Just in case.

Twenty-Two

Calgary has started to melt, and the smell of wet soil fills Sadie's nostrils; a fast warm chinook wind blows her hair in her eyes. She raises her face into the warm air, breathes deeply, knows it won't last. It's not even the end of March. Calgarians will see minus twenty again.

Sadie and Lucinda walk across campus, past the student union building and towards the Phys Ed complex. Undergrads pour out of the buildings into the sun's warmth, prematurely wearing shorts and pushing their sleeves up over their shoulders, splaying their bodies across benches, playing Frisbee on the wet grass, skidding across the patches of snow. Sadie wants to rest in the sunshine too. "Want to stop, Lucinda? Time? I've got half an hour before my cage shift." She slows her pace and points at a green bench where two boys pack books into knapsacks, rushing off to class.

Both boys wear mirrored glasses and have just the slightest hint of sunburn on the tips of their noses. One of them smiles at Sadie and Lucinda, and waves his arm over the abandoned bench as if he's prepared it just for them. "Enjoy, my ladies."

In Calgary, everyone is friendlier during a chinook.

Lucinda, a broad woman just a few years older than Sadie, pushes her sleeve up to examine her digital watch. "Sure. Let's stop for a bit. The babysitter can wait—," she looks at the watch again. "—another half an hour."

They ease themselves onto the bench, the wood still surprisingly cool through Sadie's sweatpants. Lucinda wrinkles her eyebrows, her gaze dropping below Sadie's face, and Sadie realizes that she's inadvertently massaging a nagging muscle twinge in her right shoulder.

"Oh. No—don't worry. It's fine. Just a bit stiff."

"Have you been icing?"

"Every day, Mom!"

Lucinda refuses to laugh. "I'm not your mom, but I don't want to be stuck listening to you whine when you're injured for the Olympics. Remember—keeping yourself healthy is the most important thing now."

"I know, I know." She sits on her hands to keep them away from her shoulders.

Lucinda pulls off a heavy green cardigan. She wears a matching sleeveless knit underneath. Sadie notices that the skin hangs loose around her armpits and her upper arms are still big but no longer defined. Sadie looks away, watches the shirtless boys jumping for the Frisbee.

"So are you ready for The Show?" Lucinda holds a hand over her eyes to block the sun and seems to address her question to the jumping young men rather than to Sadie.

"Mmm. We still have all summer. Training's going well, though. Back on track." Sadie keeps each of her sentences slow and even.

"Can I give you some advice?"

Sadie turns, surprised. Since when did Lucinda ask for permission to give advice? "Yeah, of course. Sure."

"Don't . . ." Lucinda scratches her knee, pinches her mouth into a tight line. "It's not like any other meet. It's not just about swimming." She chews on her bottom lip. "Honestly, the best you can do is go there to have fun."

Fun? Sadie is dumbstruck. She stares at Lucinda for a moment, then turns, embarrassed, back to the boys. One of them slides barefooted across a stretch of icy snow.

"Enjoy the opening ceremonies. Go see the bands. Take the

athlete passes to watch other events. Tour your family around the athletes' village. Go to all the gala festivities you can fit in."

"What are you talking about?"

"Sadie, no one cares unless you get a medal. Realistically, what are your chances of placing top three? In an Olympic year?"

Sadie's breathing stops; she moves her hand to the bench and pushes away from it to stand, but Lucinda grabs her arm.

"Your best time is what? 8:32? 8:35? You'll need closer to 8:25 to get a medal—that's a lot of time to take off in one meet. Anything less than a medal at the Olympics is a failure. You know that." She squeezes Sadie's arm. "You worked hard for your spot—you might as well enjoy it. Think of it as a very exclusive party. That's what I wish I'd done."

"A party?" Sadie tries to laugh. "Look—I'm training . . ." And what? She leaves the sentence unfinished. This conversation is not one she can get her mind around. She studies Lucinda's face—looks for something she's missed. Maybe she's going through post-partum depression.

"In 1996 I made it into the final for my eight hundred free. Top eight in the world—shot at a medal. Just before my swim, Marcus calls me over. He wasn't the Olympic team coach, but he'd been my college coach. I trusted him as much as anyone. You know what he said? He said—'You don't have a chance at a medal, go for a TV swim, put on a show, make it look like you could win, give folks back home a few minutes of thrill.'" Lucinda picks up a twig from the ground and fiddles with it. "That's what he told me—go out as hard as you can. Give the Canadians something to cheer about. So that's what I did." Lucinda breaks tiny pieces off the stick. "All those years trying to get perfect pacing. Here's my biggest swim of my life, and I throw it all out." She drops the pieces of stick to the ground, watches them slide between her fingers. "I did hang in there for awhile. First two hundred metres, I was still at the front. That's the worst part—Marcus and Alex Baumann were commentating for CBC. I watched the tape later that night back in the athletes' dorm. Alex says something about Lucinda Fryer being a surprise and making a run for a medal, and Marcus smugly smiles, with his stupid big rug of hair and sideburns to his chin, and says, 'Oh she won't be around for long. She can't hold this pace.' On TV for the whole nation to hear, that's what he says." She dusts her hands off. "My TV swim . . ."

Sadie doesn't say anything, just digs her toe into a wet hole she's made in the grass.

"Just know—it's not real. It's all spectacle." Lucinda pulls her green cardigan over her shoulders, drops the last bit of twig, rubbing her arms warm as a cloud slides over the sun. "I set a Canadian record that swim. The fastest anyone in Canada had ever swum that event. But it didn't matter. The press only wanted to know why I didn't get a medal."

Sadie hears Lucinda's words only as distant echo. She waits for more, for a tirade on the injustices of steroid use, on fair-playing Canadians not standing a chance. She's heard this speech before. After 1996, Lucinda was on a roll about the Chinese women. As if the rampant drug use wasn't enough, some women were impregnating themselves in advance of the Games so their bodies would naturally grow stronger, then just before the competition, they'd abort.

"Canadians are not committed enough to win," Lucinda had said.

Sadie had retorted, "You call that commitment?"

"They're doing what it takes to win," Lucinda had repeated. "Would we do that to win? And if we're not trying to win, what's the point? By definition, the goal of any race is to win."

Lucinda prepares to leave. Sadie watches her slide her flabby arms into the green tubes and check her watch. She has dyed her short hair a dark red, and Sadie thinks the green shirt and red hair make her look like a sad pumpkin. She's a bigger but less solid version of her former self, a flabbier version.

"I should get back for the sitter. It's been good to see you, Sadie." She cups a hand over each of Sadie's shoulders. "Sorry. It's just . . . there are things I wish someone would've told me." She bends down and kisses Sadie on one cheek and then the other, swings her purse over her shoulder, and strides across the grass, dodging sunbathers.

As Lucinda walks away, Sadie leans back into the green bench, rubbing her shoulder, feeling the sun on her face, and watching the boys run after the Frisbee.

Twenty-Three

"**W**hat do you mean weirder than usual?" asks Digger. He and Fly are seated at the kitchen table in his basement apartment, speaking in low voices. Ben is in the bathroom.

"Like really fucking freaky weird, man." Fly isn't bouncing around like his normal self but stares intently in Digger's eyes. "So I'm driving by his place, and I see him wandering around the parking lot, I pull in. 'Hey, Benny, What's up?' I say. Nothing. He's just walking in circles. So again I say, 'Big Benny Man, whatchya doing?' He doesn't even look at me. I park the car and get out. I walk right over to him, grab his arm. 'Hey Ben, what's going on?' He looks at me like he doesn't even know me. That's when I see—he's holding his arm funny, like it's injured. I look—and it's fucking cut. Not sliced up the vein like he really meant it. But little nicks and cuts all along the inside of his arm, like he was sure as hell thinking about it. I lost it. 'Ben, what the fuck? What the fuck?!' That just freaked him out more. He bolted. So I got it together, bolted after him, got him in a full nelson hold and pushed him in the car. I didn't know what the hell to do with him. I'm a wrestler, not a friggin' psychiatrist, for Chrissakes." Fly takes a deep breath, the first since Digger has seen him. "So I brought him here. I thought, maybe the hospital? Maybe Saul's? But I brought him here first. What're we gonna do, Dig?" He runs his hand through his hair, pulls. "This is scaring the shit out of me, I'll tell you that. When we got here, there was no sign of you; I tried to act all casual, like it was any old day and we was dropping by for a visit. Let ourselves in, offered him a beer. He wasn't as skittish as in the parking lot, but he still didn't say much."

Digger closes his eyes. Tries to make sense of Fly's story. "How long ago did he go in the bathroom?"

"Awww, shit!! You don't think he'd do anything in there?" Fly springs up, sends his chair toppling backwards.

"Calm, Fly, calm. Probably not. It sounds like he's sending out warning signs more than anything." But Digger follows Fly to the bathroom door.

They press their ears to the door, Digger unsure what they're listening for. "This is ridiculous," Digger whispers to Fly. "Hey Ben, how're you doing? Need anything?" He shrugs at Fly.

They hear a rattle from inside and both spring away from the door. Digger backs slowly towards the couch, wondering what would constitute "looking normal" in this situation.

Ben steps out of the bathroom, and he has a face full of shaving cream. He's lathered on at least half the can; cream covers the skin from just below his eyes right down to his collarbone. He's naked except a hand towel wrapped around his wide waist. He walks towards them, his movement sure but his eyes stretched wide, both hands gripping the towel.

Fly's hands are back in his hair. He looks at Digger, panicked. *Fix this, now!* his eyes shriek.

"Benny, what's going on, man?" says Digger in his best imitation of casual.

"A shower and a shave," he says. "A shower and a shave. My old man always said—'Having a bad time? You just need a shower and a shave. A shower and a shave will put you right.'" He doesn't look at them as he talks, but makes his way to the couch in the living room. He sits, trying to keep his groin covered with the tiny towel. "A shower and a shave. A shower and a shave." He rocks back and forth in time—"a shower and a shave, a shower and a shave." Tears pool along his lower eyelids.

Digger sits beside him, puts an arm around his naked shoulder.

"It's okay, buddy, it's okay."

"No." Ben looks at him. "No. Nothing is okay."

Digger doesn't know what to say. He tightens his grip on Ben's shoulder. Fly hasn't moved from his spot outside the bathroom door.

Ben's head falls heavy. Some of the shaving cream splatters to the floor and some runs down his bare chest. "I just wanted to go, Digger. I wanted to go."

Digger wishes he could say—next time, you'll go next time. But Digger, Ben, Fly all know they're too old for next time. Fly has lowered himself to the floor and sits cross-legged on the carpet, hands on his forehead.

"I just wanted to go," Ben repeats as his tears shape rivers of shaving cream down his fluffy white face. "I wanted. To go."

Twenty-Four

The water feels heavy and Sadie's arms even heavier. She must force her arms through every stroke, consciously rip her body over for every turn. She wants to get out, get out and sink herself into the hot tub, close her eyes and rest her head while the hot water loosens her tired muscles. Marcus has switched them to a long course pool in preparation for the Games, and the fifty-metre lengths feel too long, the water too rough and choppy. When she finally reaches the end, her feet are only allowed to touch the wall for a split second before she faces another infinitesimal length. Katie's fingers tickle Sadie's toes off every wall, and Sadie suspects the younger swimmer could sprint by her but hangs back to show respect for Sadie's veteran status. She could offer to let Katie go ahead for the practice. She could, but she won't.

"Sadie, there's no snap in your stroke. Pick it up. You're off pace," Marcus barks from the edge.

"I'm tired, Marcus." Sadie's hand rests on the edge, but she doesn't look up from the water. Her voice sounds flat. It's not a whine—just a statement of simple fact, one she figures Marcus ought to have picked up on himself.

"Then it's even more important to hold your stroke together. You'll be tired in your race."

"Not this tired." She blows into her goggles and wipes each lens with a thumb. "Not after a taper. I feel like I've been run over by an SUV. Like I'm swimming in quicksand." She snaps her goggles back on her face and massages the niggling twinge in her right shoulder.

Marcus has no time to respond, because the red hand hits the top and Sadie splashes off again, thrashing through the water. This time Katie's fingers reach Sadie's heels, and when they come into the wall she's prepared for Marcus's, "Katie, you go ahead."

Sadie's own relief surprises her. *Yes, Katie,* she thinks, *you go ahead.*

But she and Katie don't make eye contact when they change positions. Red top and Katie pushes off, strong and smooth, with Sadie's aching arms battering the water just to keep within five seconds of Katie's toes. If she could just get closer, she thinks, she could draft off Katie's wake, let Katie drag her along for a while, but she can't keep close enough.

Marcus doesn't say much to Sadie during the practice. His comments are aimed more at Katie, whose body seems to skim the surface of the water, shooting into the wall just seconds off personal best meet times.

Finally the practice ends and Sadie hauls her body from the pool, thinks she's made a clean break for the shower room when she hears Marcus.

"Sadie. Whoa! I need a second with you."

She turns slowly. "I know, I know. Bad practice."

"It wasn't that bad. You've been swimming hard, hitting the weights hard. You'll be tired. The main thing is to keep your spirits up through this final push." One hand holds his clipboard and the other massages the back of his neck, as if this final push wears on him too.

"No lecture?" She forces a smile, pulling off her red plastic cap, wincing as it tears at her hair. "It'll be hard to keep my spirits up with the rookies passing me at practice. With Lucinda telling me it's all a waste of time."

"Katie is not a junior. She's getting fast. She's put in her time, a solid apprenticeship behind the nation's best." He smiles to reinforce that he's handing out a rare compliment. "I expect her to break onto the national scene this year." He stops talking and scratches the back of his neck.

Yes, Sadie thinks, *wrong pep talk.*

"Don't think about Katie," he continues. "Think Sadie. You're in a different training phase, more fatigued. As you should be. Remember: we have a plan and we're executing it." With these words, he puts his palm on Sadie's head like a priest giving a blessing.

In the shower, Sadie leans her head against the wall, closes her eyes, and lets the hot water soothe the ache across her neck, through her shoulders. Marcus ignored her comment about Lucinda altogether. "When it comes to bitterness, grapefruit has nothing over Lucinda," she'd heard him say before.

"Y'okay, Sade?"

She opens her eyes to see Katie, a swimsuit hanging from one hand and a bottle of shampoo in the other.

"Sure," she says, tossing her head as if she can shake loose the fatigue that's gripped her mind, her body. "Just tired. Good practice today, Katie. You were flying."

"Thanks!"

A smile lifts Katie's features, and Sadie is caught off guard by the effect of her compliment. She turns off the water and follows Katie to the change room.

"Any dates with Russ?" Sadie blurts, plopping her wet body on the bench facing her locker, desperate to talk about anything other than Katie beating her at practice.

"He's not a bad guy," Katie says, her head buried deep in her locker, her arm tossing clothes onto the bench behind her. "At least so far—he's been real sweet. I told him I've been warned: first sign of the typical jock bullshit, I'm gone." She pulls her head from the locker, turns to her pile of clothes. "Hey—I've seen you around a lot with that wrestler. What's going on there?" She pulls a T-shirt on over her damp and sticky skin.

"Oh—Digger?" Sadie still sits undressed, facing her open locker, the pile of clothes too far to reach. "He's . . ." she finally lifts herself from the bench, grabs some socks off the bottom pile. "This locker's a disgrace. We're friends, I guess. Weight training partners?" She shrugs, bends over to pull up a sock. It's already soaked from the

135

sloppy floor and she changes her mind, throwing it in her gym bag and looking again to her locker for a suitable article of clothing. "I like him. He's not smooth and polished like other guys around this building. If anything, he's guaranteed to say the wrong thing most of the time. But I kind of like that. He's—" She pauses, pulling out a pair of sweatpants, then feels the pressure of silence and finishes her sentence quickly, shaking her wet hair "—I dunno. We're just at the same place right now."

"No action?" Katie asks, slamming her locker door and clicking its lock.

"No. No action," Sadie answers, head stuck in the neck of her sweatshirt. "Life is like swimming: done alone."

Katie slicks back her wet hair and pulls on a ball cap, waiting for an explanation.

Sadie herself wonders what she means, something about independence, about needing no one. Wouldn't that make life easier, the road to her Olympic medal more direct? "It's a line from Ethel Wilson's *Swamp Angel*. Never mind. With Digger, the timing's off. We're both pretty consumed with training right now. And a buddy of his—" She stands and tries to hold all the clothes, shoes, flutter boards, pull buoys inside her locker while she forces the door shut. "—Well, kinda cracked up. Had a bit of a meltdown. So lately we've mostly been visiting him in the psych ward. I'm keeping Digger company on his suicide watch." She swings her gym bag over her shoulder to follow Katie out of the change room.

"Eeeps! Romantic—" Katie stops at the water fountain, bends down for a long drink.

"It's okay. We're just keeping each other company. It's not about romance. Romance takes too much energy. So does sex." She sighs.

"There's a little party at Russ's parents' tonight. They're outta town and Russ is house-sitting. Just a casual hot tubbing sort of deal. You two can come—if you want an excuse to hang out with him somewhere other than the psych ward."

They've reached the change room's exit doors. "Yeah, maybe," Sadie answers, pushing her body into the heavy doors.

"Then there's the big Fernie weekend."

"Fernie weekend?"

Katie pauses, about to veer towards the cage. "Yeah, some girl on the volleyball team won a gift certificate for a big condo at the ski hill. Saturday night. Everyone's going. You should come." She squeezes Sadie's arm, waves as she bounces off. "I know some of the wrestler guys are going. It'll be fun."

Sadie's shift doesn't start for another hour, so she pushes the heavy door to the basement, where she plans to catch the end of Digger's wrestling practice. She walks down the quiet, dark stairwell slowly, the hollow silence reminding her of the depths of the swimming pool. Fernie? God, a skiing weekend—how foreign. Something other people do.

The noise of the sweatbox hits her before its smell. Whistles. Groans. Yells. Bodies thudding against the mat. Claps. The room swarms with sweating men and smells like them. But overriding the salty smell of sweat is the pungent aroma of vinegar. Sadie sees one other spectator, a young boy sitting on a rolled-up mat, his back against the concrete wall and his legs swung over the roll of mat while his butt slides down the crack between it and the wall. Sadie swings her own legs over the mat beside him.

"What's with the vinegar?" she asks, touching her nose.

He points his head to a mop pail filled with clear liquid and sitting at their feet. "They wash the mats with it. So the guys don't get ringworm."

Sadie nods and turns her eyes towards the middle of that mat where Digger wrestles with a giant brown guy whose stance reminds her of a grizzly bear. Thick black hair covers his back, lying flat to his skin, and his eyebrows are so bushy they seem to take up most of his face. She can't believe how soaked in sweat Digger is—his wet shirt slaps against his body and his hair looks as if he's just dunked his head in a swimming pool. Sweat streams down his face and he blinks often to keep the salt out of his eyes. No break though—the coach with the big cauliflower ears stays on him.

"That's it, Digger. Don't let up now," he yells through cupped hands.

In less than a minute, he yells again. "You gotta go for it when it's there. No slowing down." The coach works harder than most of the wrestlers, his face red and beads of sweat forming on his forehead. "Take every opportunity," he yells, bent over with both hands on his knees. "Don't expect him to give you another. Take it now." Then, "Go. Go. Go."

As far as the coach is concerned, Digger is the only one in the room. Sadie guesses that's because no one else is going to the Olympics.

Chlorine and sweat tickle the skin around Sadie's ears in the hot room. Her skin breaks a sweat and itches under her sweatshirt. She scratches and watches, wishing she could pull her heavy sweatshirt over her head, but she's naked underneath.

Digger doesn't look at her. No one does, though they must've seen her come in. Each man looks only at his opponent. She watches, impressed with Digger's speed, strength, and stamina. She wonders if he is showing off for her and then feels her skin grow hotter, fans her neck with her hand. He wins every takedown—takes a right leg one time, a left leg the next, and then both together on the third time. He makes it look easy, and the grizzly bear's face grows darker, his stance more hunched. Still, he can't get a paw on Digger's leg or near his body. Sadie wonders if anyone could.

Finally, Saul ends practice, blowing his whistle and turning his back on his wrestlers. Digger does a few extra moves with the bear, going over the steps slowly and repeatedly. The bear nods his big head and holds up a paw. Then Digger stops to chat with Fly. Fly bounces around him, apparently unaffected by the intense workout. Digger swats Fly's hand like he would at a real fly and eventually sweeps Fly up over his head and brings him down with his back pinned to the mat. The two lie on the ground, laughing. Next, Digger gets a towel from his gym bag and stands wiping his face and neck with it while he talks in a low voice to Saul. Sadie waits and watches, her head heavy against the concrete wall. Finally, he makes his way to her on the blue rolled mat.

"Wow," she says. "You're good."

He laughs. "You thought I might not be?" He drops his gym bag on the floor, shuffles around for a clean shirt and changes into it.

"Well, maybe not that good."

He sits next to her, wiping his face on his clean sleeve. "How was your practice?"

"Ugh. Brutal. Cement arms."

He studies her face. Their shoulders touch and neither moves away, though both are hot and sticky. "You look like the fun has gone out of your run."

She scrunches up her face. "What?"

"It's something we used to say. When I was an undergrad, someone on the cross-country team dared me to run a marathon—42.2 kilometres. So I did. Most marathon runners are well into their thirties and skinny as skeletons. Here's me, this beefy twenty-year-old kid clodding along with them. But they let me train alongside. Sunday mornings we'd do our long runs—four hours long! For the first two or so hours, everyone chatting, all social. Then, the group would go dead silent, too exhausted and miserable to talk. At that point, someone would always announce, 'The fun has left the run.' We'd struggle along in silence through to the end—no noise except our breath and pounding feet." He raises a leg and lets his foot fall hard against the mat for emphasis.

"Hmmm. Well this is certainly one hell of a marathon," Sadie says, hating the petulant lilt of her voice.

"Yes—and you're coming to its grand finale. The best part. Don't let the fun fall out of your run," Digger speaks in a soft, soothing voice. He pushes her hair off her face.

"But don't you ever   " She rubs her temples. "It's just, now that I'm getting so close to the finish line, I can't help but wonder what's behind it."

She watches her words hit him and bounce to the floor. He won't let them penetrate. They're the only ones left in the room, and they listen to the sound of water in the pipes above them.

"You need a holiday," he finally says.

"A holiday?" She laughs. "When would you suggest I take a holiday?"

"Well." He looks at his watch. "When's your last practice for the weekend?"

"Saturday morning," she says slowly, not sure where this is going. "Tomorrow."

"Great. How about tomorrow, then?"

She looks for a sign he's joking. "Serious?"

"There's a big party in Fernie this weekend. Fly's been bugging me to go. Says I need a break from the sweatbox and the psych ward. He's going early tomorrow morning to get in a day of skiing. I can't go for a whole weekend. Gotta do weights tomorrow morning. But if you wanna drive out with me tomorrow, we could meet everyone there. Go for one night. I think some of your swimming buddies'll be there." He's talking fast, as if he's scared he might change his mind if he rests on a single word. "A weekend mountain retreat. We'll just go for Saturday night."

Sadie says nothing, wonders if the "just" is to convince himself, wonders if he can handle twenty-four hours away from the sweatbox.

"I guess it's a big condo—everyone's just bringing sleeping bags and Therm-a-Rests. Crashing wherever. I said no to Fly at first, but he gave me his best C'MON! No one can resist Fly's C'MON." He lifts her hand from the mat, tugs on her fingers. "C'mon!"

She looks at him, trying to determine whether to take him seriously or not. "I have two shifts at the cage. And Marcus will kill me if I ski."

"Someone can cover your shifts. And we won't ski. We'll just après-ski."

When she doesn't say anything, he smiles and raises his hand for a high-five, indicating that the problem has been solved. She lifts her palm to his, slowly, like a child comparing size. Their fingertips touch, each pad pressing softly. The fleshy heels of their hands push into each other. Their eyes move at the same time to their palms pressed together and they realize that they are an exact match.

Twenty-Five

*D*igger memorizes the streets that lead the way to Ben at The Centre. He rarely has occasion to venture outside his little northwest nucleus, so tightly does his life circle around his training at the University of Calgary. Now that he's quit his biweekly jaunt downtown to work the door at The Drink, he can nearly always be found within a ten-minute radius of the U of C's Phys Ed building. He didn't realize how small his Calgary was until he started his daily trips to the northeast to visit his buddy in the Mental Health Unit. Today, the seventh day of Ben's confinement, Digger finds his way without one wrong turn.

He parks his 1986 RX-7 in guest parking and unfolds himself from it. The RX-7 was cool back in 1986 when he got it as a gift from his dad, a splurge after some investments skyrocketed. "A star athlete needs a star vehicle."

Now rust has eaten holes in both the doors and a host of scratches and dents scatter the body, but he can't afford to replace it, despite the damage it's doing to his back. Fly has taken to referring to it as "The Slipped-Disc Mobile." Digger's hand floats to the pain in his lower back as he climbs the steps to the sliding hospital doors. Yes, indeed, the Slipped-Disc Mobile.

He nods to the lipsticked lady at the reception desk and pushes the up arrow at the elevator. She must recognize him, because she goes back to reading her book. The hospital atmosphere, human voices replaced by beeping machines, makes him nervous and he realizes he's holding his breath, sure the sour air swims with germs. Inside the elevator, he takes a deep breath but chokes on the smell. He hates the smell of hospitals, believes he's smelling death even though he knows it's just antiseptic mixed with stale bodies, bodies not getting enough fresh air and exercise.

On the fifth floor, he steps out of the elevator and nods to the fat man sitting behind a computer at the central station.

"He's looking better today," the man says. "He'll be happy to see you."

Digger raises his hand in a wave of acknowledgement but doesn't say anything, too intimidated by the hush, by the drugged faces he imagines watching him from every room.

Ben's room is four doors down from the desk, and Digger rounds the corner slowly, always afraid of what he might see in Ben's bed. But today Ben's eyes land surely on Digger's face, lucid.

"Well—hey! Big Man! Welcome back to earth," Digger says a little louder than he intended.

"Hey," Ben repeats, looking down at his sheets, pulling them tight across his chest.

Digger can see that Ben is embarrassed and looks quickly away, studies the landscape painting next to the door, two deer chomping on grass, spectacular mountain scene behind them. Ben is still in a private room and Digger's happy for that, doesn't know if he could handle making conversation with real crazy people. Ben has been reading. On his side table sits an orange, hardcover copy of *The Teachings of Buddha* with a bookmark placed a third of the way in, and next to that an untouched Styrofoam cup of green hospital Jell-O. Digger imagines a giant Jell-O-making machine, like something out of *Charlie and the Chocolate Factory*, working unceasingly in the basements of hospitals across the country. He sits down next to the side table.

"So you're reading. Does that mean they cut off your supply?" So far this week, Ben has been way too high to read.

Ben cracks his first smile. "Yeah, they're drying me out a bit." He runs his hand along the metal bar at the side of his bed. Forward and back, forward and back, forward and back. The motion makes Digger dizzy and he has to sit on his own hands to keep himself from reaching out and stopping Ben's. "I mean, they're still playing around with doses, but they started me in counselling today, so they wanted me to be somewhat alert."

"Counselling? All right! That's good news. We gotta get you outta here, man. I'm getting desperate for friends. I even got roped into some hot tub party at a basketball player's house tonight."

"Hanging out with the b-ball boys?" Ben exhales a small huff that vaguely resembles laughter.

"I dunno," Digger shakes his head. "He's seeing a friend of Sadie's or something. I guess she thought we could use a change from hanging out at the psych ward." He watches for Ben's laugh, sees the hand moving on the metal bar—back and forth, back and forth, back and forth. "Sorry, Ben. Trying to be funny." He bounces his clenched fist against his own forehead. "I'm not so good with psychward etiquette. This all falls far outside my repertoire. But I'm doing my best, okay?" He reaches out like he might pat Ben's head or his shoulder, but his hand stops halfway, as if he's forgotten what he meant to do with it. "So tell me, what'd you and the counsellor talk about?" He brings his hand to rest between his mouth and his nose so he can breathe in the smell of his own skin rather than the smell of Ben and sickness.

"Usual psychobabble." Ben's face, in contrast to his running hand, is very still, almost motionless. "He figures that the root of my 'episode' is disappointment at not making the Olympics."

"He needs a Ph.D. to figure that out?" Digger addresses his question to Ben's hand rather than his face, since the hand is what seems most alive.

Ben continues as if Digger hasn't spoken, "He says I need to learn to focus on the process rather than the end, says that I need to recognize that the value of my experience in sports was in the process." The hand strokes faster and faster. "I said—how about if someone took away your medical license, nabbed your Ph.D., and said, 'Hope you enjoyed the process'? How would you like that, I said."

143

The hand slows a little and Digger is able to take his eyes away from it, looks at Ben's face. "And what did doc say to that?"

"He said we were talking about me, not him, and maybe we had accomplished enough for today." Ben smiles for the second time in a week. "He gave me this to read." He gestures with his elbow at the orange book without letting go of the metal bar. "He says he wants to talk about religion tomorrow, says he sees a similarity between a priest and an elite athlete. Single-minded devotion and all of that."

Digger feels like he's lost the train of the conversation. "Mmm, and what'd you say to that?"

"I said—maybe like a priest who turns thirty and discovers there's no God." The knuckles on the moving hand are turning white from effort. "Or there is a God and He just doesn't give a shit about anyone over twenty-five."

Digger scratches his ear. "So this therapy is really cheering you up then?"

Ben studies the bed sheets pulled tight around his chest, and Digger can see his eyes are welling up.

"You're going to be okay, Ben." He knows he's said the same words a dozen times in the last week, and wishes he could think of anything else to say. He reaches out and stops the moving hand, squeezes it and holds it tight.

Twenty-Six

Steam rises around Sadie's face and she ties her frizzed hair on top of her head to stop it itching the back of her neck. She soaks in Russ's parents' hot tub with three other girls—Katie and two women off the U of C basketball team. Digger plays table soccer in the basement with Fly and a bunch of Russ's basketball buddies. Sadie leans her head back on the tub's edge and looks up at the full moon.

"Ahhh, take me away," she says, closing her eyes.

Shouts from the match downstairs reverberate up to the girls outside.

"Such boys. All games. You'd think with a hot tub full of barely clothed beautiful women, they'd rather be out here," pouts Katie. She lifts a cool, dewy beer bottle to her lips and takes three long swallows. "Can't let it get warm." She downs the rest of it in one smooth motion.

A lanky basketball player named Karen pulls her long body out of the water and props herself on the highest seat in the tub to cool down. She pulls in her limbs, trying to make room for the others, her elbows and knees jutting above the water's surface. Sadie notes the smoothness of Karen's legs and reminds herself to keep her furry calves fully submerged, hidden.

"We need more drinks," Karen says ,eyeing the empty bottle in her hand. "Remember, we're training for the real party, tomorrow night. Fernie-palooza."

"I'll go," Katie volunteers. She jumps out of the tub wearing a tiny blue bikini—her legs are shaved too, Sadie notes—and tiptoes through the snow to the back door, opens it a crack, and shouts down the stairs, "The ladies need more drinks!"

Sadie coolly observes, thinking Katie too bold, too obvious. She doesn't yet realize how cute she is, that she doesn't have to work so hard to attract. Sadie bets that by next Christmas, Katie will have fucked her way through half the varsity teams.

"Ladies need more drinks," Sadie hears Digger yell. "Ladies need more drinks," Russ yells. In moments, one of the nameless basketball players ducks his head through the doorframe and hands Katie a fresh six-pack. She takes it from him with a curtsy and hurries back to the warm water.

She hands a beer to everyone. "And two to spare." Then, on the second thought, "One for the fetcher," and she guzzles a full bottle before jumping into the hot tub and opening another.

"Hmmm, even a twenty-year-old in a bikini didn't get those guys out here?" Karen says, sliding her body back into the water. "What're they doing?"

"Foosball," says Katie. "Table soccer or naked women—not even a toss-up, apparently." Her eyes scan the yard as she drinks her beer.

"Heterosexual jocks are all latent homosexuals," Sadie says, her head still leaned back, her eyes closed. "They're good enough guys once you understand that. They just like each other more than they like women."

The three other women laugh. Stella—a short basketball guard with a nearly shaved head—laughs the loudest. "That's what I tell Jeff! He drops me in a second if Russ calls. Russ this, Russ that. He tells me I should be happy, that the best way to judge the quality of a potential boyfriend is how he treats his friends. Therefore, he's a great boyfriend, right? Right—I say—a great boyfriend to Russ!" She laughs, rubbing a beer bottle against her neck and face.

"Boys, boys, boys . . ." Katie slurs. "Let's talk about anything else." She takes a noisy slurp of beer. "You'll never guess who asked me out, Sades. Bogdan!"

Sadie feels acidic jealousy rolling about her stomach, even though she herself has never considered going out with Bogdan. Katie's just arrived and has already taken over the place. "Hmmm, I feared you were going to say Marcus," Sadie says coolly.

"Ewww! Gross!" Katie laughs, leaning her head back and opening her jaw so wide Sadie can see the roof of her mouth, imagines seeing right down her dark throat.

"I think Marcus is kinda hot," says Stella, "for an older guy."

"Mmm, nice pecs," agrees Karen.

"Are you going to go out with him?" Sadie asks, ignoring the other two.

"Ick! Marcus?!"

"No—Bogdan."

"Nah. Well, I dunno. Probably eventually. Chances are—" She twirls a bottle around her fingers.

"I thought you're going out with Russ?" Sadie asks, sitting upright now, eyes squinting at Katie through the steam.

"I'm not that naïve. I know how it works around here. You need a backup. And a backup for your backup." She jumps out of the water, ignoring Sadie's glare and splashing Karen. "Let's roll in the snow," she blurts, dropping the empty bottle on the ground. "Hot/cold therapy. It's good for the muscles."

"No way," says Karen. "But you go right ahead. I'm way too comfy in here."

"Anyone dare me?" Katie asks.

"Look at that snow," says Sadie, letting her body fall back under the water, closing her eyes. "I'd rather spend an extra two hours with Marcus. Marcus and Bogdan. In a bad mood."

It rained during the warm spell, then froze again. A hard crust covers the icy snow.

"Five bucks? Five bucks if I roll in the snow?" Katie says, already jogging to a white spot.

"Sure, I'll give you five bucks if you roll in that," says Stella, letting her empty bottle drop in the snow beside Katie's. "You gotta stay in, though. It can't just be a quick roll."

Katie wobbles to the middle of the yard, the beer hampering her balance, and tries to keep her smile as the icy snow scrapes her shins. She stands in the middle of the yard, snow up to mid-calf, tiny patches of baby blue material covering her breasts and crotch, the rest of her glowing bright white in the moonlight. "This spot good enough?"

Everyone nods. "A hardcore masochist," laughs Stella. "Have to be to swim four hours a day, I guess."

"Or to go out with Russ," Sadie mutters under her breath, pretending not to watch.

Katie lifts her hands high above her head, one hand atop the other, biceps pressed against her ears, and bends her knees to gently lay her body down on the ice. Sadie notices that it's a perfect streamline position. Katie rolls her naked body over in the snow once, "That's once."

Then again. "Twice," she forces out in a gasp.

And again. "Three times," she shouts, victorious.

Sadie imagines the snow scraping across the soft skin on Katie's bare belly. Then Katie stands, brushes herself off as if she's been rolling in the sand, stumbles a little, and stomps back towards the hot tub with her lopsided grin.

"That'll be five bucks." She holds a hand out to Stella.

Stella slaps it in a high-five. "I'll get it to you when we're out of here." She hands Katie the last beer; Katie holds the bottle to her lips and guzzles.

Sadie laughs, reclining back into her closed-eyed position. "If those guys only knew what they were missing." She scrapes frost off the frozen hair hanging on her forehead. "Nearly nude women rolling in the snow."

"Speaking of those guys," says Katie. "We need more drinks."

"I'll go," Karen says. "My turn." She swings a long leg over the edge of the tub, steps straight off the deck and to the ground, bypassing the stairs. Outside the tub, she tugs on her bikini top, pushing her small breasts high, striving for more exposure. "Let's see if I can get them out here."

The other women watch through the windows as Karen enters

the door, yelling, "Ladies need more drinks," and jogs down the stairs wearing nothing but the strategically arranged bikini.

Stella laughs. "That'll have to get them."

Moments later, Karen returns by herself, carrying a new six-pack. She sighs, plopping her body back in the water. "That settles it—"

"—They're gay," all four women finish in unison.

"And that would explain why they all want anal sex all the time," Stella says, laughing along with the rest.

Katie chokes on her beer. "What?!"

The rest laugh louder.

Stella turns red. "Oh, Karen, you dirty girl. I can't believe you said that."

Each of the girls lifts a bottle to her lips.

"Who wants to race?" Katie raises her beer in the air and then presses it to her lips, leaning her head way back.

"Okay—my turn for some hot/cold therapy," says Sadie, ignoring Katie's new contest and looking for a soft patch of snow. She hops out into the cold—too startled to worry about hiding her furry legs—and runs for a soft spot in a sheltered corner, rolls once, short and fast, then runs back to the tub. "Holy shit, that's cold," she laughs, plunging her body back in the hot water.

"Well, now we all have to go," Karen says, already swinging a leg out of the tub. "Ready, Stell?" Stella heads for the hot tub stairs and both run to Sadie's soft spot in the snow.

"I still get my five bucks," Katie pouts. "I went first."

"You'll get it, you'll get it." Stella hugs herself warm, hurrying back into the pool.

"We need beer, whose turn?" Katie asks, swinging her empty bottle like a pendulum in front of her face. There's still one left from the last pack and it's clear Katie wants an excuse to go see the boys.

"You go," says Karen. "We all just got back in the tub. I'm not going back in the cold."

Katie sinks into the water up to her chin. "I already went."

"I'll give you another five bucks," says Stella, dropping her bottle onto the snow beside the growing pile. She twists open the last bottle.

Karen and Sadie laugh.

"You can't buy me," Katie slurs.

"Yeah right," laughs Sadie. "We've all seen what you'll do for five bucks, Kates."

Katie bites her lip, trying not to laugh. "Okay, make it ten if I can get them out here?"

"Done!" Stella answers.

Katie jumps out of the tub, yanks her bikini bottom high over her hips, and in a single smooth motion pulls the top over her head. She swings it like a lasso and it lands in the middle of the tub, splashing warm, heavily chlorinated water into Stella's face. Ignoring Stella's glare, Katie strikes a pose, jutting out a hip and holding her hands high above her head. She pivots towards the door.

"If that doesn't get them out here—" Karen says, resting her head on one edge of the tub and stretching her long leg to raise a heel out onto the opposite edge.

The three women watch as Katie walks inside the house, "Ladies need more drinks!" She runs down the stairs.

They wait. In five minutes, Digger and Fly come outside wearing their red leather Dinos Wrestling jackets.

"Ready to go?" asks Digger. "We got a big trip tomorrow."

"Is Katie okay?" Sadie asks, lifting her shoulders out of the hot water.

"Oh yeah," grins Fly. "Your friend Russ will take care of her."

Sadie feels herself cringe at the lilt Fly gives the word friend. No secrets in the Phys Ed building.

Digger grabs a towel from the pile beside the door, holds it open. Sadie pulls herself out of the tub and steps into it.

Twenty-Seven

*D*igger checks the small map scribbled on the back of a pool
schedule and pulls the Slipped-Disc Mobile into Sadie's cul-
de-sac. He stops the car behind her rusted brown Toyota, crumples
the map into a small ball, and stuffs it into the ashtray. The car
might be a wreck, but he likes it neat. He creaks open his door
and grips the top of the door frame, preparing to pull himself out
of the low reclined seat, when he sees Sadie jogging out the front
door. Good. He lets his weight fall back into the seat, waves out
the front windshield. Sadie smiles in response. She's wearing a red
Dinos toque pulled low down to her eyes despite the fact that the
sun is shining and Calgary again feels distinctly spring-like. A small
backpack is slung over her right shoulder, and Digger's relieved
she's a light packer. His tiny car is already near to full, shoeboxes
taking up half the back seat and most of the hatchback. Each box
is stuffed with wrestling shoes he's supposed to sell to supplement
his carding income.

She opens the door and bends herself into the car.

"Welcome to my luxury sports car."

Sadie laughs, adjusting the seat, pulling her legs in after the rest
of her body.

"Seat belts," Digger says, pointing to a buckle that's fallen
down between the seats. "This model is pre-airbags. A classic, you
might say."

Sadie buckles in while Digger backs out, and they're off with a celebratory blast of the engine as Digger brings his foot down hard on the gas pedal.

"A road trip!" Sadie smiles. "You have no idea how long it's been since I went somewhere that was an actual holiday and not a swim meet."

"Oh, I think I have some idea." Digger says, adjusting his rearview mirror. "How was practice this morning?"

"Great for me." She pulls off her toque and ruffles her hair. The smell of chlorine permeates the small car. "It was rough for Katie, though. The flip turns weren't treating her so well."

"I bet." He lets his back slide low into the seat, settling in for a long ride.

"She barfed in the gutter thirty minutes into practice, but Marcus wouldn't let her stop. Kept the little speedball off my feet. For today at least."

Digger drives south on Macleod Trail, winding through the heavy traffic and passing an endless strip of restaurants, coffee shops, and discount stores. Sadie has slipped off her boots and propped her stockinged feet on the dashboard, her knees pulled into her chest.

He notices that she's massaging her shoulder, hard, as if she's digging her fingers deep into the muscle, touching bone. "Sore shoulder?"

"Swimmers always have sore shoulders." She smiles and lets go of her shoulder, absently curls a piece of hair around the tip of her nose. "God, this city is getting huge. It sprawls and sprawls. Makes our little corner of it seem pretty insignificant." Her forehead is stuck against the passenger window and she stares.

He can't imagine himself or any of the other wrestlers discussing their own insignificance. He resists teasing her, repeating her words, because he's afraid she'll mistake his ribbing for mockery, afraid she'll start talking like Ben or Fly.

"What d'you think about when you race?" he asks her.

"Nothing," she says, without lifting her forehead off the cool window.

"Nothing?"

"Absolutely."

"Me too—all body, no brain, right?"

They're out of town now and he's holding an even ninety kilometres an hour. A steady stream of cars passes them in the outside lane.

"Autopilot. You put in all those hours training so that when it comes to competition, you can go on autopilot. But I wouldn't say it's no brain—more like mind control, turning off the senses you don't need. Zoom in. Close the doors to everything else."

"What do you hear?" he asks.

Signs along the highway advertise hotels in Okotoks.

"Nothing." Her face still presses against the window as she counts the billboards passing by. "I shut off my ears."

"Yeah, me too. Just blank air. The world disappears. All those people cheering and I don't hear a word."

He swings the car right on the turn-off for Okotoks.

"They cheer for themselves," she says, lifting her head from the glass. Digger notices the pressure of the window has left a red mark in the dead centre of her forehead. She looks around Okotoks, a sleepy bedroom community where each monstrosity of a house looks exactly like the next. She tells him that when she was growing up in Calgary, suburban kids used to call this commuter town "Smoke-a-tokes."

As they pull out of Okotoks onto Highway 22 to Black Diamond, Sadie slaps both hands on her knees, announcing, "Here's a thought for you—"

Digger has known her for less than two months and already he has grown used to her onslaught of "thoughts."

"I read somewhere that a life oriented towards leisure is a life oriented towards death." She speaks quickly, as if she's afraid she'll lose him if she dawdles. "Because death is the ultimate form of leisure. The Great Rest."

He nods.

"But recreation is the opposite, right? Re-creation. Regeneration. Rebirth. Recreation affirms life. Renews life."

He shifts the clutch and speeds up for the highway to Black Diamond.

"So where does sport fit? Are elite athletes killing themselves or making themselves more alive?"

"Hmmm. Is there a right answer? A prize?" He smiles, looking sideways from the road to her.

"Unfortunately, I think it's gotta be the first," she says, giving his knee a playful shove to show she's not ignoring his flirtation. "Death through over-exertion instead of leisure's death through inertia. Sport delivers death through a slow wearing-out and killing of body parts."

"Holy doom and gloom, lady! Talk about worst-case scenario. Olympic athletes get what everybody wants. Immortality. A gold medalist's name lives forever."

She pinches her bottom lip between her thumb and her index finger, but she doesn't say anything for a few minutes.

She smiles. "Guess we'd better win ourselves some gold medals then." She balls her hand into a tight fist and wipes the condensation off the inside of the window. The weather's darkened as they've gained distance from Calgary. Heavy slush falls from the sky, splatters the window. "Visibility's not great, hey?"

"It's alright," he says, flipping on the windshield wipers. "Where'd you hear that quote anyway? About a life of leisure?"

"Bathroom wall."

His eyes move from the road to her.

"It was written on a bathroom wall."

He laughs. "That's it—we're done with Sadie's Thoughts of the Day! You're making me think too much. A bathroom wall? We're on holidays!" He pushes a Tragically Hip CD into the stereo. "No more thinking about wrestling, swimming, or sports of any kind. I don't want to hear so much as a curling rock for the rest of the weekend." He turns up the volume. "Relax. Look at the mountains." He points towards their hazy silhouettes far in the distance.

Sadie watches the mountains, listening to the Tragically Hip compete with the motor's hum.

"When I was a kid, I went to these wrestling camps in the States," says Digger into the silence. "None of us was even in high school yet. Just kids. And we ran, wrestled, and lifted weights fourteen hours a day. Looking back, it was child abuse. Men yelling at us. Hitting us. Telling us if we couldn't handle it, we should go back to our mommies. Calling us names if we wanted to stop. *Loser, wimp,*—" He looks at her, embarrassed. "—*pussy.* We were just kids. I remember fathers kicking their sons, kicking them hard in the ribs. *Quitter. Good for nothing.*"

He pauses, flicking the windshield wipers up a gear.

"Hell," Sadie announces, running her fingers over her lips, looking out the window away from Digger.

"Yep," he answers. "Still, would I be as good now if I hadn't done that then? I don't know. I wouldn't change a thing. In case the answer is no. But when I think on my childhood, that's all I remember. There must have been something else. But those camps, they're what I remember."

He feels Sadie's hand at the back of his neck but won't look at her, knows his face is growing red—partly from his confession, partly from her unexpected touch. She massages the tight knots in his muscles.

"That okay?" she asks quietly.

He smiles his answer and removes a hand from the steering wheel, pats her knee briefly. She wonders if they might pass out of the "no action" stage she's been so insistent upon. A weekend away together without following through on all this flirtation seems unlikely. Then again—they'll be packed into a condo with hordes of drunk, snoring jocks. They might be safe yet. She massages his neck hard until her own hand goes numb.

Soon they come to a four-way stop and Digger realizes they're already in Black Diamond. He turns left onto the bare stretch to Longview. Sadie flips absently through his glovebox. Before he can stop her, her fingers close on a white envelope. Too late.

"Pictures! Can I look?" But she's already pulling them out.

"Those—they're, they're kind of a joke," he says, talking faster than usual. There goes his chance of this turning into anything other than a friendship. "Brace yourself." He turns his eyes back to the road, using his peripheral vision to monitor her reaction.

As she looks at the first picture, he turns up the stereo, tries to think of something else. In the photo, Fly poses wearing women's lingerie. His knees are close together and he leans forward with a hand on each. His lips pout into the camera. Thin spaghetti straps stretch across his shoulders and the pink lacey lingerie pulls at his chest and across his hips, comes down to his mid-thighs. His shoulders press together to create a kind of cleavage in the neckline dip where cleavage is meant to be. This faux cleavage combined with the jut of his hip, which creates the illusion of a waist, makes him look almost feminine, almost delicate. Sadie whistles under her breath and flips to the next picture. In it, Digger wears the pink teddy. On him, the fabric stretches farther, his pecs bulging out the sides. The lingerie barely covers the top of his thighs. He stands with one hand on his hip, the other lifted palm-up to an imagined hair-do. His smile teeters on the verge of breaking into a laugh.

"Very Marilyn Monroe," says Sadie, flipping to the final photo.

This time she laughs. Here, Ben—in all his bulk—is squeezed into the teddy. He bends forward to hide the fact that the pink material doesn't quite make it to the top of his legs. The pink looks like a hanky across his wide chest, his nipples naked and the spaghetti straps buried in his fury chest. He tilts his chin towards his chest, eyes opened wide into the camera. On Ben, the lingerie covers him like a doily.

Sadie spreads the pictures out in a fan and studies each as if she is an old man playing cards for nickels. Finally, she piles them neatly together, puts them back into the envelope and back into the glove compartment. Snapping the glovebox closed, she turns to Digger.

"Explanation. Please."

He reaches for the volume knob and lowers it, then scratches his ear. "Are you sure you want to know?"

"I'm very sure I want to know."

He bites his lip, chasing away a smile. "We were in Iran for a tournament. So bored. Nothing to do but play cards in our dorm room—"

"So bored that it seemed like a good idea to wear women's lingerie?"

"Patience! I'm getting there." He clutches, slows down as they drive through Longview—a small town infamous for its police radar traps. "My girlfriend at the time had packed my bag for me and when I got there, I couldn't find my red singlet, just my blue one. So I'm ripping through my bag in a panic. No singlet. But out comes this little lace stretchy thing, soaked in Obsession perfume. The guys were both there; they both saw it. Actually, they smelled it before they saw it. So I ask, 'What the hell am I supposed to do with this?' My whole bag smells like women's perfume. All my wrestling gear—like women's perfume. Fly grabs the lingerie from me and says, 'Oh, believe me—I know what you're supposed to do with it,' and he starts—well, you know Fly, you can imagine what he started doing—pretending the lingerie was his own blow-up girlfriend. Ben is watching and laughing away. Of course, he's gotta get in on it too, so he says, 'I bet we're supposed to wear it. She knew we'd be bored. She sent it for entertainment.' Next thing, Fly's pulling it over his head, striking poses. Pretty damn hilarious, you have to admit. So you can see how it progressed from there." Deep dimples dig themselves into his cheeks. "In Iran, you have to make your own fun." He speeds up again on the other side of Longview. "The girlfriend wasn't too happy, though. Apparently, she'd never worn the thing and was planning to . . . well, planning to use it when I got back. That changed. No one was using it for anything after Fly and Ben had stretched it to shit."

Sadie still hasn't said anything.

"Before Fly got his hands on it," Digger continues. "Ben thought maybe I should actually use it in Iran, that maybe I was meant to wrestle in it instead of the red singlet."

Holding his breath, he turns to look at Sadie and feels immense relief when he sees she's biting the insides of her cheeks to stop herself from laughing. He takes a breath.

"And people think swimmers are weird," she says. "I thought wrestlers' quirks were all ear-related."

She flips out the Tragically Hip and changes to Spirit of the West, leans back. "So what's next on the Tour De Digger?"

"Just blank highway from here to the Frank Slide. We are now officially in the middle of nowhere."

"Frank Slide!" Her feet push against the dashboard, knees to her chest, and she looks so like a little kid curled up in the front seat. "I used to love the Frank Slide. We'd drive through on family vacations all the time. One day it's a town, the next day it's a pile of enormous rocks. I never drive by without imaging the lives of those people—no control over their own futures. Do you know the myth?"

He shakes his head, relieved that it was so easy to get off the lingerie topic.

"The myth is that everyone in the town was killed except a little baby called Frank. He somehow slid into a crevice between two rocks and was found there by rescuers doing the cleanup." She's absently rubbing the back of his neck again, staring at the empty road ahead. "Not true," she continues. "I believed it for years. But then I went to the interpretive centre. Lots of people lived," Sadie says unhappily. "I know—weird to be disappointed. But to believe something for so long and then find out you're wrong—that's upsetting. The town was always called Frank, even before the slide. There was no invincible baby."

She pauses and rests her head back against the window. It's still more than a hundred kilometres to Crowsnest Pass and the Slide so they're going to need another topic. Digger enjoys the silence for now, not worried about long, awkward lulls because he knows she'll come up with something else. For a while, they're quiet, occasionally tapping one another to point out a homey ranch down in the valley or white-capped mountains in the distance.

"Do you read sci-fi?" she asks suddenly.

"When I was a kid. Lately—I don't—I haven't really—no, honestly, I really don't read at all anymore. Truthfully, I just wrestle. That's pretty much my life—all there's time for. Pretty brutish, huh?" He notices the snowfall growing heavier and turns up the windshield wipers, praying she doesn't think him shallow or stupid. He resolves to read more.

"Well, there's this old story. All the countries in the world are having a contest to see who can be the first to get a man on the moon. They try and they try but no one can do it. Then finally, the Russians realize there's a glitch in the contest rules. *Aha,* they think, *it doesn't say we have to bring the man back from the moon.* So off they send their man to the moon. They win the contest! The whole country celebrates! No one cares about the poor stranded astronaut." She pauses, waiting for Digger's reaction.

Clumps of heavy slush dot the highway and snow pounds the windshield. Digger slows the car. There are now other vehicles on the road, both in the oncoming lane and behind him, all plodding through the slush just as slowly.

"Why do I feel like you're waiting for a specific response?" asks Digger. "Like someone's forgotten to give me my script?"

"Do you see the metaphor?" Sadie asks.

"Metaphor for what?" He squints at the road in front of him.

"For the Olympics. Astronaut, athlete. Moon, Olympics. Countries take their athletes to these great heights in the name of glory, but when they're done with them—"

"Sadie!" Suddenly, his full attention has turned to her. "You need to snap out of this anti-Olympics thing you have going on. You didn't come this far to psych yourself out."

"I know, I know," she says, pulling her red toque back on, down over her eyebrows. "I need to block the image of Lucinda with a baby on her hip and scowl on her face. Her and her TV swim. I was never like this. It's when my grandma died. I just started thinking too much, started questioning things that I'd always accepted as fact."

"Exactly. You're thinking too much. Try thinking of yourself going fast. Think of yourself winning."

Snow covers everything now, the white road indistinguishable from the white ditch, from the white air. A snowplough's blinking lights head towards them in the oncoming lane. Both look at it, wondering how it turned from spring back to winter so quickly.

Then Digger's heart booms—headlights are coming straight at

him, to the right of the plow. Snow's too damn heavy; he can't see, he can only see the blur of the headlights. Ditch. He tries to yank the wheel hard towards it. Not enough time. The thud of metal on metal jolts him, the car. The car spins, blurring colours. Metal scrapes on metal, drags across pavement. His arm swings out to cover Sadie. The car jolts to a stop; his shoulders and neck snap forward, his forehead hitting something hard. Lifting his head from the wheel, he sees Sadie's eyes wide open, but staring straight ahead. A warm trickle on his face. Reaching towards it, he already knows that it's only from his nose. It's always bleeding. Bleeds if he sneezes too hard. Through his broken windshield, he sees the crumpled hood. Sadie's still frozen, he shakes her shoulders, nothing, he slaps her hard across her right cheek, she coughs, then vomits, brown gunk falling down her chin, onto the front of her shirt, but now she's making choking noises, the car's smoking, there's a face at the window.

"Get her out of the car! We have to get her out of the car! She's choking! There's fire!"

The people move too slowly, but at the same time too quickly; now Sadie's lying on the snow-covered asphalt at the side of the road, red Dinos parka draped over her, his leather jacket a pillow under her head. A woman kneels behind her, her black mitts on the snow, her fingers holding Sadie's head at the temples.

"I'm trained in first aid. We've called for help. An ambulance will be here soon. Just hang in there, honey. You're going to be fine." The stranger talks to Sadie, and Digger wonders if Sadie's in there, if she can hear. He should hold her head; he should talk to her. He sees the driver of the other vehicle—a man in his early twenties, rubbing his face, he paces in tiny circles, "It's all my fault! Stupid! Stupid!" He smacks his own head with each "Stupid."

Yes, thinks Digger, yes it's all your fault. His blood rushes to his head; he wants to charge. He feels a hand on his arm.

"She's conscious," says a man in snowpants and a big fur hat. "In and out."

Digger lunges to her side.

"She says she's going to the Olympics," says the woman holding

Sadie's head between her two palms—one pressed into each of Sadie's temples.

"She is." Digger nods. "She—" he bites off the *was* rising in his throat "—is."

"I can feel my toes," says Sadie, awake again. The voice sounds quiet and high-pitched, nothing like her own. "That means I'm not paralyzed, right?"

"We're going to help you. Help is on its way," says the woman kneeling at her head.

"But that means I'm not paralyzed, right? I'm going to the Olympics."

The snow blows hard now, but Digger doesn't feel the cold at all. Sadie distracts all his senses—Sadie telling everyone she is going to the Olympics, Sadie insisting she can feel her toes and therefore isn't paralyzed, Sadie with a mousey little voice not her own.

He holds his face above hers so she can see him. And her eyes do clear for a moment. The reassuring lady lets go of Sadie's temples, excuses herself to give Digger and Sadie privacy.

"This isn't supposed to happen," says Sadie, looking straight at Digger, her voice apologetic.

She's sorry, thinks Digger, that she's been reduced to a cliché, that she can't think of anything else to say. But then her mouth falls lax and her face rolls towards the wet pavement. Quickly, the woman with black mitts returns, placing a palm on each of Sadie's temples, pulling to provide traction and stability for Sadie's neck.

"You're going to be all right, sweetie. Just hang in there."

Digger realizes both his hands are clasped to his face, just like the other driver, circling in his "stupids." He needs to do something, but what? A woman has called the ambulance, covered Sadie, holds her head. He stands back, kicking at the slush and watching.

Now, the ambulance arrives, the paramedics shove him out of the way with feeble assurances. One policeman interviews him, another hands him Sadie's red parka soaked with sour vomit. He rolls it in a ball and shoves it in the corner of his hatchback, where it will be towed away with the rest of the wreckage. Tomorrow, he'll go to the wreckers and pick up the boxes full of wrestling shoes, the case of his CDs, and all the paperwork jammed into his glove compartment.

After the paramedics load Sadie into the ambulance, a round-faced, pale paramedic tells Digger he can ride with them to the hospital in Black Diamond. Digger steps up into the back of the ambulance and makes himself as small as he can, scrunched into a corner with his back pressed against the door. He listens to Sadie beg for painkillers. It's in her back, she tells them, intense pain. That means she's not paralyzed, right?

The moon-faced paramedic grows stern. "No painkillers until you've seen a doctor. We don't know the extent of the internal trauma you've sustained. Ingesting medication could be fatal." He softens and holds a hand to her forehead. "Just hang tough. We're almost there."

She is tough. Digger knows she's tough. But she's diminished, whining, weak, looking to others for help. He forces her image out of his mind and estimates the kilometres back to Black Diamond.

While ambulance attendants unload Sadie's stretcher at the hospital, Digger skulks into a corner of the waiting room. But he can't sit still, paces restlessly between the coffee and soda pop vending machines, back and forth and back and forth. The hospital is so small and the walls so thin that he can hear every word said in the Emergency Room.

"Likely spinal fracture. Internal trauma," says a curt and efficient voice. "Stomach distended."

"It could be constipation caused by a high-protein diet," says a woman's voice. "She says she's competing in the Olympics."

"Was." The response is a single exhalation as much as it is a word.

"Feel this. Hard as rock. It's more serious than constipation, that's for sure," says a younger male voice.

Digger cannot hear Sadie's voice, but he knows by the doctor's responses that she's talking. Sometimes. He pictures her wide eyes, stunned, pleading. He sits and grabs a magazine. Anything. He flips pages, his eyes not taking in any of the words but only playing with the shiny colours.

"Should we notify your parents?" asks a voice behind the wall.

Her answer is too quiet for Digger to hear.

"Well, we're sure they would want to be notified. Someone will have to call them."

"Should we have your friend call them?" the woman's voice asks.

Digger holds his breath, listening, but still cannot hear Sadie's response.

"You'd prefer a doctor calls them, then?"

Guilt gnaws at Digger's innards, but he's relieved to hear a doctor will call.

"Okay, we're going to do some x-rays and then we'll ship you back to Calgary, to the Foothills Hospital."

He hears Sadie moan as they shift her body for x-rays.

She must be asking her questions about paralysis again. The answers are non-committal: "We're here to help you," "Everyone is going to do their best," "Just relax and try not to worry."

Every word sharpens the gnawing at his insides. He almost wishes he were the one who was hurt.

Almost.

He stands again and resumes pacing, walking circles past the pop machine, the empty bulletin board, the coffee maker, the doorway to Sadie. As he passes the vending machine, he spots his faint reflection in the glass, transparent over the Snickers and Mars bars, and wonders how this weekend has veered so far from his plan.

Twenty-Eight

$\mathcal{S}$adie hardly slept that night, wheeled from one examination table to the next, carted into another ambulance, shipped to Calgary, x-rayed and re-x-rayed. Now, she lies in the Foothills Hospital, a place she knows too well.

"Do you have to do that? It's going to scare the hell out of my parents." She stares at the ceiling. When she moves her eyes from side to side, she can see she's wearing a steel neck brace. A pinch-faced nurse tapes her head to the brace—two long pieces of tape stuck to the middle of her forehead and stretched to opposite sides of the brace, one taped above her left ear, the other above her right.

"We can't have you moving. Not until you've seen the neuro-surgeon."

"Fine. I promise, I won't move." Sadie no longer drowns in pain as she did yesterday in the ambulance, but she figures this reprieve might have something to do with the morphine drip standing at her bedside. Since the nurses set her up in this room in the trauma ward, the pain has only whispered at her from a distance. *You're hurt. You're wrecked. You're broken.*

"I don't go on anyone's word but the neurosurgeon's. Not ever before and not now." The nurse doesn't smile. No emotion registers in her voice. Only boredom.

"I can tell you right now I don't have a broken neck. The tape is overkill." The restraints trap her. She must look ridiculous. If only the nurse would just untape her head, she'd feel better, less caged. She closes her eyes.

"The tape and the brace stay until Dr. Hock says so," the nurse concludes, her footsteps thudding out of the room.

Sadie would not be able to describe her new room. She can't look to the right nor the left. She only sees the ceiling, a white blank. She knows, though, that she is not alone in the room. There are two or maybe three others, moaning and pleading for morphine, asking to be rolled from one side to the other. The lights have been off and the blinds drawn since she arrived. There has also been no sign of her parents yet.

She doesn't know if she sleeps or not. No dreams, no coherent thoughts, just the blank white ceiling and the nagging, faraway pain in her lower back, and the boring, predictable wish that this could all be a very bad dream.

Mechanical noises drown out human voices, the nurses and doctors mere shadows behind the more imperative beeps, buzzes, and drips. And all the time an urgent feeling nags at her, tells her that she has forgotten something, that she is supposed to be somewhere else. *Later*, she thinks, letting her lids fall closed, *I'll get it later.*

When sunlight finally comes through the window, she feels a tap on her shoulder. She opens her eyes to the same blank ceiling.

"Hello, Sadie. I am Dr. Mitchell. I am the physician regarding your general health and then you will be seeing Dr. Hock regarding your spine."

She hears him fumble through some paper.

"That was quite a crash you had. You're lucky to be alive."

"Lucky?" Sadie says in a flat voice to the ceiling. "Lucky is not exactly what I feel right now."

She hears more flipping paper, the click of his pen, a muffled cough, and, embarrassed by the silence, she says, "I used to think four was my lucky number. I'll need a new one."

Dr. Mitchell is still flipping pages. "Four?"

"April. Fourth month."

He hangs a clipboard at the foot of the bed. "Maybe luck

doesn't have a lot to do with it." His tone is no-nonsense. He has no time for lucky and unlucky numbers. "Being so fit worked in your favour," he says. "If you didn't have the muscle mass you do, that car likely would have crushed you. The passenger side of the vehicle, as is most often the case, took all of the impact. Even in a head-on collision, the drivers instinctually veer slightly to protect themselves and the passenger sides collide. Happens every time."

His "as is most often the case" and "every time" remind Sadie that, to him, this is just another day at the office. To Sadie, she is the main character in her own tragedy, but to this doctor she's just a name to be checked off the daily list of chores.

"I hear you're an Olympian."

She groans—this time in embarrassment, not in pain. "You're the sixth person who's said that to me since I got here. Is that all I talked about last night?"

"It was obviously at the forefront of your mind." His voice is softer. For the first time, Sadie wishes she could see him.

Then his tone becomes automated again. "Your internal trauma is minimal. There's not a lot I can do for you. Only time will help you there. Your main concern, though, is your spine, and therefore with Dr. Hock. He's in surgery today and won't be able to see your x-rays— or you—until tonight, or even tomorrow. Until then, the nurses will have to keep you immobile. We have prescribed you regular doses of morphine to manage the pain." He relays this information as if it is no more emotional than the weather report: cloudy periods today; your back's likely broken; wind from the north.

During his speech, Sadie has closed her eyes. After a few moments, she hears him briskly stepping away.

The next time she opens her eyes, her parents stand above her.

"Hi, baby," her father says, and for the first time since the crash, she feels she might cry.

"I hurt my back," she says in her new, mousy voice. But she stops herself from adding, "Daddy." *I hurt my back, Daddy* is what she wants to say.

Then her mother's cool hands are on her forehead.

"That feels good." *That feels good, Mommy.* "Oh no," Sadie moans. "The morphine is making me nauseous."

If she vomits, she won't be able to roll her head to the side; she will choke.

"What can I do for you?" Sadie wonders where her mother's Head Nurse voice has gone. Suddenly she's the one waiting for instructions.

"Just hold your hands on my forehead. That's good. It's cool. I'm so hot. So hot and sick." Her voice whispers from the pillow.

Her father's face above her looks angry, his eyebrows too close together.

"Where's the doctor?" he snaps at his wife, before turning to look for a nurse. "What's being done for my daughter? Can she at least get some bloody Gravol before she chokes on her own vomit?"

Sadie pictures her mother wearing the long fur coat—a soft, dry, cool sleeve rubbing against her hot and clammy cheek. But her mother's arm is bare. Her mother says it's too warm for fur. Sadie thinks of the snowy highway heading towards Fernie and can't believe that it's spring just outside her window.

"It wasn't our fault," says Sadie. "The accident. The guy was in our lane." She's overwhelmed by a need to apologize. People were counting on her. She feels the sweeping flood of remorse fill her insides. "He was going the wrong way. We were going the right way."

"Shhh, honey, shhh." Her mother has found ice and rubs a cube across Sadie's forehead, along her hairline, then uses a rough white cloth to wipe away the water before it trickles into her ears.

"I dreamt about Grandma," she says with her eyes closed, feeling the cold tickle on her skin. "She was alive, but so sick, so so sick. And nobody would help her. She wanted me. She called and cried for me. But I was gone. I was in Sydney. I wanted to help her. I should have helped her."

"Shhh, honey, shhh," her mother says again.

And her father again speaks roughly to the nurse. "What's wrong with my daughter? You're giving her too much morphine. She's having nightmares. I won't tolerate her having nightmares. As if her condition isn't bad enough without nightmares. Where is the doctor?" Her mother and father, she notes, have switched roles, him bitching, her pampering.

Sadie feels the cool water bead on her skin, and imagines herself curled up on the floor of the pool, looking up through the water to the surface, her father's lips moving without a sound.

Twenty-Nine

$\mathcal{D}$igger's footsteps resound in the empty hallways of the Foothills Hospital. He has spent more time in hospitals this last few months than in all his thirty years' worth of months combined. He shuts his nose, breathes through his mouth, and looks to the ground.

He has not seen Sadie since the accident, almost three days now. She's still in the trauma ward so, technically, visits are restricted to family. But once he was ready to find out, he called her mother and found out that no one really enforces the rules. Friends are allowed in for short visits.

He coerced Fly—bribed him with beer—into coming along for moral support. But Fly has stopped in the coffee shop downstairs, urging Digger to go ahead for some "preliminary alone time."

"Go on. I'll be there in five." Seeing Digger shuffle circles in the hallway, lingering outside the coffee shop, Fly'd given him a shove in the direction of the elevators. "Go! You're a big kid. You'll be fine. Five minutes."

Digger doesn't know why being badly hurt and recovering in a hospital makes Sadie so inexplicably terrifying, but his head feels detached from his neck and his hands far away from his body, everything disjointed and out of his control. He's scared to round the corner, scared to see Sadie's face. He's reminded of his first visit to Ben, the new Ben. The diminished Ben. Then, like now, he felt responsible. Partially.

Only worry about what you can control, Saul always tells him. And he definitely cannot control snowstorms, cannot control oncoming vehicles in the wrong lane. He takes a deep breath and rounds the corner.

The room contains three beds. Three beds and one nurse. In the trauma ward, patients require constant supervision, a nurse's station pushed into the corner, a nurse always ready. The nurse huddles over a stack of paper on the desk. She looks up at Digger and nods silently before turning back to her documents.

Sadie's bed is the closest to the door. She lies on her back, face to the ceiling, a metal cage around her head. He walks slowly towards her, half hoping she won't open her eyes. Maybe he could just leave a note.

"Hi there. I'd recognize that shuffle anywhere," she says without opening her eyes. Her voice sounds shallow and raspy.

He wonders if she really does know it's him, or if she's expecting someone else. He stands. Still. "We weren't allowed to bring flowers." He studies his empty hands. "Or chocolates. Not while you're still in the trauma ward."

"No worries. A little company is what I need more than anything." She has opened her eyes and blinks at the ceiling. She looks pale and thin, sunken into the mattress, but he doesn't see any wounds or scars.

"I know. Sorry. I should've come sooner—"

"Relax," she makes a soft laughing noise, then winces, grabbing her side. "I'm just saying thanks. Thanks for coming."

"Fly came too. He's downstairs, probably eating junk." His laughter has a nervous edge, as if they are strangers. He sits in a seat close to her pillow where she can see him in her peripheral vision through the cage of her neck brace.

"I just wish I could roll over. I can't stand another minute of looking at this ceiling." She closes her eyes again.

"Any word on when you'll . . . when you can . . ." His voice trails off. Like everyone else, he's afraid to ponder too closely the possibilities of what she may and may not be able to do. He doesn't mention walking. He won't mention swimming.

"The neurosurgeon was supposed to see my x-rays two days ago and come take this stupid contraption off my head. I still haven't seen him. Everyone tells me he'll be here any minute, that he's a very busy man. So I just stare at the ceiling and wait. How are you?" Her tone brightens with the last question, and he thinks that if she could move, she would've shaken her hair abruptly before asking it, tossed her head as if shaking away a particularly relentless mosquito. "Any aches and bruises?"

"No. Nothing. I'm good. A little blood on my clothes is all." He knows there's apology in his voice, and he wants to hear her say, *it's okay, it's not your fault.* He remembers the young policeman who knocked at his apartment door the day after the accident. The guy was younger than Digger himself, though the uniform and wedding band made him seem so much older. Before he left, he told Digger it was normal for the driver to protect himself, to instinctively yank the wheel in the direction that would minimize impact to the driver's side, however slightly. A head-on collision was never *exactly* a head-on collision—always a little off-centre. Digger knew from the hospital reports that Sadie's left side was injured the worst—so close to where he sat. Inches. Yet he's fine.

The nurse from the corner comes to the bed. Without speaking, she checks the IV stand at Sadie's side and writes something on the clipboard located at the foot of the bed.

"Wrestling still?" Sadie asks.

Digger listens for accusation in her voice, but the question sounds as neutral as if she has asked what he had for breakfast. The nurse returns to her corner, and Digger reaches over, rests his hand against Sadie's forehead.

"Thanks."

"Yep, wrestling is fine. On Monday, my first practice back, my rib cage felt a little bruised and sore, my back tight. I covered it up, though. Saul was pissed enough at me, even without knowing I hurt myself. But now, I'm good as gold. We're off to Pan America Championships in Colombia next weekend. That'll be the final warm-up meet before the Olympics." He stops abruptly on the last word. He got carried away talking about wrestling, forgot where he was, and now he has said too much. He feels his face growing hot; he scratches the back of his neck.

The nurse shuffles paper in the corner, footsteps rush by in the hallway. "It's okay, Tom," Sadie finally says. "You can talk. It's okay." A single tear rolls out the side of her eye and trickles towards her ear. "Everyone censors themselves around me. As if I don't know. As if I hurt my brain, not my back. You're the first friend or relative who's mentioned the Olympics since I got here."

Not knowing what to say, he reaches for her hand and holds it tight. The strength she musters to squeeze it back surprises him. "You'll be all right," he says. He says it like he believes it, though he's not sure what "all right" could mean in this context.

She closes her eyes and after a few minutes he thinks she is sleeping, but her eyes open, quick and alert, when the hard clacking sound of cowboy boots enters the room.

"Good afternoon, Ms. Jorgenson," says a freckled man of no more than five feet, even in the cowboy boots. "Dr. Hock at your service. Finally."

Digger drops Sadie's hand and shuffles himself and his chair away from her bed into the curtains.

"First, let's get this silly thing off of you." Dr. Hock unbuckles the neck brace and slides it over her head, setting it to rest on the floor. "It's not even your upper vertebrae that are fractured. I don't know what good this torture device was meant to do."

Next, he swings a briefcase off his shoulder to the ground and pulls out a big manila envelope. He clutches the envelope before himself as if it is an Easter surprise. "Well, I have good news and bad news." He pulls the x-rays out of their envelope and holds them up to the light. "The good news: you're alive—"

"I already knew that. You'd better have more." Sadie squints her eyes at him, more activity than Digger has seen from her yet.

"And no damage to the spinal column!" he says with a big smile, and Digger sees that he has dimples too. A five-foot freckled doctor with dimples? It's almost too much. Digger would laugh if he were somewhere other than the trauma ward.

"Can we save the bad news for another day?" Sadie's facial features lift upwards in a laugh, such a contrast from her earlier expression that she looks almost flirtatious.

"Hey, it took three days to get me here this time. Are you sure you could wait another three?" Doctor Doogie Howser, as Digger has come to think of him, flirts back.

"It depends. How bad is bad? Maybe we can just call it quits at the good news. You scrap that file of terror, and I walk out of here a free woman?"

"We doctors have a lot of power." He winks. "But not that much power." He turns his attention back to the x-rays. "So the bad news is, you have crushed your L1 vertebra. The good news is that I am a very good surgeon and I'm going to fix it for you." He smiles as if he has just asked her out on a date.

"A crushed L1? You better be really good," Sadie says, her tone no longer light.

"Oh, I *am* really good. The surgery will be about seventeen hours. And I'm not going to lie to you: whenever we have to operate that close to the spinal column, it's dangerous. Even with a surgeon as good as me," he smiles.

"Seventeen hours of surgery. Ah, no thanks. Really, I feel quite a bit better than that. Are you sure?"

"The surgery will be split into two parts—half attacking the bone from the front, another half attacking it from the back."

"When?" Digger's voice comes deep from within the curtains. He hears the aggressiveness of the one word but can't soften it. The other questions—*How soon will this be done? What are the chances, statistically, of it working? Is there a chance of paralysis? Are there other options? Is surgery absolutely necessary?*—ricochet around his head but he can't get them out. "Is she going to be paralyzed?" he glares at the doctor as if this is all his fault.

Dr. Hock's eyes move to Digger for the first time. Then back to Sadie. "There is always a chance of paralysis with spinal surgery.

Any time there is a knife that close to the spinal column, it's a high-risk procedure. But I promise you, I will do my best to have you walking again."

"Paralysis?" Sadie's voice is whiny, but almost playfully whiny, as if she cannot really grant any credence to this conversation. "Really, I feel a lot better than that," she says again. "Perhaps there's been a mistake."

"Your L1 is not the best vertebra for this to have happened to. We'd be in better form if the fracture had occurred higher up, but—"

"Wait, wait, wait!" Sadie's objections are not playful this time. "I was told in Black Diamond that it was my L3, not my L1."

Dr. Hock looks stumped for the first time. "One moment." His cowboy boots clank out of the room. Digger and Sadie have time to say nothing. Dr. Hock is back in less than two minutes. "Well, I have some good news and some good news. The good news, for you, is that it's the girl in the next room who has a crushed L1. You, my dear, have a fractured L3 and you can try walking tomorrow. With any luck, we will have you up, fitted into a clamshell back brace, and out of here by the end of the week. You will have to come back in a month or so to get the brace refitted, since your volume is sure to increase. But other than that, you're out of here. Unless I can interest you in that surgery. After all, I really *am* quite good." He laughs and hurries the x-rays back into their envelope and into his briefcase. Before Sadie can respond, his cowboy boots stomp off, loud in the stunned silence.

"So I broke my back, but just a little bit," Sadie says to the ceiling.

"Did that just happen?" asks Digger, on the brink of laughter; he'd be roaring with laughter if Fly were telling this story in the sauna.

Just then Fly finally enters the room, tucking a half-eaten chocolate bar into his breast pocket. "Hey, Crash! Look at you, good as new. There's not a scratch on ya! It'd take more than a speeding car to crush that fine body, eh? You and me have something in common now—you're a crash test dummy and I'm this guy's throwing dummy." He nods his head sideways at Digger. "Yep, we're the invincible ones." He raises his hand to her as if she's just won a big race.

Sadie lifts her arm to meet Fly's high-five. The first time in three days that she's moved her own body.

Thirty

Sadie lies in bed on top of the covers wearing a pair of navy blue running shorts and a long-sleeved white T-shirt with STEPS TO SYDNEY inscribed across the chest. She's immersed in a rat-eared copy of *Paradise Lost*. Her mother pulled it out of Sadie's boxes of undergrad junk, then brought it to the hospital, snatching away the issue of *Cosmo* that Sadie was letting her eyes play with. She's deep into the words now, awed by the perfect completion of each of Milton's lines.

Sufficient to have stood   though free to fall

And

Order from disorder sprung.

She marvels over the way each line balances so exactly, yet so precariously, on its fulcrum, perfect but vulnerable, ready with the slightest movement to swing in the wrong direction. Stand/fall. Order/disorder. Each character imbued with the freedom to choose, but inevitably choosing wrong.

The nurses have unhooked her from her morphine drip but still bring her two perfectly round tablets every four hours. The opium-based drug makes her itch like a heroin addict. This morning she walked for the first time. A noteworthy achievement, since she needed help rolling over just last night. But at nine o'clock sharp, the stern-faced nurse—Roberta, her nametag reads, though she's never introduced herself—handed her a towel. "You can take a shower."

"I can? By myself? Now?" Her body felt unused. She had grown almost comfortable with her confinement to the bed, was unsure about testing her beaten bone cage.

The nurse nodded and pointed the way to the shower room.

Sadie's first steps were those of a toddler. She tested the ground with her foot before each step, shifted her weight oh so tentatively, held her hand to the wall, unsure of her own balance. Moving hurt her everywhere—her back, her ribs, her neck, her shoulder. Still, movement was movement and she stood proudly straight by the time she reached the shower.

Under the stream of water, little black dots invaded her vision and she held the wall as if the flow of liquid were enough to knock her over. The water pressure felt rough on her bruised flesh, but it was a good pain, she told herself, a pain of progress. When the water hit a sore spot on her ribs, the ache was such a surprise she dropped the soap. She looked at that white bar on the tiled floor and knew bending down and picking it up would be impossible. She finished the shower without her soap.

She thought about her hairy legs, though she couldn't move her body enough to see them. Even if she were physically able, she would not be ready to shave them. Not yet.

And now—wearing her own swimming sweats and T-shirt, free of all the hospital's wires, tubes, and monitors—she runs a hand down her sides, pulls each knee to a ninety degree angle, twists her torso, her chest pointing out over one hip, then the other. Shaky but liberated. Her fingers gently explore her body, always finding new areas of injury, a bruised rib, a torn rotator cuff, a sprained elbow. The accident wrenched and ripped her whole left side. But she can stand, she can walk, she is ready—she thinks—to test what else this battered body can still do for her.

Meanwhile, slowly—line by line—she makes her way through Milton and remembers sleeping on *Read for Your Life* at the cage. Finally, she's not too tired to read. At the sound of soft footsteps, she looks up from her book to see a lime green polyester shirt in the doorway. "Oh my God, Ben! You're out!"

"Yeah, I thought I'd clear a space for you. You might need it worse than I do."

She laughs as he reaches for a chair.

"So I took Dr. Fly's advice," he says, pulling his seat right close to her bedside.

She lifts one eyebrow, afraid to ask. "Which is?"

"Take two pills of suck it up and don't call me in the morning."

They both laugh, Sadie weakly with her ribs and chest aching, Ben quietly into his shirt sleeve so as not to disturb the other patients. "You okay?" Ben asks.

She shrugs and feels the familiar tears. "Don't worry. I'm okay. I'm alive." She shrugs again. "It doesn't hurt when I lie down. Sitting kills."

"And what's the . . . prognosis?"

So he too is afraid to mention the Olympics head-on. "No one seems to know for sure. I'll be wearing a back brace for a while. Maybe one month. Maybe three months." She opens her book of poetry. Closes it. "The Olympics is in four months."

Ben nods. Opens his mouth, then closes it again.

"Maybe I can still go. I haven't tried swimming yet."

"Maybe." Ben doesn't even try to sound like he believes that possibility.

She smiles to stop herself from crying. "We athletes are experts at lying to ourselves and believing it. It's the one thing we practice every day."

Almost imperceptibly, Ben nods.

"To think of all that training," Sadie says. She reaches for a glass of water on her side table, winces at the sharp sting to her neck and shoulder. Ben passes her the water. "All of those years. For nothing." She can still see her Olympic Dream, but it's like seeing her home town from an airplane—the miniature play houses, the insects that are really moving cars, the tiny splashes of blue that even the imagination cannot conceive of as backyard swimming pools filled with children, filled with life.

"It wasn't for nothing!" Ben leaps from his chair, flips it around, and sits again, leaning intensely over the chair's back. "You were training for your life. If you weren't so fit and so strong, you could be paralyzed. You could be dead. You thought you were training for the Olympics, but really you were training for your life." He stares at her but she says nothing. "Which is more important?"

Still Sadie has no answer.

"Things work out the way they are meant to work out. Everything—"

"The way they are meant to work out?" Sadie's words are slow and even and come from a long way away. She cannot believe he has said this to her. Not now. Not here.

"Yes, but not always in the way we think they will or the way we plan for." A wet glow glistens in Ben's eyes and Sadie sees that he's still not well. She remembers Digger telling her about Ben's *Book of Buddha*, and she hopes he's not going to get religious on her. Ben's still talking, unaware that she's been reading his eyes, evaluating his mental health.

"Focusing on the end in sport will just make you crazy. Take Digger. Saturated with anger. So, he's got some bad draws, got shortchanged a bit on media attention. And it would have been nice if he were an Olympian before now. But that anger. It'll kill him. Or somebody else." He shakes his head, flicking away a bad thought. "So you, too, need to think about the process. It's like you were training for—"

"My life. Right. I get it." She nods politely, as if Ben is a door-to-door Jehovah's Witness. "Let's go for a walk."

"You can walk?" He forgets his speech, steps to her bedside.

"With your help. Slowly. I'm not going to make it to Sydney if I can't make it down the hall, am I?" She reaches out her arm, shy and unaccustomed to asking for assistance. She slides her legs off the bed so that her feet touch the cool tiles on the floor. He puts one arm around her back and a hand on her arm, moves to help lift her to her feet, but jumps away when he sees her wince.

"It's okay. It's going to hurt." She lifts her T-shirt and shows him the deep purple swelling on her rib cage, pushes up her sleeve so he can see the red abrasion from her elbow to her shoulder. "I'm going to stand, though. Are you going to help? It'll take a lot longer and be a lot more painful if you don't."

Ben steps back. "That's some serious bruising. Have you had your ribs x-rayed?"

"Yes." She snaps, impatient. "It's just bruising. Help me up. Please. Now."

He steps towards her again. "Sorry. Your ribs were just a bit of a shock. You hardly looked hurt when I came in."

She holds up the back of her hand. The skin from her wrist to her knuckles is covered with tiny deep cuts. "My only visible wounds. From the windshield. The rest I can cover up."

He puts his arms around her again and helps her to her bare feet, this time ignoring her groans and the scrunched-up look on her face.

"Thanks." They walk carefully out of the room and down the nearly empty hallway. In the trauma ward, most patients are confined to their rooms. Ben stays by her side, keeps her pace. "Sorry," she says. "I move like my grandmother."

"Don't apologize."

"I just had to get out of that room. Did you see the other patients? Geez! The Grim Reaper's always hovering in there." She stops to lean against the wall, tired. "The guy next to me was working on a family farm when a threshing machine rolled onto him. Crushed pelvis. Who knows what else? He goes through morphine pills like popcorn. And he's always begging his mom, 'When can I go back to work? They need me on the farm. I have to work on the farm'." She pushes off the wall to her feet again. "Man! I'm just thinking, Buddy, relax! You're hurt. The farm will wait." She stops again, looks down the hallway and takes a deep breath, fills her cheeks with air. She holds the air for a count of three, then releases, long and slow through her teeth. Ben follows her as she turns around and heads back to the room, one slow step at a time. "Then the lady across from me in her eighties was hit by a car while she was standing in a crosswalk. She'll never walk again. Only conscious enough to ask for more painkillers."

"Cars. The number of injuries due to cars," Ben says. He shakes his head as he takes Sadie's arm, lets her rest her weight on him all the way back to her bed. "It makes sense, though. Cars transform us into dinosaurs. Seriously, when we're driving, our brain to body mass ratio is equivalent to that of a dinosaur. Why wouldn't we be stupid and aggressive?"

"Down with cars," she agrees, as she lays herself gently down on the bed, being sure to put her weight on her good shoulder. Ben lifts her legs up to the mattress. She closes her eyes.

"Should I go?"

"Mmm, I think so," she says, her eyes squished tight. She hears the sound of apology in her voice again. "Can you ask the nurse for some morphine on the way out? It's time." She relaxes her head against the pillow and listens to the throbbing in her spine.

Thirty-One

Digger and Fly sit in the shade under the overhang of the gymnasium's entrance. They flew to Colombia yesterday, weigh in today, and will wrestle tomorrow. Fly was called on last minute to fill in the sixty-nine kilogram Canadian spot when the regular team member tweaked an ankle at the last practice. The air hangs hot and sticky humid, but Digger's skin shows no trace of sweat. He made weight ten minutes ago and has no sweat left. He holds a bottle of blue juice in anticipation; he'll drink it as soon as he attends official weigh-in. Eight more minutes.

"Geezus, Digs. That stuff looks like antifreeze. How can that be good for you?" Fly holds bottled water.

"You're the health expert all of a sudden?" Digger rolls his eyes at Fly and then turns his attention back to the parking lot, where a team of Americans wearing plastic suits do jumping jacks in the midday tropical sun. They avoid the little shade offered by the surrounding palm trees. Nothing in their rigid faces says vacation.

"Look at those morons," says Fly. "They're going to heat stroke themselves before the tourney even starts." He pours a little of his water over his own forehead, rubs the water on his face onto the back of his neck, not letting any touch his lips.

"Fine line between tough and stupid," says Digger without smiling.

Fly shakes his head. "Relax, Digger. You got your game face on already. Take it easy. Meet starts *tomorrow*."

"Those 'morons' are the ones who'll be filling the podium at the Olympics. That's our main competition right there. Watch and learn." While he says this, his eyes do not leave the Americans. Covered head to toe in their silver shining suits, they look like an army of space creatures warming up for an intergalactic war.

Their coach has set up a scale to the side of the parking lot and as the athletes make weight, they throw off their plastic coverings and the soaking, sweaty clothes underneath. Stripped to their underwear and towelling off each other's sweaty skin, all hard, bulking muscle, they look less like Martians and more like ancient Roman gods of war.

"Holy shit! Look at that guy," whispers Fly. "He's got a chest like a horse's ass. Boom! Boom!" He holds a hand over one of his pecs with each boom.

"Check out their eighty-five kilo guy," agrees Digger. "He's got twice as much muscle as last year. Lookit his legs!"

"'Roids?" Fly says this even more quietly. The last thing he wants is another team to hear him firing the accusation of steroids.

Digger twists his mouth to the side. "What else? How much weight training would you have to do to grow like that in a year?"

Fly jumps to his feet. "Yeah well, people probably think I'm on the juice too." He rips off his shirt and strikes a pose. "Read 'em and weep, sucker." He kisses his own bicep.

Digger throws his full Gatorade bottle at Fly's head. "The only thing on steroids is your mouth." He stands and follows Fly into the airless gymnasium and away from the American spectacle.

Back at the hotel, their teammates sprawl across unmade beds, fanning themselves with old newspapers, trying to stay sheltered from the hot sun, a hostile force out to steal what little energy they have left. The building has no air conditioning. Dressed in nothing but gym shorts, Digger and Fly roam from room to room, trying to find the coolest spot.

"This place is a dive," says Fly, kicking a garden fence that surrounds a plot of weeds in the hotel's inner courtyard.

"We're not on vacation, Fly. It's not s'pose to be a five-star Ramada." Digger does not look at him while he speaks.

"Geez, glad to see your mood hasn't improved at all. I pity the poor bastard who has to wrestle your grouchy ass tomorrow."

Digger keeps walking, kicks at the garden path, dust flying in the air.

"I'm not saying I expect the Holiday Inn," Fly continues. "I'm just saying we'd perform better if we had better accommodation. People at home get all jealous of our so-called world travel. If they only knew. I'd rather wrestle in Toronto or Calgary. At least there, I know what I'm eating and what I'm sleeping on. And that's all I'm saying. Okay, Your Censorship?"

Digger rubs the back of his own neck, feels a muscle knot the size of an egg in each of his traps. He huffs air through his nose and lifts the corners of his mouth into a pseudo-smile. "Yeah, okay. I guess." He play punches Fly in the shoulder. "I'm just a little tight. This is it. The last chance to see what I got before The Show."

Fly sees a spot of shade and stops to lean against a tree. "It's cooler here than in the rooms. At least there's a breeze." They both slide down the tree's trunk and sit in the dust, legs spread out in front of them. "You're probably a bit distracted by Sadie too."

Digger feels his face muscles grow solid. "I'm not distracted."

"Holy fuck, Digger. That vein in your temple's gonna bust. Relax!" Fly holds up his hands as if protecting himself from attack. "I can't say anything right today, can I? I just mean it would be normal to be worried. It'd be only human to be thinking about how she's doing."

Digger reties his shoelaces. "I can be human when it's over." He looks at Fly. "Too much has gone into this. I can't lose it now." He leans his back against the tree and closes his eyes. "Conversation over."

Fly sighs. Digger can hear him fidgeting, picking at the weeds, throwing rocks at the sidewalk. *Let him believe whatever he wants,* thinks Digger, *this is my time, the only time I've got, I won't let myself be derailed by something I can't control. Think wrestling, stay relaxed*, he coaches himself. He opens his eyes. "You think I'm self-centred," he says. "What is a successful athlete if not self-centred? To win is to be selfish. Every day an athlete has to make sure he gets the best food, best sleep, and best workouts possible. That's all. What's the Olympic motto? *Citius, Altius, Fortius.* Swifter, Higher, Stronger. It doesn't say anything about nicer. I'll worry about my manners when it's over." He closes his eyes again, stretches his neck to the left and then to the right, clasps the back of his scalp and pushes his head forward until his chin touches his chest, tries to loosen his neck muscles. "Anyway, Sadie and me—we're just friends. I have no . . . I'm not obligated."

Fly says nothing.

"Guys! Guys!" Scotty the Body, the team's fifty-five kilogram wrestler, runs at them full speed with a huge smile on his face. "Get this! Get this!"

"Whoa, man! Slow down." Fly jumps to his feet but bounces in slow motion compared to Scotty. "You're saying everything twice, guy. Once will do." Fly dusts his hands off on his shorts, looks at Scotty. "Okay. Breathe. Then talk."

"You gotta check out this massage room! I go in for a little pre-tournament work over. It's pretty good; she's massaging nice and deep. Then she tells me, roll over on your back. I do as I'm told." He shows nearly all of his teeth in his smile. "Next thing you know, I feel her sliding my drawers down! And she grabs my unit! I swear to God! Grabs my unit!"

"Say it once, Body. You're double talking again." But Fly is bouncing now too. The two of them are like a couple of bees trapped in a bottle.

"She jerked me off! Right there! Just like that! I swear."

"No way, man! No way!"

"Say it once, Fly. You made the rule—follow it," says Digger. Neither Scotty nor Fly turns towards his voice.

"Then she grabs a Kleenex, cleans me up, pulls up my drawers like nothing has happened. Says, 'Thank you, sir.' Just like that. 'Thank you, sir.'"

"Is she hot?" Fly grabs his gym bag and stands at Scotty's side, prodding him back in the direction he came, ready to follow.

"God, no! She looks like my grandmother! But a hand job is a hand job."

Fly laughs. "Is she into it?"

"Into it? Nuh-uh. That'd be sick. Watching her face, you'd think she was pulling an asparagus stock. Let's go!"

"How much?" As they walk, Fly rips through his gym bag, looking for his wallet.

"Five bucks." They both pick up speed and then, remembering Digger, look back over their shoulders.

"You comin', Digs?"

"I," he says, pulling himself into a cross-legged position, "am here to wrestle." He closes his eyes and leans back against the tree and imagines himself nose to nose with an American who has the chest of a horse.

Thirty-Two

Sadie's life in the hospital consists of waiting, and the passivity does not suit her. She grows crosser by the day and knows that the nurses like her less and less. "I *need* morphine," she whines at them. When they bring it, she snaps, "This stuff makes me barf. Bring Gravol." She hates the sound of her own voice, but only stops when her mother shows up issuing commands.

"You don't need morphine anymore. It'll make you constipated and miserable. God knows you don't need any help on that front." She turns to the nurses without waiting for a response. "Switch her to ibuprofen, 222s if she really needs them. And if she keeps up this whining and snapping, duct tape her mouth shut." Sadie can't see whether or not she winks with this last command.

She sees impatience even in her father's eyes, but his big shoulders shrug it off and he lets her snap at him, brings her books, straightens her blankets, sneaks her lattes. "My poor girl." His tolerance makes her even more cross.

They also serve who only stand and wait, she reads in Milton. Serve what? And since when did she want to serve anyway? She misses her predictable clichés.

She has been fitted with a clamshell back brace, a thick white plaster contraption that she wears under her clothes and tightens with Velcro straps until she can barely breathe. It looks like hockey equipment and she feels like a bulky defenseman lumbering down the hallway. It digs into her breasts at one end, her hips at the other, itches her stomach. Sweat tickles down her rib cage and the brace sticks to her skin.

Hot, itchy, uncomfortable, cranky, and in pain—no wonder she's gotten no visitors other than her parents in the last week. Her mom's probably warning people away. Fine. She does not want to see anyone anyway. Let them stay away.

She thinks of Digger competing at Pan Ams in Colombia. She wouldn't mind seeing him, maybe. But what could he want with her now? A crippled girl, struggling to walk like some ill-fated Dickens character. Their lives have forked. She would be nothing but dead weight to him now. *Let him go*, she thinks.

They had gotten close, but now her memory of him is hazy, like an open water swimmer who has ventured so far towards the horizon that the land has grown faint, so like a mirage that she begins to wonder if it was ever real at all.

Two orderlies, young pimply men dressed in white coats, bound into her room.

"Luxury Limousines Are Us," the taller one says, sliding a single bed on wheels up to Sadie's bed. "Hop on. Door-to-door service."

"I didn't order a limousine," Sadie says. She hears the pout in her voice and hates herself for it. "Unless it's a limousine out of here." Hates it but cannot stop.

"Nope. Not today, my lady. This limo is headed for x-ray." He shrugs, lifting the left corner of his mouth towards his ear. "Those are the instructions from above. I just follow them."

"Yeah, don't shoot the drivers," says the shorter one, taking her arm and leading her onto the wheel-a-bed.

She lies back on the bed and watches the lights zoom past her, a continuous streak of white, each blurring into the next. Her drivers seem to have forgotten about her and talk to each other above her head. She won't let herself listen to them, but lets their words blur together like the lights above her.

At x-ray, they stop and leave her bed in a line of others. Dropped off at the curb like yesterday's garbage, she thinks, detesting her own melodramatic self-pity. She closes her eyes and tries to sleep. If only she could sleep until it was time to go home to the pool.

When her bed arrives at the front of the line, it could be ten minutes or an hour later. Sadie can no longer attach any meaning to time. An x-ray technician pulls on her bed, smiling down at her.

"Hi," she says, willing herself to be pleasant, or at least not so unpleasant.

"Hello," says a young man in a snot green pajama shirt with matching pants. "My name is Sam. We're going to see if we can help you out with your pain," he adds, studying a chart that he's picked off the sidebar of her bed. "Bad accident, hey?" He hangs the clipboard back on her bed and his eyes travel from her head to her foot. "Amazing. You don't really look hurt. You're lucky your face wasn't cut up."

"Mmm. Lucky," she forces herself to say as he wheels her bed under two large circular lights.

"Want a rundown of today's procedure? Basically, we're going to freeze the nerves in your back. In three of your vertebrae. The x-ray," he says tapping the machine above him, "is to make sure we're guiding the needle to the right spot. We'll also be injecting steroid solution to promote healing, and the needle has to go all the way to the area between the joints. So, we have a lot of body to get through. A lot of tissue." He smiles. "It will be a little unpleasant."

"What isn't?"

He asks her to roll onto her side. Then he opens her hospital gown and wipes her back with disinfectant. Another man, a stranger, joins him, works at his side. Once they begin working, they do not talk to her at all. She feels like a car.

"Our income in Canada just isn't on par with the US salaries," complains Sam.

"Yeah, but there are so many things you can do to supplement. It just requires a little imagination." The nameless assistant talks while Sadie feels the needle prick her skin, force itself deep into her back. Her breath catches.

"Take my wife," the same voice continues. "She's making a load of cash off glue. Every time we go to the States, we just zip a couple boxes of Crazy Glue back over the border. Then we sanitize it and resell it as Medical Glue. You can't beat that mark-up."

Another needle pricks Sadie and this time she's ready for the hard push that follows the sharp sting.

"So there are opportunities. Just waiting to be taken advantage of."

Sadie holds her breath, waiting for the third prick, but cannot help jumping when she feels it. A hand pats her shoulder.

"How many more patients today?" asks the glue smuggler.

"God knows," says Sam. "Did you see the line-up of beds out there? Too bad we don't get paid by the patient."

With that, he withdraws the needle and puts his other hand on Sadie's head. "There you go. All done for today. Easy as pie. We'll put you out in the hallway and give the orderlies a shout to pick you up and take you back to your room."

Parked back in the hallway, Sadie closes her eyes and tries to lull herself to sleep by counting imaginary lengths.

Thirty-Three

$\mathcal{A}$ gymnasium in Colombia is no different than a gymnasium anywhere else in the world. Whatever the country, a gymnasium has cement walls, high ceilings, and hard floors. A gymnasium smells of human sweat and stale air, and reverberates with shouting voices. Right now, Digger and Fly could easily be in downtown Toronto, even though they lie on warm-up mats in Bogota, Colombia.

Digger is the only Canadian left in the tournament. The Americans beat the rest out. Digger, though, got a good draw: his horse-chested American landed on the other side of the pool and they will meet in the final.

"I've been watching him, Digs," says Fly, sitting upright, stretching his fingers to his toes. "He's strong, but he's slow. Not that you're any blazing streak of light, but you've got more staying power, better technique."

"Okay, Coach Fly," mumbles Digger, the same lines from yesterday still carved deep into the space between his eyebrows. Fly hops to his feet to help Digger stretch. Digger still lies on the mat, face to the ceiling, and holds one leg up for Fly. Fly pushes the foot. Digger's knee should touch his face, but his leg barely passes the ninety-degree mark. Fly keeps pushing, but it's like trying to move a cement wall. Digger says nothing.

Bang. Bang. Bang. Fly drops the foot. Even Digger's face lines loosen as he turns to look. *Bang. Bang.*

"What the hell?" Fly steps away from Digger.

Digger pulls himself up into a sitting position. "It's coming from there." He points at a thick steel exit door. The noise comes from the other side of the locked door, the side where the lightweights currently fight for gold medals. *Bang. Bang. Bang.* The wrestlers warming up near Digger and Fly look to the door, then shrug. Speaking Russian, they continue their stretches.

"I gotta see. You comin'?" Fly weaves around the pairs of men stretching and jogging on the warm-up mats and sprints towards the other exit door on the far end of the wall.

Digger looks to the Russians but then back to the banging door. He hops to his feet and runs to catch Fly, chases him through the far door into the tournament zone.

On the other side of the wall, referees' whistles, coaches' yells, wrestlers' falls, and the announcer's booming voice compete with each other. One mat lies in the centre of the gym, a gold match in progress, the stands around the perimeter packed with screaming fans. Athletes and coaches line the sides of the mat, bent over, hands to their mouths, shouting. Fly and Digger weave their way through the athletes, coaches, and referees to the exit door that was shaking with bangs.

Facing the door, they see the eighty-five kilogram, roidal American, Digger's opponent in today's final. He wears the same plastic silver suit he wore yesterday, hood up. He's bent over at a ninety-degree angle and repeatedly runs head first into the steel door. *Bang.* Back up. *Bang.* Back up. *Bang.* Back up. His head hits dead centre each time. Without reaction, without emotion, he backs away and charges it again. *Bang.* And again. *Bang.* And again. *Bang.*

Fly puts his hands on his hips and shakes his head. "Knock knock."

"Who's there?" Digger bites away the unfamiliar feeling of a smile, the first real one since he's arrived in Colombia.

"Psycho—"

"Psycho who?" Digger asks, his face all smile now.

"Psychopath, man, psychopath! What's with these Americans?" He glances sideways at a group of US wrestlers cheering on a teammate at the mat next to them and lowers his voice. "Completely wacko."

Digger stares at the American in his silver suit, and holds a hand to his mouth to stop his laughter. The American continues to ram his head into the door, oblivious to Fly and Digger watching. "Completely," Digger agrees. "I saw that guy at Worlds two years ago in Toronto. A friggin' hundred degrees out and we're wrestling in an un-air-conditioned hockey arena. Toronto in August: so hot and humid you couldn't breathe. The whole tournament was a gong show—referees sliding in puddles of sweat, falling on their asses. And there's this guy, warming up in his plastics. Running the arena stairs dressed in layers of sweat clothes and then plastics." He shakes his head.

"Wasn't he the one crying at the last Olympics?" Fly still stares at the American.

"Yep. On the podium, bawling like a baby. Silver medal. Threw it on the ground and stomped on it. Americans—second place is the first loser. After he lost the final match, he started blubbering, his face pressed to the dirty mat, and he was still sobbing when the ceremonies started an—"

Digger feels a heavy hand drop on the back of his neck. Saul sticks his head between theirs, one hand on Digger's neck, the other on Fly's.

"You here to spectate or compete?" Saul barks at Digger. "Back into the warm-up room. Finish stretching." He steers them by their necks, pushes them back towards the other door, and they go. But Digger notices, with one last look over his shoulder, that Saul too has stopped to gawk at the silver attack on the steel door.

Thirty-Four

ed welts stand out on Sadie's skin, down her arms and legs.
The nurses have ignored her mom, and when Sadie presses
hard enough, they still give her morphine, which makes her itch all
over, but without it, her neck and scalp hurt so badly she can't open
her eyes, and the sharp, throbbing pain in her lower spine makes her
want to wail. She chooses to itch.

She's still in the hospital. Still. She's still in pain, still on morphine,
still clutches her lower back in pain on a simple walk to the end of the
hallway and back, and she's still in the bloody trauma ward. Still.

Today, she has a new visitor. A heavily rouged woman in her
sixties perches on the edge of a chair at Sadie's bedside, back straight,
face serious, pen poised.

This is her mother's idea. A lawyer. "You have to protect herself,
have to be sure you are adequately recompensed for what you've
gone through. If you don't get a lawyer, the other driver's insurance
company will not give you what you have coming."

"Aw, Dot, can't we wait until she's out of the hospital at least?"
her dad had asked, hovering at the foot of her bed.

"No, Bill," Dot pronounced. "No, we cannot."

"Do you think money can make up for what I've lost?" Sadie
snarled, slamming her *Paradise Lost* on the bedside table.

"It's better than nothing," Dot answered and hired the lawyer,
Fran Oglevey. The ER doctors assured Dot that Fran was the best

in personal injury law. "It's just a preliminary consultation. You'll understand that when you're feeling better."

Sadie thought she ought to explain that she'd hurt her back, not her brain, that she wasn't going to understand things differently no matter how she felt, but remembering the utter lack of success she'd had explaining that to anyone else, she kept quiet.

Now, she's face to face with Fran Oglevey, circling to pick her rewards from the road kill.

"The way this works," Fran cheerfully explains, "is you don't pay a cent up front. Then when we're all done, I take 40 per cent of your settlement. That saves you fiddling with expenses in the years it will take to reach an agreement. Any physiotherapy, acupuncture, psychiatric counselling . . . *anything*, I pay. With an advance on your settlement." She relays this information like a Gap sales girl informing a customer of a two-for-one T-shirt sale. "So." Fran blots the excess ink off the tip of her pen onto the yellow lined paper on her lap. "Let's start at the beginning. What was your income before the accident?" She smiles, ready to record Sadie's answer. She leans forward, poising her pen above the pad of paper on her lap and her burgundy blazer pulls tight, wrinkles around the elbows and shoulders. She's painted her lips burgundy to match the suit and sprayed her hair so the ends bend under in a perfect curl.

"Income? I was an athlete."

"Yes. Yes, I understand that." She still smiles, and Sadie wonders if her teeth are getting dry. Maybe she smears them with Vaseline like a gymnast or a figure skater. "But a very successful athlete, an Olympian. We can include endorsements, awards, all those winnings under the heading of income." She taps her pen on the still-blank paper.

Sadie stops herself short of rolling her eyes, of laughing out loud at Fran Oglevey's ignorance. "Amateur athletes do not get monetary awards; there are no winnings. Endorsements? Seen a lot of swimmers on TV commercials?" Sadie takes a deep breath, sharp pain stabs her lower spine. She winces. A cool bar of discomfort roots itself up her neck and through the base of her skull.

"Well—" Fran's eyelids close and she counts on her fingers as she reviews some private stock of video footage. "—there were those two fellows on the egg commercials."

"Hmm." Sadie can't help being impressed that this woman remembers Alex Baumann and Victor Davis, however vaguely. "They were different. Olympic champions. World record holders."

"Okay." Fran rubs her chin. She still hasn't recorded anything on the pad in her lap. "We can get figures for that. Find out what they were paid—as a hypothetical." She looks at Sadie. "What were your chances of winning in Sydney?"

"Winning?" Sadie's voice registers surprise at the bluntness of the question.

"Yes." Pen waiting.

This woman has never swum a lap in her life, probably never broken a sweat: what does she know about winning in Sydney? "I had a chance. It was a goal."

"Okay. But on paper, what was the likelihood? What was your record?"

"Record?" Sadie feels a nerve twitching beneath her right eye. "Sport isn't about what happens on paper. If the 'likelihood' mattered, no one would have to show up to race," says Sadie.

Fran says nothing but sits waiting, a little speck of lipstick on her front tooth.

"Last year, I was tenth at Worlds," Sadie continues. "That was my best showing so far."

Fran's pen doesn't move. It's the first time Sadie has been embarrassed at being tenth best in the world.

"This season's training had been going really well. I was getting faster all the time." Sadie is disgusted at her own attempt to convince this lawyer. "Until my grandmother died," she admits. She looks down at the woman's feet squished into burgundy shoes that match the suit, forces herself to shut up.

"Okay." Fran taps the lid of her pen on her notebook. "Let's leave standings out of it for now. Let's leave all the athletics out of it for now. I understand you have a university education. What's your degree in?"

196

"English."

"Okay. Any experience in the field?"

"What field?"

Fran taps her pen, chews her lip. "I guess you don't have an education degree with that?" When Sadie shakes her head, she continues. "Any writing experience? Editing? Part-time jobs?"

"I work in the cage at the university. Or did before the accident." The doctor told her she won't be bending over for four months, and thus ruled out going back to work. "Folding towels. I work out six hours a day. What else am I going to do?" Sadie holds her life out for a judgment.

"Wage?" The paper on Fran's knee is still blank.

"Minimum."

Fran clicks her pen closed, slides it behind her ear, a sheathed sword. "Okay. Let's leave it at that for now. All we need is a preliminary statement. Something to get us started. But I have to let you know— in any motor vehicle accident, the award for personal damages is . . . well . . . has a rather low ceiling. If we are going to make a claim of any significance, our case has to be built on how the accident has affected your income. We have to make a list of money to which you would have been entitled had you not . . . experienced this misfortune." She extends a hand and Sadie reluctantly meets it, limp.

Fran tucks the unused pad of paper into her shoulder bag and Sadie listens to her burgundy heels click out of the room, then leans back and lets herself scratch her arms, her legs, under her nightshirt, ignoring the new welts she makes on her already irritated skin. Now she knows what it is to have her life quantified, to have its value measured. Deemed worthless.

Thirty-Five

A wood-panelled station wagon slowly rounds the Jorgensons' cul-de-sac and eases its way into their driveway. Digger feels as if the car is driving itself: if he followed his own first instinct, he'd back the car right out of here. The visit was more Ben's idea than his. Ben sits quietly in the back seat. Fly bounces in the front, pouring a purple Slinky back and forth from one hand to the other.

"It'd be a perfect day for the Slipped-Disc Mobile," he says, setting the Slinky on the dashboard and watching it drop onto his lap. "Summertime requires a sunroof!" He makes a hill of his legs from the seat to the floor and tries to get the slinky to climb down it. "Chicks dig sunroofs. I'm not sure how much chicks dig wood-panelled station wagons." It's a beautiful day in late May—the kind of day that anticipates the dry prairie summer just around the corner.

Digger says nothing. He watches the curtains in the Jorgensons' front window sweep shut and he suspects Sadie has seen them pulling into the driveway. He wonders if she enjoys these visits, or if they are just a reminder of everything she has lost.

During a visit to the hospital, he had struggled to think of something positive to say. "At least your face wasn't cut up," was all he could come up with. "You don't look hurt."

She'd snapped, told him that he was the hundredth person to say this to her. "I'd rather my face was cut. I'd rather be hurt on the outside than the inside. At least I could swim."

Digger realized his comment was superficial, stupid, but there was no right thing to say. And he knew that, put in Sadie's position, back broken and stuck in bed, he'd be no easier to get along with. Probably worse. He would've smashed Dr. Doogie Howser's nose right through his freckled face.

Fly bounds up the front steps and rings the doorbell, tapping out the tune of "Hi-Ho the Dairy-O" while the purple Slinky dangles from his free hand. Ben and Digger file up behind him on the steps.

Sadie's mother opens the door. She wears her hospital pajama uniform, but Digger can't tell if she's just come home or just leaving. "Well, I hope Sadie's pleasanter to you than she's been to us lately. Feel free to try your luck." She points them down a dark hallway to the living room. Digger looks for some family resemblance, some trace of Sadie in her mother's eyes or mouth. The shoulders maybe. Really, he has a hard time remembering Sadie's face at all, so hard has he worked to block the image of her pale, vomit-caked skin against the wet pavement of Highway 22.

The living room, like the rest of the house, is hushed. A hospital bed has been wheeled to the centre of the room. Sadie lies on the bed with her eyes closed. When he last saw her at the Foothills, she wore gym shorts and sneakers, looked ready to head out for her daily run. Now, cocooned under a sheet in the middle of the day, cloistered from the prairie sun, she looks like something's been taken from her, looks the way he'd feared she would when he first visited her at the hospital.

"Hi there," he hears himself whisper.

"Hi guys," she says, opening her eyes. Her voice is alert enough that he knows she wasn't sleeping. The three of them stand huddled around her bed. She pulls herself into a sitting position, studies her knees, looking embarrassed. Digger notes, for the first time, the décor. A floral chesterfield sits against one wall, the rest of the room cluttered with faded but matching chairs. Pictures of Sadie, from infancy to high school, cover the walls and scatter the end tables. The most recent of the photographs is an eight by ten of Sadie's university graduation, placed on a dusty ledge in the corner.

She forces herself to sit up, wincing. "A hospital bed in the living room. I feel like an invalid." She runs a hand over her hair, tucks some loose strands behind her ears, a losing battle against the matted knots that cover her scalp. "Sitting hurts though."

"Then don't sit!" Fly's voice booms, exaggerated in comparison to Digger and Sadie's whispers. "Hell, if I had an excuse to lie in bed all day and have people wait on me, I'd take it! Enjoy it while you can; you'll be jogging out of here soon enough."

Sadie's lips turn up slightly, but Digger can't tell if it's a smile or a grimace. "Dr. Fly," she says and looks at Ben, who smiles back.

"Want to play with my Slinky? A youthful attitude is the best antidote to suffering." Fly hands her the purple toy.

She laughs at Fly, reaches for the toy, lets it slide from one palm to the other. It's good to see her laughing, thinks Digger, but then he notices her face scrunch in pain as the laughter shakes her body.

"Have a seat. You're all making me claustrophobic," she says. "Want something to eat or drink?" She pulls the sheet off her body, slides her feet to the floor. Digger feels a stab of guilt as he notices her still-furry legs.

"Fly always wants something to eat," says Ben, easing himself into the floral chesterfield.

"Actually, now that you mention it, I am a little peckish. What do you have?" Fly rubs his belly.

Sadie pushes her body to standing, clasping her hands to her lower back, and waves them to follow her into the kitchen—bright yellow walls smattered with pictures of sunflowers. Her mother, at the end of washing dishes at the sink, looks at them briefly but doesn't stop her work for introductions. Sadie ignores her. Her mother places the last washed dish in the rack, pulls out the plug to drain the water, then dries her hands methodically on a yellow tea towel hanging on the cupboard next to the sink and leaves without saying a word.

"She's so worried about giving me space," says Sadie. "It's her house. If I deserved my own space, I'd have my own house." She sets the Slinky on top of the refrigerator and pulls open the door with what looks like a considerable effort. "Or maybe she's just sick of me and staying away. Carrot cake?"

"Sure!" answers Fly.

"Like he'd ever say no," says Digger, stepping in beside Sadie so he can lift the cake from the fridge for her. "You relax. Point me in the right direction—plates, forks, glasses? You shouldn't be waiting on us."

Sadie leans against the counter and directs him in the snack preparations.

Fly and Ben grab stools and pull them up to the island while Digger busies himself cutting generous slices of cake—at Sadie's coaching—and pouring mugs full of milk for everyone.

"Cream cheese icing!" says Fly, watching Digger cut the cake. "Yum-meee! I could eat a whole bowl full of it!"

"Sugar and butter—your two favourite food groups," says Ben, staring at the orange-flecked cake with its substantial layer of fluffy white icing.

"Have a seat, Sade, I've got it under control," says Digger, letting his eyes fall directly on hers for the first time since the accident. They rest there for a moment and then he starts handing out cake. His whole body looks more relaxed, his muscles less tensed, now that he has a job to do.

"Sitting hurts. I'm officially a leaner now." He feels his jaw clench, the telling throb in his temple, and she must see him tighten, because she continues. "This is good, though. I'm comfy. In the company of three hotties. Being waited on by a future Gold Medallist." Suddenly everyone's quiet, only the sound of clinking forks. Sadie looks at Fly, Ben, Digger. "You're the last of us left, Digger. Now it's just Digger's Quest for the Gold." She looks at Ben as if she expects him to comment, but he stares at his cake, breaks it into little pieces with his fork.

"One step closer!" says Fly, oblivious to the awkwardness. "Pan American Champion, baby!"

"Mmm-hmmm, I read that in the paper," says Sadie, looking at

Digger. "I was wondering how long you'd take to tell me." She sees Digger's fork stop partway to his mouth, and too late notes the hard edge to her voice. Everything out of her mouth is an accusation.

"I don't know how much you want to hear."

"I want to hear."

"Well, hear this," Fly continues, ignoring the growing tension, "Digger stomped all over the American. Made him whimper like a run-over dog."

"I wouldn't call five to three a stomping, Fly." Digger won't meet anyone's eyes as he pushes his fork onto his cake, watches it mush up through the tines.

"I read that you did well too, Fly."

"Nah, I was just third," he answers, shovelling cake into his mouth. "Not even first loser."

Sadie shakes her head, then winces, her hand grabbing her neck.

"Y'okay?" Ben's voice is quiet, serious.

"Yeah, I just—my spine makes noise every time I move. It freaks me out more than anything. I snap, crackle, and pop. Like someone filled my head with Rice Krispies." She gives her neck a hard rub, then lets her hand fall to her side. "At least my shoulders don't hurt anymore," she forces a laugh. "The wonders a bit of rest will do. Congratulations, guys. That's a good pre-Olympics meet, Digger." She pronounces each word clearly, not letting her eyes leave his face, as if to convince him of her sincerity. "Momentum's with you now."

He nods.

"I, for one, will be watching you on TV. Cheering my heart out."

He smiles his thanks but can't help hearing the "on TV" as an accusation. He looks away and shoves the rest of his carrot cake into his mouth in three big scoops. Looking at his watch, he grabs his mug of milk, downs it in one long swallow. Suddenly, he can't get out of here soon enough.

Thirty-Six

Sadie's dad has wheeled the bed out of the living room. Uncomfortable or not, Sadie has decided she will not spend her days in a hospital bed. She's pulled the curtains open and light trickles into the dusty room. Sadie now meets her visitors at the door. She has a pillow and blanket on the floor and when she gets too sore from standing or sitting, she lies there, tries to stretch, lifts her knees into her chest, pulls her head away from her shoulders, feels her spine as something not belonging to her, a thing imposed upon her. The hard floor beneath her back keeps her alert.

Today, Lucinda and Marcus sit in the living room on the floral chesterfield, one at each end. Dust rises up into the sunlight as they seat themselves. It's the first time she has seen Lucinda since the day they watched boys playing Frisbee on the wet U of C grass under the spring sun. Marcus's eyes leap around the room, from framed photograph to framed photograph, and Lucinda's fingernail traces and retraces the outline of a single flower on the arm of the chesterfield, but Sadie has become accustomed to the pained smiles, the fidgeting. *Relax*, she wants to say, *I'm still me.*

Sadie lies on the carpeted floor, knees to her chest, and looks up at them. Seeing Marcus, she thinks of a dream she had last night. She was in the passenger seat of an RX-7 and Marcus was behind the wheel, having a fist-waving screaming match with the driver in the next lane. The faster they went, the less blurred the other driver's features became, the more she resembled Lucinda. Both cars raced for the same parking spot; Sadie, pressing her palms against the dashboard, choked on a scream for them to stop. Marcus stepped on the gas in a mad rush for the spot, but the other driver did the same. Suddenly, a parked car alongside the spot came into view, Bogdan and Katie necking madly in the driver's seat. Marcus and Lucinda aimed straight for them. As Sadie tried to grab the wheel, both cars crashed full force into Bogdan's car, and Sadie felt a hard, familiar jolt before waking.

"How're practices going?" she asks Marcus. "Katie still getting faster by the day?"

"Yep, she's picking up the slack, keeping Bogdan in line for you," he says, as if he actually believes Sadie might come back. "She had a good showing at Nationals in Montreal. Won the eight hundred free, actually."

Sadie knows this, of course, has read about it in the Calgary Herald. Marcus must be nervous, talking too much, saying exactly what she doesn't want to hear, compulsively stroking his sideburns. Sadie has never seen him shaken like this. In fact, except for Eva's funeral, she's rarely seen him outside his kingdom in the University of Calgary aquatic building.

"She dedicated her swim to you, actually." He's still talking. "'My mentor and inspiration,' she said."

"Hmm. Took my medal and then dedicated it back to me," Sadie says, then makes herself laugh. Even to her, the laughter sounds tinny and unconvincing.

Lucinda cuts in. "What about you? How're your treatments going? You look better than I expected. You've got good colour in your face."

Sadie rolls to a sitting position, lets out an involuntary squeal as sharp pain knots the muscles in her lower back. Awkwardly, she rolls onto her hands and knees, and laughs to find herself in such an ungainly pose before her guests. She uses the arm of the couch to drag herself to standing. "It's weird not being able to make my body do the simplest things I want. We're at odds—me and my body. It's become my instrument of torture." She tries sitting in the La-Z-Boy but immediately changes her mind, leans against the corner wall.

Marcus's and Lucinda's eyes fly about the room. Sadie sees they find it hard to watch her, and she looks instead to the layer of dust on the coffee tables. Her mother has quit cleaning the room, refusing to clean around Sadie, whom she says is as capable as anyone of swishing a cloth over the furniture now and then.

"My latest treatment," says Sadie, writing her name in the dust on a nearby table, "you wouldn't believe it. Some of the cures are worse than the illness. This guy specializes in re-tightening ligaments. He injects a fluid into the injured ligament. With a needle. Of course, it's always needles. Then, he pumps as much saline solution as he can into the ligament. Tell me that doesn't hurt? The idea is to re-injure the ligament, to remind the body that it needs to keep healing. I get twenty needles a session. Three sessions a week. And this guy does that full time. Needles all day long." She rubs her name off the tabletop with her balled-up fist, looks at Marcus and Lucinda. "I call him Dr. Sadistikov."

"Will that work?" asks Marcus, his coach's face back on.

"They tell me it will. I'm ready to try anything at this point. I just want to be better." The last sentence strikes her as asininely self-evident and she wishes she could take it back. "I can't live on my parents' floor forever. And . . . swimming . . ."

Lucinda stands up from the chesterfield. "Why don't I make us some tea? Is that okay?"

Sadie nods and follows her into the kitchen. Lucinda knows her way around from the years they swam together, the many post-workout breakfasts. She puts the kettle on to boil and picks a raspberry teabag from Sadie's mother's collection. Lucinda works her way through the cupboards, collecting cups and saucers and spoons and cream and sugar and napkins. She arranges everything neatly on a big wooden serving tray. Sadie leans quietly against the cupboard, watching. When the kettle whistles, Marcus joins the two women. He perches at the island and flips through a U of C newspaper.

"Did you read that garbage?!" Sadie breaks the silence, hears a force in her voice replacing the whiny sulk she's been using since the accident. "Some ivory tower professor tearing apart elite sport."

Marcus flips to the article called "Has the Olympics Passed Its Expiry Date?" He's obviously familiar with the article. A five-by-seven black and white picture of one of his colleagues fills most of the page. "Ah, yes, Professor Lute."

Sadie looks over Marcus's shoulder at the picture. Professor Lute is ageless in the way of the obsessively fit. He could be thirty-five or fifty-five. Impossible to guess. Thick black-rimmed glasses cover much of his face, and Sadie wonders if he really needs them or if they are just part of his professorial equipment. "See what he says about the Olympics? That it's an outdated model. That sport should be based on a cooperative model, not a competitive one. Cooperative? Bullshit!"

Lucinda quietly sets steaming cups of tea on the table.

Sadie doesn't look up but continues speaking over the steaming cup in front of her. "He says the way elite sport is now, it only rewards freakishness. Freakishness! That we turn people into national heroes just because they have size seventeen feet and can move water faster than everyone else."

Professor Lute's face looks mockingly up at her, and she grabs the paper from Marcus and flings it shut.

"He says—get this, this is my favourite—" She throws the paper open again, reading from the article. "He says that Olympic events are so 'ridiculously rarefied and stupidly specialized' as to be pointless. Ridiculously rarefied and stupidly specialized? Give me a break! What does he think he is? Isn't he a Professor of Ridiculous Rarities? Academics are the masters of the stupidly specialized."

She stops because of the laughter on Marcus's face.

"What? What's so funny?"

"Welcome back," he says. "It's good to see that old ferocity." He lifts the cup of tea to his lips. "You'll be back in the pool yet."

Lucinda stirs her spoon in her tea, around and around and around, the spoon clinking the glass mug with each turn. The clinking rattles Sadie's nerves.

"Lucinda, don't tell me you agree with this man?" Sadie grabs the hand, stops the swirling.

"Well, no, of course not, but as a mother, I mean . . . how? I don't know how that would work. A cooperative model? It's very . . . very theoretical. Would I want my kids to suffer the pain we did? To wreck their shoulders? Their knees? To more or less ignore their university educations? For what?" She puts her spoon down, sips her tea. "It's obviously just a theory. I don't know how it could be put into practice."

Sadie looks at her, waiting for more.

"That's all." Lucinda pushes up the sleeves of her green cardigan, the same cardigan she wore the day they watched the topless boys playing Frisbee at the university.

Sadie stares at Lucinda and realizes she feels no connection to this woman. Her air of defeat, even victimization, her feeble attempts to mask that deflation with abrasive practicality, her "you might as well just have fun at the Olympics" lectures. Sadie will never be that. In fact, looking at Lucinda, Sadie somehow knows that she will swim again. Maybe not at The Show. But she will swim and she will swim fast.

Thirty-Seven

*T*he office door clicks shut behind Digger. He's in Saul's office, Saul perched on the corner of his desk, wearing his usual uniform of baggy gray sweatpants and a red Dinos Wrestling T-shirt. He has a ring full of keys in his left hand, and Digger hopes he's not going to stick one of them into his ear, go for the infamous eargasm.

Team pictures and gold plaques cover the office walls, trophies engraved with dates that reach back over the last two decades. A window behind Saul looks into the centre of the building, down into a pit where undergraduates sprawl, drinking Starbucks lattes and highlighting bright yellow sentences in hardcover textbooks. Digger notices a petite girl dressed in pink lying with her head in a pudgy guy's lap. She holds a textbook in the air and reads from it while the man leans back and drinks coffee. Digger has walked by "The Pit" many times on his way to the weight room, but never in all his years on campus has he lounged in it.

Today, Digger showed up late for practice. He took Sadie to her appointment with Dr. Sadistikov. She's okay to drive now, but she's scared in traffic, gripping the door the whole time, and her back muscles seize in pain when she squishes her body into a car. So he said he'd take her and he did.

The appointment ran late and when he got back to the sweatbox, the wrestlers had already warmed up, done drills, and started to scrimmage. Saul didn't say anything, just laid his index finger across the face of his watch, then pointed at an empty corner of the room where he wanted Digger to warm up.

For the rest of the practice, Saul ignored him. Digger thought of all those other sessions when Saul's eyes followed no one but him for the entire two hours, critiquing every move, noting every small error. He thought of Saul's incessant demands and how he would've given anything to have Saul focus on someone else, just for five minutes.

But today, Saul did not look at him, did not talk to him. Digger wanted to call to Saul, to prod him—*How does this look? How am I doing at this?*

But he took the reprimand in silence. And at the end of practice, he got two words.

"Digs. Meeting." Saul pointed at the ceiling to indicate his second-floor office.

Now, Digger leans against the closed door, hair damp and smelling of soap. Maybe he should've left Sadie at the doctor's office with cab fare, told her he'd call her after practice. She would've understood. He'd slipped up.

Saul stares at the keys in his hand, flipping through them one by one, rubbing his index finger along the carved edge of each.

"Sorry I was late, Saul. Unacceptable, I know." Still, Saul doesn't look up from his keys. "It won't happen again."

"We don't have time for it to happen again." The keys drop with a clank to the desktop beside Saul. He crosses his arms over his chest, covering the wrestling dinosaur on his shirt. "We leave for Sydney in a month." He looks Digger hard in the face. "You're spending too much time with the crippled girl."

The words hit Digger, as he knows they are meant to. "How I spend my time out of the room is irrelevant. Do you think I'm not 100 per cent committed? That I don't bring everything I have to that sweatbox every day?" He works harder than anyone else in that room, and he knows Saul sees it, day after day.

"You were late. Today. Thirty minutes late."

"Once. Once in how many years?"

"But why now? Why let things slide this close?"

Digger says nothing, lets his eyes fall to the floor. He hears Saul open a drawer, shuffle through some folders.

"Look at this." Saul passes him a piece of paper. TOM STAPLETON is written in block capitals across the top in Saul's steady hand. Next to it, the date is recorded—1996. The rest of the sheet is in Digger's handwriting, small neat letters, exactly spaced and easy to read. Digger's list of goals. "Olympic Champion" is at the top, underlined three times, three stars in front of it and three stars after.

"I know," says Digger.

"You're so close." Saul takes the paper from him and puts it back in the folder. "A select few get this close." He squeezes his eyes shut as if confronted with intense pain. "You know who you're going to be if you don't get a medal, Digger? Nobody. A fat, old guy like me with fucked-up ears, fucked-up joints, fucked-up teeth. But worse than me. I work in wrestling, in the small world where people give a shit about some college matches I won decades ago. There are no more jobs like mine—three salaried coaching jobs in the country and they're taken. You're shit outta luck. So when this is all over, what? You're an insurance salesman with butt-ugly ears? Slobbering over your beer, like your dad, explaining to everyone how you almost won an Olympic medal?"

Digger grows hot and itchy at the mention of his drunken dad, but Saul doesn't pause for a response.

"You're too close for that. Get a medal and people notice. You won't have to spend your life dreaming up reasons why you didn't." He grabs his keys from the desktop, clenches them in his hand. "Too busy diddling around with some injured girl. Isn't the Olympics bigger than that?" This time he looks at Digger and Digger nods his head ever so slightly, almost embarrassed to admit that the question needs an answer. "You owe it to yourself to finish this job, Digger. You owe it to yourself and to me. The two of us have invested a great deal in this dream. A lot of time. A lot of energy. A lot of heart." He pauses, extends his hand, meets Digger's eyes. "Let's see what we can do to see that the investment pays off. In full."

Digger meets Saul's hand, grips it hard, not trusting himself to speak.

Saul smiles, "That's my boy," and reaches his other hand around to pat Digger between the shoulder blades. "Thatta boy!"

Digger is suddenly surrounded by Saul's arms, chest, paunch. Digger returns the hug, patting Saul's back. "We'll do this, coach. We'll do it."

He clicks Saul's door quietly behind him, thinking there's only one more summer of wrestling. Almost there. He can fix the other things when he gets back.

Thirty-Eight

*R*ainforest noises chirp over Sadie's body. She lies on her back on a gym mat, eyes closed. She is part of a semicircle of mats, all faced towards a man in loose-fitting purple pants and a graying ponytail. But at least her clamshell brace is gone. She and Dr. Hock had their own private ceremony in his office, a ceremony that began and ended with her dumping her brace in his trash can. And so now here she is, starting a beginner yoga class.

"I have to do *something*," she told Dr. Hock.

"Start easy," was his reply.

This is easy. Her left hand sits loosely on her abdomen. She breathes in through her right nostril, out through her left. She wonders how anyone can call this a workout.

Under the chatter of the rainforest comes the instructor's soft, expressionless voice. Unlike with Marcus's orders, she can choose to let these words in, or just let them wash over her, smoothe her skin. "People today are not in harmony with their bodies," says the ponytailed man. "They treat their bodies like machines. Machines that can be pushed to do a variety of functions. They grind the gears." He lifts his body into a cross-legged position and gestures that Sadie and the other students should do the same. His hands sit in prayer position at his chest. As he inhales, his hands move up and over his head. When he exhales, they come down to the floor and then back, palm-to-palm at his chest. Once everyone mimics his actions, his voice continues.

"They squeal their brakes. Have you heard the saying, 'Drive it like you stole it'? Rental cars. That's how people treat their bodies."

Sadie tries to sit straighter, hopes it will lessen the pain in her lower back. The instructor moves onto all fours, arches his back like a scared cat, holds the arch for a few seconds, and then flattens his back again. Everyone in the semicircle copies this motion and repeats it.

He must see Sadie's pain, because he comes to her, lays his hand flat on the base of her spine. His hand's heat warms her through her clothes.

"Your hands—" she whispers. "So warm."

"I have been blessed with healing hands." He places the palm of his other hand on the back of her neck. She closes her eyes, lets his heat soothe her. He raises his voice so the others can hear, then continues talking. "Drive it like you stole it. The body is treated no better than a rental car. There is no respect. There is no awareness of the connection between mind and body." He pats Sadie's back and returns to his mat at the front of the semicircle, resumes the pose of a cat. "You see people on those machines—" He pushes his toes into the mat, lifts his hips into the air, aiming his rear end at the ceiling, stretching one leg in the air, holding as he counts ten breaths, then stretching the other. "—those cardio machines—pushing their bodies as hard as they'll go, and the people exercising while reading a magazine at the same time. They don't listen to their bodies, don't hear what their bodies tell them."

Sadie cannot do the pose. She finds yoga so slow, so lacking any competitive element. Yet she cannot hold her foot in the air, not for fifteen seconds. He sees her struggling and quietly slides to her mat again. No one turns to look, but she hates being singled out nonetheless.

He puts his hands on her shoulders, gestures for her to roll onto her back, lifts her right leg in the air for her. "Your spine has suffered much trauma. My hands feel it. You must be gentle. You need the support of the earth beneath you." He gestures for her to alternate her legs, to stretch her left side. "Don't do anything that hurts," he whispers in her ear before returning to the front of the room.

Don't do anything that hurts? She remembers being twelve and doing her first truly challenging swimming set, 12 x 200 on three minutes. Remembers it exactly, her shoulders throbbing in pain, shooting sharp stingers down her arm. Her lungs aching for air. That hurt. She had looked up at her coach and told him so. "It hurts," she'd said, clutching a cramp in her side. "It's supposed to hurt," he responded. "That's the only way you get better."

She curls her knees into her chest and rocks her head side to side, listening to it crack and pop. She notices the boy next to her, moppy hair and a beaded necklace. A hippy, she thinks, trying to imagine Bogdan going to a yoga class. Or Digger or Fly or Russ. The boy sits up straight, takes a deep breath, then folds himself in half as if he has no bones. He easily places his head on the floor between his knees. As he lifts his body back to sitting, he sees her staring and smiles. She scowls back. She hates this. It's stupid. She sits and tries to bend forward, but a sharp pain at the base of her spine grabs her, makes her breath catch in her chest. She rolls onto her side in the fetal position and watches the moppy-haired boy grow blurry.

Soon, a hand is on her back. "You have had enough for today," says the instructor's soft voice. "More than enough. Come back, though. A little bit more each time." He smiles his soft smile, and she lifts herself to go. At the door, she grabs her knapsack and swings it over her shoulder. It holds nothing but a bottle of water, her copy of *Paradise Lost*, and a collection of Browning, but the bag feels heavy on her neck.

As she climbs the dark and dusty staircase to Baron's Court, her legs feel so weak they tremble, and she bangs her fist on the cold cement wall, letting sobs shake her body. But at the top, when she meets the heavy steel door, she takes a deep breath, dries her eyes on her sleeve, and pushes through. Immediately, she's glad she managed to straighten her face, because there sit Katie and Bogdan, eating bagels with cream cheese and struggling over the campus newspaper's weekly crossword.

"Sade! Hey!" Bogdan smiles and waves, the first to see her.

"Up and around!" Katie says when she looks up at Sadie walking towards their table.

"Join us! Sit! Sit!" Bogdan pushes the papers and food aside, makes a space for her.

She feels awkward and fussed over, a visitor rather than part of the group. "Hi, guys. Thanks. I'll stand though." She rests her body on the railing next to their table. "I'm a better leaner than a sitter these days."

"Oops. Sorry," says Bogdan, his smile flattening.

"Not your fault," says Sadie, pulling the bottle of water from her knapsack and taking a long drink. "Everyone seems to be apologizing to me these days. Everyone except the jackass who hit me, that is." She smiles, but no one else does. "So!" She looks around the table, tries to determine if Katie and Bogdan have become more than swimming partners. "How are you guys? What's new?"

The silence, the tangible discomfort, threatens to pull her under, fill her lungs, drown her. She understands their dilemma. Their lives are swimming—nothing else—so how are they to answer her question in a way that doesn't make her feel left out?

"Katie! I heard you won Nationals. Congrats!" She tries to prompt Katie, to bring the swimmers to life, to remind them how to act like themselves.

"Uh-huh," Katie says smiling, uncertainly, like a child who is proud of herself but has been instructed not to brag. "I did."

"That's great! Who was there? Who'd you beat?"

"Pretty much everyone was there." Katie sounds defensive now, as if Sadie was implying it was a weak Nationals, as it often is in an Olympic year. "Everyone but you."

"Awesome." Sadie knows she's never uttered the word with less enthusiasm. She adjusts her weight against the steel railing. A knotted pain travels from her lower back, across her hips, into her legs. "Well done."

"Yep," says Katie, piling the newspaper pages on the table in front of her into a tidy heap. "Now, it's my spot to defend. Four years. Watch for me in 2004." She smiles, trying to meet Bogdan's eyes, but his eyes are on Sadie, watching her wiggle in pain.

"You know what I heard Mark Tewksbury say once?" Sadie stands straight, stretches her neck. "I heard him say that the Olympics leaves its athletes broken souls." She feels as though Lucinda has quantum leapt into her body. But it's a fact. She did hear Mark Tewksbury say just that, though at the time she was quick to put it out of her thoughts. What dusty, neglected corner of her brain it has risen from now she cannot imagine. She sees Katie look quickly to Bogdan, him shake his head ever so slightly. "I suspect it's true," Sadie hears herself add.

With the words out of her mouth, there's nothing left to do but take her broken soul and leave. So she leaves.

Thirty-Nine

*T*wo days before Digger leaves for Sydney, he drives his wood-panelled station wagon to a TV studio in downtown Calgary for an interview. He and two other athletes—a runner and a gymnast—are going to appear on the Calgary Morning Show. Fly slouches in the passenger seat, eating apple crullers.

"Way too early, guy," says Fly, his mouth full of dough. "Only for you would I get out of bed before seven. I wanna see this shit live!"

Digger turns off Memorial Drive and winds his rattling car through downtown Calgary, clunks into the station parking lot. "If I were you, Fly, I would've stayed in bed. The interview will probably last fifteen minutes max."

"Fifteen minutes of fame! And that's only the start of it for you. That's even before your gold medal."

"I guess you can always go back to bed after. If you're not too revved up from all that sugar." He eyes the empty Tim Horton's box on Fly's lap. Half a dozen crullers in a twelve-minute drive.

"Just don't let the other two hog all the air time! Don't let them give wrestling the short shrift." Fly yells this last part loud over the morning rush-hour traffic.

"Don't remember signing you on as Press Manager." Digger pulls the keys out of the ignition and reaches into the back seat for his gym bag.

"Well, I have to worry about everything now that we've lost Benny to the dark side. You're down to one chief assistant."

Ben has taken to hanging out with the Buddhist Association on campus, attending prayer sessions, wearing nothing but self-effacing beige, and shaving his hair close to his scalp, eschewing his previous attachment to his curly hair as a sign of worldly vanity. He claims to have renounced alcohol, women, and sport, and Digger wonders if his beige shirts are lined with horse hair.

When Ben first started drifting away from them, towards the Buddhists, Fly pointed out that Ben had always been a bit of a fanatic. Now that wrestling was done for him, he simply needed something new to which he could attach this fanaticism.

"He's always been a nut," was Fly's explanation.

"He's a nut?" Digger had responded. "Careful—remember every time you point a finger, three point back."

Now Fly says, "You should've asked Ben for his purple velour shirt. That would've gotten the viewing public's attention. No way a runner or gymnast would be able to upstage you."

As it is, Digger wears his national team gear. Both he and Fly are quiet as they enter the station's front office. A receptionist with a hushed voice points them towards the studio, indicating that they should hurry. Inside, the other athletes are already on stage, sitting stiffly on a plush white couch. They wear the same clothes as Digger, red and white nylon pants and jacket, a Canada goose sprawled across the chest and down one arm, a Canadian flag covering the top half of the back.

A woman wearing a painted face and a lime green power suit sits on an armchair opposite them, but does not look at them. She busily checks her microphone, consults her notes, and points various technicians here and there, sending them for this and that. Digger has never seen someone look so busy while sitting. He hands his coffee cup to Fly and approaches the stage. When he reaches the top of the steps, the woman looks up at him from her armchair.

"And you are—" She looks down at her clipboard.

"Tom—"

"Stapleton. Right. Check." She makes a mark on the clipboard and sets it down on her lap, turning to address a young woman who hands her a glass of water.

"But people call me—"

"Just sit on the couch." She points across from her, as if he may have missed it. "Between the other two. Your sport is—"

"Wrestling," he finishes, filling in her pause, as he backs towards the couch.

"Right. Check." And she's summoning another technician, insisting she needs fewer lights and a fan.

He squeezes between a very young and very skinny girl gymnast on one side and a tall male runner he recognizes from U of C on the other. They all lift their lips in a faint smile at each other, then simultaneously wipe the palms of their hands on their nylon pants.

They are saved from having to make conversation, because the show's star suddenly turns her attention to them. "You can't go wrong," she says. "Just follow my lead. We have seven minutes. Anyone can last seven minutes. Smile, answer the questions, and everything will be fine. Actually, let's have you stand: show off your athletic physiques. Someone get this couch out of here," she yells over her shoulder. Before the athletes have had time to stand, two men are at the ends of the couch, ready to follow orders. Digger and his companions hurry off, throwing obliging smiles in their hostess's direction. She turns the back of her head to them again as a short man in a suit and high-top red running shoes sprints onto stage, his eyes fixed on Digger. "Your ear! Is the other one better? That's going to be distracting for the viewers."

Digger turns his head to the left so the little man in red shoes can assess his other ear. He thinks of the story he likes to tell the kids about his ears melting in a fire, but no one has asked what happened, so he says nothing.

"Hmm. Not much better, but I guess it will have to do. Change spots with her." He points at the girl gymnast. "Don't let that mangled ear face the camera." He studies it again, distaste crinkling his face. "Whatever you do."

He whispers something to the host on his way back and she laughs, re-clipping her microphone, straightening her skirt, then patting her hairdo. Digger can feel his palms sweating. He rubs them against his thighs one more time. He would rather be in the sweatbox, swapping takedowns with Ben, or even at mat centre with a 'roidal American. Then a man's voice counts down, "Four, three, two!" He gestures "one," then points silently at the hostess.

Music sounds and their hostess introduces them. There is a warmth and energy in her voice that was not there ten seconds earlier. Suddenly, she is interested in the three athletes in her studio. Nothing, says her facial expression, could be more interesting.

"Today we are honoured with the company of three Olympians who will be representing Calgary and representing Canada at the 2000 Games in Sydney, Australia. First we have Sherri Bennett, a gymnast."

Sherri steps forward with her arms waving above her head. She is all smiles and dimples. To Digger's surprise, while the faux audience is still clapping, Sherri does a cartwheel, then a back walkover before stepping back into line.

"Next we have Michael Drake, who will represent Canada in the four hundred metre hurdles." Michael steps forward, flashes the camera a Colgate smile, bows his head, and steps back.

"And last—but not least—Thomas Stippleton, a wrestler!"

Stapleton! Digger thinks, unable to correct her, his mouth so dried out that his lips stick to his teeth.

She laughs and walks flirtatiously closer to Digger. "I guess we won't ask you for a demonstration like young Sherri here! We will all have to watch ourselves around a world-calibre strongman like you." She playfully squeezes his bicep, and then, subtly and out of the camera's range, pulls on his elbow so his body rotates to ensure his worst ear is facing away from the camera.

"How about you, Michael? Care to give us a little talent show?" She points down the stage, where two hurdles have been placed.

Digger sees the back of Michael's neck go red, but he obliges, shaking his legs to loosen the muscles and then running a light jog towards the hurdles, clearing them both easily.

"As easy as that," smiles their hostess, hiking up her skirt, pretending she might try the hurdles herself. "Ha! I would kill myself trying that. Most of us would. But then, you three are not most of us, are you? You are amongst the world's best athletes. Sherri, I'm told that you have your sights set on gold, and that your classmates are sending you off with an extra-special good luck charm?"

On cue, Sherri pulls a beaded necklace out of her pocket. "Everyone in my class painted me a bead," she says in a squeaky voice that grates on Digger's nerves. "These three are from my best friends." She lays the necklace across her palm and holds it before her. The cameraman zooms in on the three beads, each bearing a set of initials. The hostess ties the necklace around Sherri's neck, and Sherri promises to wear it the whole time and to bring back a medal for her teacher at the gymnastic club's independent school. Gymnasts, she explains, don't have time for real school.

"Why don't you give us and your classmates a little preview of that gold medal performance?"

Sherri smiles in response. In a flash, her tracksuit is off and she's wearing nothing but a skintight bodysuit. The bottom half is white, the top half red, and a goose covers the chest and most of her right arm.

"What would you like to see?" She smiles up into the hostess's face, and Digger wonders if Sherri's cheeks are getting sore yet.

"Well, what have you got? Something fancy? Something involving air and somersaults, I think. What do you think?" She addresses the pretend audience and is answered with a burst of machine generated cheers, whistles, and claps. "Air and somersaults it is, then," the hostess announces.

Sherri steps towards two mats laid out along the front of the stage. She takes a deep breath, smiles, and transforms herself into pure energy. Fly multiplied by a million and finally airborne for real. She's running, she's flying. Hands over feet, hands over feet. She is in the air. Her hands grab her knees and she rotates backwards. Over once. Over twice.

Yes, but she only weighs eighty pounds, thinks Digger. It wouldn't be that hard to fly if you only weighed eighty pounds.

The clap machine rages again and the hostess beams at her new star, "Encore! Encore!"

Sherri is in motion again. This time she does two back handsprings and then a backwards somersault high in the air. Digger claps.

"Well, Sherri Bennett, and Michael Drake and Thomas Stippleton, I, along with all of Calgary and all of Canada, will be watching you in Sydney, cheering you on to the gold!"

Music blares again and the hostess flicks her microphone off. Her eyes briefly land on the athletes. "Good work. Thanks for coming." She looks to the cameraman, "Where'd Bridget go? I need a coffee! Someone yell for her to bring me a coffee."

Coming off the stage, Digger won't meet Fly's eyes. He does, though, grab the cold cup of coffee thrust into his path as he walks by. He takes one sip, then drops the cup in the garbage can at the door.

They walk out of the studio, Fly close on Digger's heels. They get in the car, both doors slam loudly, and Digger pulls through the maze of cars and onto Memorial Drive. The traffic crawls in all three lanes; horns blare as drivers fight for a spot in what they hope is a faster lane. It no longer matters; Digger is in no rush. Neither of them talks and neither of them moves to turn on the radio. They just sit in silence, Digger's hands tight on the steering wheel and Fly's eyes fastened on his passenger window.

"That was bullshit, man," Fly finally says.

Digger nods, but he doesn't trust himself to speak. *It's Stapleton,* he wanted to say. *How hard is Stapleton?*

Forty

The U of C locker room is both dirtier and smellier than Sadie
remembers. The floor is slippery with slime and scattered with
wads of hair, Kleenex, gum. As usual, the air is heavy with the scent
of chlorine, but underneath there's a sharp trace of human sweat and
moldy towels. Apparently, you can get used to anything, and Sadie
has simply gotten unused to the locker room in her three and a half
months away from the pool. Now, she takes small breaths through her
mouth, avoiding the smell and hurrying to get on to the pool deck.

Hurrying, that is, as much as she can. Getting into a swimsuit
proves to be more of a challenge than she expected. She still cannot
bend over without supporting her weight. The muscles in her lower
back are too injured and weak to hold her. She braces herself against
a locker door with one hand and tries to loop a leg hole over her foot
with the other. Naked, hopping on one foot, and clinging with all her
might to a locker door, she feels like a fool. *Please*, she thinks, *Don't
let Katie walk in. Don't let Katie see me like this.* Once a role model, a
mentor, a competitor, now reduced to this. Her body shakes—with
a laugh or a sob?—but she holds her breath and directs all her energy
on the dilemma presented by her swimsuit.

Once she gets one leg in a hole, she shuffles to a wooden bench
and sits to lift the other leg in. Already breathing hard and feeling a
little faint, she stands and yanks the Lycra up over her hips and chest,
wiggling her torso to squeeze everything in. Her post-accident body

is not as trim as her pre-accident one. Before, this suit was a second skin, a sleek surface for water to speed across. Now, the straps dig into her back, and excess flesh pushes out of the leg holes, around the chest.

She sighs, grabs a towel out of her locker, wraps it around herself, and walks onto deck.

She has no intention of swimming today. Yesterday, she told her physiotherapist she was ready to get back in the water. The physio shook her head. Pulling an acupuncture needle from Sadie's neck, she said, "No. Not swimming. It'll be too easy for you to get lulled into over-exerting yourself. That will only set us back."

"How about water jogging," Sadie had offered as a compromise. She needed the pool.

The physio eyed her warily. "Only if you wear a floatation device." She reached around Sadie's head to pull a needle out of her lower scalp. "I mean it."

A lifejacket? Sadie would rather drown.

On deck, she sees Marcus. Bogdan and Katie are in the far lane, swimming up one side and back the other, a tight train, chugging round and round the same track. Evening practice? That means it must be four in the afternoon already. She has a hard time keeping track of the day's passing now that she has lost her lifelong schedule of training times, constant feedings, and strategic power naps. But she is building a new structure—one that, at present, is based upon physiotherapy appointments and rehabilitation sessions. A routine of regeneration.

She quickly turns away before Marcus sees her looking, before Marcus sees her at all. She no longer belongs to that group and does not want to be held captive by one of his attempts at small talk. She does not know how to shape her face in response to his sympathetic stares.

Instead, she walks towards the diving tank, where professors and university staff swim their post-work widths. A lifeguard sits up in the guard chair and smiles down at Sadie. He would have known her before, would have seen her swimming at the other end every morning, every evening. And he would have heard about her accident. A front-page article in the campus newspaper—*Olympian's Dreams Crushed in Head-On Collision*—has ensured that everyone has heard. Now she's a campus celebrity of sorts, though not at all in the way she had imagined. She forces herself to smile back, and then looks towards the bin of float belts for water jogging. *A lifejacket?* No. Really, she would rather drown. She'll try it without first.

Holding onto the steel pole alongside the guard chair, she awkwardly lowers herself down to the deck and sits with her legs dangling into the water. She imagines the lifeguard disgusted at her still unshaven legs, and absently runs her hands over the fur as she remembers her old practice ritual: a quick plunge and then feet over head, feet over head, feet over head. Today's entrance will have less flare. She eases her body into the water, clutching the edge, hating the slow, cold, wet crawl up her body, the steady seep through her tight suit. Once she's in the water up to her neck, she rests her elbows on the edge and pulls her hair into a tight bun on top of her head.

Now. How to do this? Water jogging. Just jogging in the water, right? *How hard can it be?* she thinks. She has seen people do it. Hundreds of people. Laughed at them, in fact. *If you're going to get in the water, just swim, for God's sake,* she'd once believed. She lets her elbows slide off the edge and her legs instinctively slip into whip kick, keeping her afloat.

"Okay, here goes," she says to no one as she faces the opposite side of the pool. She moves her arms and legs in a running motion. Step. Step. Step. Her heart beats faster and louder but she hardly moves, could return to the pool ledge in two or three quick and easy strokes if she were swimming. Step. Her neck is the first to register the pain—a sharp shooting into the back of her scalp, down her right arm. She hears her physio's voice: *Just make sure you wear a lifejacket.* Step. Step. Maybe she will warm up; maybe it will get easier. On her right, a retired professor she recognizes from the philosophy department swims past her, his arms jerky above the water. He fights the water instead of letting it carry him. His splashes catch Sadie in the face. She uses an arm to wipe her eyes, relying on her legs alone to hold her up. Her breathing grows loud in her own ears. How hard can it be? Step. Now her lower back is aching too, a dull thudthudthud in her buttocks, but she's almost at the wall. Her heart pounds in her ears. She lets her legs float up from under her body, does three head-up breaststrokes, and grabs the edge. Head-up breaststroke? Like an old lady in a flowered shower cap. Still, she's grateful for the edge. She holds tight and tries to catch her breath. Twenty-five yards and her scalp already itches with sweat, her neck aching, her back throbbing.

She will need a float belt. She would get out of the pool and walk back to the other side for one, but the idea of getting her body out of the pool is even more daunting than the idea of water jogging back. She considers her options. Float on her back? That would leave her neck exposed. What if someone swims into her or she bangs her head at the other wall? The possibility of any impact to her neck panics her, makes her teary-eyed. Head-up breaststroke? She promised her physio she wouldn't swim. Water jog? She rotates her neck and it makes loud cracking noises. Twenty-five yards has never looked so far.

Maybe head-up breaststroke doesn't really count as swimming, she decides, starting her move to the other side, the whole way picturing herself in a bold flowered cap.

At the edge, she smiles up at the lifeguard. "Would you mind passing me one of those float belt thingies?"

"Sure. No problem." He jumps from his seat to the floor in a single motion, easily bypassing the chair's ladder, grabs a belt from the bin, tosses it to her, and is back in his chair in one swinging step.

"Thanks." She looks at the belt. A lifejacket it is. She pulls it into the water, wraps it around her waist, and fastens it tight. Water jogging, take two. First, though, she folds her arms on the deck and lays her head in them, closes her eyes. Just a little rest.

The lifeguard's powerful leap off the chair, his strong legs, remind her of Digger. She hasn't spoken to him in a month. Almost exactly. They both just quit calling. The visits stopped. They are on two different tracks; she knew she was only a drain on his momentum. Maybe after Sydney, and after she has recovered, they can try again.

Leaving him be was her gift to him, but also her gift to herself.

But three days ago, she bought him a good luck card, sent it in the mail. In the store, picking a card, she had stood until her back sent shrill warning alarms shooting down her legs. She read every single card and then read them again. In the end, the one she got didn't even say anything about luck. On the front it read: "Life Is A Journey." And on the inside: "Enjoy The Road, Wherever It Ends." At the bottom, she had printed her name and *I'll be rooting for you. Have fun!*

"SAYYY-DEEE!! YOU'RE HERE!!"

She looks up to see Marcus standing at her elbow, smiling. "Hey," she says, trying to inject a little enthusiasm or friendliness into her voice.

"I saw you come in. You didn't come say hi."

She tries to read his face and is surprised. No sympathy there. Instead, she sees helplessness, an admission that there's no right thing for him to say or do.

"I have no place over there anymore, Marcus. I don't belong. And I don't want to be the poor crippled girl."

He squats down, rests his forearms on his knees. "You could've come over just to tell me how you're doing. I do want to know." He reaches out to her hand on the deck, wraps his hand around her wrist. "How're you doing?"

She takes a deep breath, thinks. "Okay," she says. "I'm figuring out a way to rebuild my life without swimming. Finding out who I am once the swimming is over." She pulls her hand away, rubs her eyes. "But I would have had to do that in a few months anyway."

Marcus nods his head ever so slightly, and she knows then that he agrees. That he has known as much all along. This is how it always ends, how it once ended for him too.

Forty-One

$\mathcal{A}$ single gym bag, red and black, sits in the middle of the bed, filled to overflowing, a pile of neatly folded T-shirts at the top.

Fly bounces on the edge of the bed. "Okay. Whaddya got? Plastics? Singlets? Wrestling shoes?"

"Check. Check. Check." Digger stands with his hands on his hips, staring into his closet, sure he must've forgotten something.

"Blue *and* red singlets?" Fly smiles, reminding Digger of the fiasco of the perfumed pink teddy. "You'd look a little off wrestling on national television wearing lace."

"Blue and red. Checkcheck." He turns from the closet to Fly, holds his hands in the air. "Guess I got everything."

"You'd better, because once I drop you off at the airport, you're on your own. I don't know how you're going to manage without me. I really don't. You'll see." Fly lies back on the bed, hands behind his head.

Digger smiles, zips his bag closed. "I can't believe this is it. I'm packing for the Olympics. All the . . . everything . . . and now it's really happening. And—I'm scared like a little kid. Scared. Of all things! Nervous as hell." He rubs the back of his neck, embarrassed at having said so much. He braces himself for a smart comment from Fly.

"Of course you're scared. But it's happening." The vastness of his smile blocks out the scared part. "And it couldn't happen to a more deserving guy." Fly stands and steps towards Digger, holding his hand out for a high-five. When Digger meets it, Fly's hand closes, firm, and pulls Digger in for a tight hug, three solid slaps on his back. "Go get 'em, big guy! Go get 'em." Releasing Digger, he slides his hand in his pocket. "Here. I got you this." He opens his balled fist.

Digger takes the smooth black pebble out of the centre of Fly's palm. "A rock?"

"It's a touchstone. To remind you—you're the true thing." Fly shrugs. "Take it. For luck."

Digger rubs the back of his hand to the smooth surface. "I will. That's—that's . . . great. Fly—thanks. I . . . it's—"

"Yeah. Yeah. I know, at a loss for words. I have that effect on people. Anyway, you're a man of action, not words. Just thank me before the whole country when you're delivering your gold medal acceptance speech."

Digger unzips the side pocket of his bag and slides the rock into it, next to a brightly coloured card.

"Aha! The good-luck memento pocket. What's that? A card from your mommy?" Before Digger can re-zip the pocket, Fly has the card in his hand and is reading it. The smile falls from his face. He closes the card and slides it back in the side pocket. "Sadie."

Digger shrugs. "Came in the mail yesterday."

"So, you're taking all your good luck cards to Sydney, right? This one's nothing special? Just from a friend? Look, man, why not just call her? Get her to take you to the airport. She makes a prettier driver than me." He picks a cordless phone off Digger's nightstand, hands it to him. "One ride to the airport isn't going to distract you, is it?" He pushes the receiver into Digger's hands. "I bet she's home."

Digger takes the phone, stares at it.

"Do I have to dial the number too?"

Digger chews his bottom lip, takes a deep breath, almost smiles. "Do it!"

Digger slowly begins to push the buttons.

"I'll say it again," Fly sighs dramatically. "I don't know how you'll manage without me."

Forty-Two

*W*hen Sadie gets to Digger's house, he's sitting on the front steps, red and black gym bag at his side. He looks so much like a kid on his way to summer camp that she finds herself getting out of the car as if to swing him around in a hug and help him with his bag. But he's already jogging towards her rusted Toyota, gym bag slung over his shoulder.

"Wanna drive?" She holds the keys out to him as he throws his bag into the back seat.

"Sure." He takes the keys, letting his hand press against hers for just a moment. "Thanks for coming to get me. Short notice and everything."

"Not a problem." She ducks into the passenger seat, grabs an orthopedic support from the driver's side, and fits it behind her lower back. "I didn't expect I'd get a chance to see you before you left."

Once he's buckled in, he turns to her. "Sorry I haven't—"

"No. Don't say it. I understand."

"Really?"

"Fully." She points to the road, indicating that he should drive rather than talk.

"Then maybe you can explain it to me." He pulls the car onto the road, following orders.

"When you get back." She smiles and squeezes his forearm. "Did Fly make you call me?"

A surprised laugh escapes Digger. "Fly doesn't make me do anything."

"No, he just pushes you in the right direction now and then." She laughs. "He's the self-appointed Manager of All Things Digger."

"Sounds like you understand everything," he says, smiling and lifting one hand from the steering wheel, letting it rest on her knee.

"Nah, I just have a lot of time to think these days."

"Still. Understanding Fly, that's an achievement!"

They wind their way through the foothills, all dead and brown. It's been a hot summer and the land is thirsty. Dust hangs in the air. But it's a sunny day, and Digger and Sadie can see as far as the mountains. Sadie points out a tall scalped peak in the distance to the left of the road. "I always love when it's so clear you can see the mountains."

Their ride to the airport is too short for Sadie. She's happy to have Digger in her car, driving her car. The energy in his voice when he talks about his last month of training warms her.

"It's good to see you smile," he says. "You look—better."

"I feel better," she says simply. "Slowly but definitely surely." She nods as if to relieve him of some unnamed burden. Her right hand fidgets in her pocket, her fingernails scratching against paper. She pulls her hand from her pocket. "A poem," she says. "I brought it for you. Another good luck charm. If you're not loaded down with them already."

"Seriously?"

She feels heat sliding up her neck. Poetry? Not your usual pre Olympic gift for a wrestler. Her first instinct had been to highlight the lines near the end of the Browning poem:

> *How such a one was strong, and such was bold*
> *And such was fortunate, yet each of old*
> *Lost, lost!*

Fortunately, she'd fought off that instinct. Too dark. Too Lucinda. Instead, she'd highlighted the very final lines where Childe Rolande, knowing what he knows, eyes wide open, forges on, raises his trumpet to his lips, and blows.

"Seriously, have it. I'm done with it."

He takes the tightly folded paper from her palm and slides it into his chest pocket.

At the airport, he asks her to come inside to see him off. She stands at his side while he checks his bag, grabs a coffee. She leans against a wall—her back too sore to sit—while he makes a last trip to the washroom. When he comes back, a woman's voice announces his flight's last call for security. But rather than going, he sits down on the bench next to her, pulls out the folded paper, twirls it round and round, still doesn't open it, then slides it back into his pocket, plays with her fingers. "Wish me luck."

"You don't need luck."

He says nothing, just studies her fingers, so she adds, "I'll watch. I'll cheer." She stands, pulling on his fingers, encouraging him up from the bench, and they walk to his boarding gate, hand in hand. The other Canadian wrestlers mill about, a blur of red and white.

He turns to her, takes both her hands in his, but then seems to forget what he wants to say. He doesn't speak, but he also doesn't step away, seems glued to her hands while his teammates wait in the background.

"A search drawn out through the years," she says.

"What?"

"Nothing. Just part of the poem. In your pocket." She leans forward and places the lightest of kisses on his cheek. "Go. Show the world what Tom Stippleton is made of." She squeezes his fingers. "I mean, Stapleton."

He chews on his lower lip, a habit that instantly turns him into a twelve-year-old boy. But his eyes—narrowed and glistening—have a crazed intensity that undermines any claim to youthfulness. If anything, they remind her of Ben in his early days at the hospital. "I'm going to win," he says.

She nods, meets his eyes, knows hers are watering. "I'll cheer for you," she says again, unable to think of anything else. She drops his hands. "Call me when it's over. I'll bring you back."

He looks at her quizzically.

"I'll pick you up."

He puts a hand on her head, smoothes her hair. "I will." His hands are heavy, and suddenly the sheer bulk of him weighs on her. She pities the men forced to wrestle him.

He is, she thinks, Fitzgerald's Tom Buchanan in his prime, a man at the pinnacle of such an acute limited excellence that everything afterward will savour of anticlimax. Win or lose. And she has promised to bring him back from that?

She watches the oversized red maple leaf on his back as he walks to join his teammates, and she knows that no matter what happens in Sydney, she will need to be strong for his return.

For him, too, it will soon be over.

And for her?

She will get in her car, drive to a drugstore, and pick up some shaving cream. At her parents' place—which, for now at least, is still her place—she will draw a nice, warm bath and finally shave these hairy legs.

✐Acknowledgements

Thanks to my mom, Johnna Abdou, who believed I was a writer long before I believed I was a writer. Thanks to my dad, Frank Abdou, who fostered a love of storytelling and taught me (inadvertently, perhaps) that fact has very little to do with a good story, and truth and fact are not the same thing. Thanks to my little brother, Justin Abdou, for introducing me to the very bizarre world of Canadian Olympic Wrestling (as well as its even more bizarre cast of characters). Thanks also to Justin for teaching me how to do a gut wrench.

A warm thanks to Marcel Dirk, Darrell Bethune, and my other colleagues, who broke out the champagne when they heard the good news.

Thanks to Dr. Paul Michal for filling in a few medical details. Thanks to University of Western Ontario's Dr. Balachandra Rajan and Dr. John Leonard, who must be at least partially responsible for Milton sneaking his way into this novel.

I am unspeakably grateful to my brilliant editor, Suzette Mayr, who saved me many an embarrassment. Without Suzette, this novel would be a different, lesser book. Thanks also to Elisabeth Harvor and the Humber College mentorship program for insightful feedback right from the first draft of the first chapter, and to Lynn Coady and the Sage Hill Fiction group of summer 2004. And many thanks to all the helpful folks at NeWest.

Thanks, as always, to my computer genius friend, Kevin McIsaac, who makes house calls any time of day and accepts payment in single-malt Scotch.

The biggest thanks goes to my husband, Marty Hafke—simply because the way he looks at me makes me feel as though I could do anything.

ANGIE ABDOU was born and raised in Moose Jaw, SK. She has a Ph.D. in Canadian Literature and Creative Writing from the University of Calgary and teaches at the College of the Rockies. She lives in Fernie, BC with her husband and two children. Abdou has been speed swimming since the age of four and currently competes at the Masters level.